THE FIEND
IN THE FOG

What Reviewers Say
About Jess Faraday's Work

The Strange Case of the Big Sur Benefactor

"Clever. Clever, clever, clever! That's almost all I can say about Jess Faraday's *The Strange Case of the Big Sur Benefactor*, but...of course you know there's more. ...Faraday is a brilliant wordsmith who knows her way around the crafting of historical fiction, understanding where the balance exists between too much detail and not enough, firmly placing her readers in the time and place her stories are set without bogging down the flow of the storyline."
—*The Novel Approach*

Fool's Gold

"The plot, while complex and full of intrigue, is easy to follow, full of moments of clarity. It's told from Ira's point of view, we get to see everything through his eyes, and that works perfectly. The historical detail shines through. ...Fool's Gold is a mystery, a superbly written gay mystery and it's perfect for anyone who likes something a bit different, who wants an adventure."—*Prism Book Alliance*

"Jess Faraday's storytelling skills are flawless. From creating rich and multi-layered characters to texturing each layer of plot so it grounds the reader in the time and place of the novels, these books are not a lesson in Victorian Era or Old West history. They are each detailed yet subtle, every scene perfection, written with a finesse that draws you into the story and captivates and captures the imagination. There's a reason *The Affair of the Porcelain Dog* and *Turnbull House* both made my list of their respective years' Best Books. *Fool's Gold* will make it a three-peat in 2015. This series is full-immersion historical fiction. In a word: Outstanding."
—*The Novel Approach*

Turnbull House

"With characters who are layered with charm and complexity, settings that play out visually like a full color series of daguerreotypes on the mind, a mystery that reveals how far apart Ira and Goddard have grown since Ira walked out two years before, and a fluid prose that draws the reader into the lives of the characters and the time of the story, *Turnbull House* is as flawless a historical novel as I've ever read."—*The Novel Approach*

"*Turnbull House* was special. So addicting. I needed to read more. The characters were distinct, sexy, and believable."—*Books A to Z*

"ALL the characters are so real and believable that I feel like I've stepped back in time to Ira's world...yes, definitely as vivid as *The Affair of the Porcelain Dog*. In the end, *Turnbull House* is nearly perfect. I will be right there ready for when the third book releases. ...Ira Adler is an easy addiction for me."—*The Blogger Girls*

"Overall, while managing to be a cracking good mystery, this book is at the core about "doing the right thing" when it's not obvious what that thing is, and the ever-present potential for redemption. ...This series is really, really worth your time."—*Mrs. Rayman Reads*

The Affair of the Porcelain Dog

"*The Affair of the Porcelain Dog* is an excellent mystery. The characters are complex and in general not what they seem on first sight. Many unexpected twists and turns keep the novel intriguing right up to the end. The historical setting of late Victorian London is portrayed accurately. It is recommended for mystery collections at public libraries, especially those in gay- and lesbian-friendly areas, and college and university collections."—*Gay, Lesbian, Bisexual, and Transgender Round Table of the American Library Association*

"Jess Faraday takes you into a very bleak, dangerous, and inhuman realm. A world without mercy. But despite all this, she's able to deliver a beautiful and romantic story. ...This clever multi-layered mystery skillfully combined with some very strong characters will definitely keep you in suspense until the very end."—*Booked Up Reviews*

"The author builds a credible plot through the actions of diverse, fully-nuanced characters, which keeps the reader interested. ...Excellent first novel by a promising new author, which I give five stars out of five."—Bob Lind, *Echo Magazine*

"Sherlock Holmes Meets Oscar Wilde. Faraday has written a brilliant Victorian mystery. ...The careful plot is arranged like set of nesting boxes. With Faraday's smashing writing and research, Victorian London comes alive through the eyes of a 19th century outlier."—*The Bright List*

"Faraday's writing is strong, and the dangerously complex plot meticulously constructed. Her handling of detail is evocative, rather than finicky, so the story doesn't bog down. If you enjoy engaging Victorian mysteries and complex plots with colorful, devious characters, Jess Faraday's *Porcelain Dog* should be right up your dark London alley."—*Joyfully Jay*

The Left Hand of Justice

"[*The Left Hand of Justice*] is an exciting book with drama, romance, and mystery. The characters were interesting and strong. Once you get into the story, it is hard to put the book down."—*Curve Magazine*

"Gripping historical mystery/thriller with elements of steampunk and paranormal. The author managed to drag me back in time and entertain me with a fairly convoluted plot that was just a little bit out there."—*Library Thing*

Visit us at www.boldstrokesbooks.com

By the Author

The Affair of the Porcelain Dog

Turnbull House

Fool's Gold

The Left Hand of Justice

The Strange Case of the Big Sur Benefactor

The Fiend in the Fog

THE FIEND IN THE FOG

by
Jess Faraday

2021

THE FIEND IN THE FOG

© 2021 BY JESS FARADAY. ALL RIGHTS RESERVED.

ISBN 13: 978-1-63555-514-1

THIS TRADE PAPERBACK ORIGINAL IS PUBLISHED BY
BOLD STROKES BOOKS, INC.
P.O. BOX 249
VALLEY FALLS, NY 12185

FIRST EDITION: AUGUST 2021

CREDITS
EDITOR: SHELLEY THRASHER
PRODUCTION DESIGN: SUSAN RAMUNDO
COVER DESIGN BY TAMMY SEIDICK

Acknowledgments

A book is never the work of a single person. I first have to thank Sandy Lowe for her patience with my multiple delays and extension requests. Sometimes life happens, and it's wonderful when your publisher has your back. Many thanks also to my editor, Shelley Thrasher, who is not only eagle-eyed and possessed of an uncanny breadth and depth of knowledge, but is also really enjoyable to work with. Thanks also to BSB's team of cover designers, who have never failed to provide absolutely gorgeous covers for my books. And finally, a big thanks to my family, who, rather than resenting the amount of time and energy that my book took from me, and consequently from them, never failed to ask, when I finally sat down for the day, if I shouldn't actually be writing.

Dedication

For everyone who lives and loves in the interstices.

OUR HEROES

Four disparate groups of people, whose paths will cross in unexpected and life-altering ways.

THE CORNWALL STREET CLINIC

A clinic serving the indigent on London's East End, which has recently become the target of a mysterious and threatening presence. Its defenders include:

Nurse Abigail Gordon (Abby): Abby co-founded the clinic with her fiancé, Dr. Gideon Spencer. Abby sees herself as the clinic's protector, but she may be protecting it from the wrong thing.

Dr. Gideon Spencer: Gideon co-founded the clinic with Abby. He's a gifted physician hiding not just one but two dark secrets.

EISENSTADT HOUSE

At their family home in upper middle-class Kensington, a brother and sister fill their time with odd hobbies and a revolving cast of lovers.

Meg Eisenstadt: Meg is a crusader for justice and equality, though her inexperience in the world often hampers these efforts' success.

Nathaniel "Nat" Eisenstadt: Nat fancies himself an alchemist, and though London's occultists won't take him seriously, his latest project just might be on to something.

THE CONSORTIUM

A secretive organization devoted to occult research…and to consolidating its own power.

Lord Julius Carlyle: Lord Julius is the head of the Consortium. He oversees its research and fans the flames of competition between his two protegés, Algernon Hathaway and Dr. Jin Wylie.

Algernon Hathaway: Algie is brilliant, if blinded by ambition. His main project is the Academy of Occult Sciences, which recruits promising university students. His real passion, however, is the study of practical lycanthropy.

Dr. Jin Wylie: Jin was happy working as an alienist at Hanwell Asylum until a patient's escape saw him dismissed and disgraced. The Consortium quickly recruited him to work on the question of theoretical lycanthropy.

Bernadette Kingsley: Bernadette has a first-class degree in biology from Girton College, Cambridge. Unfortunately, positions for female scientists are few and far between. She works as a functionary for the Consortium but hopes that one day they will recognize her research.

A GANG OF SCRAPPY STREET KIDS

Garrick: Garrick, age fifteen, is the leader. Quick of fist and of temper, Garrick is coming to suspect that being a leader means more than simply keeping people in line.

Clyde: Twelve-year-old Clyde is a nimble-fingered thief with a surprisingly large vocabulary, who can seamlessly alternate between male and female personas.

Eli: Fourteen-year-old Eli has a penchant for Bible stories and Kabbalah, and is becoming the gang's voice of conscience.

Bert: Fourteen-year-old Bert is a brawny young man whose muscle conceals a sharp mind and a keen sense of observation.

CHAPTER ONE

November 1885
Whitechapel, London
Tuesday Afternoon

Garrick

"There she comes," Bert said. "Just like I told you."

Garrick leaned his shoulder against the blackened bricks of the burnt-out sugar factory. Deep shadows between the factory and the warehouse beside it made the alley the perfect place for the boys to watch the street without being seen.

"I'll be damned," Garrick said. Not that Bert's prediction surprised him. Bert didn't say a lot, but he saw everything.

Garrick followed the other boy's gaze down the street to a woman in her mid-twenties rounding the corner. Dull, grey dress; brown hair pulled back beneath a plain, dark woollen hat that was probably secondhand; heavy, flat-soled shoes; scrubbed face, earnest expression. Nice coat, though. Garrick rubbed a thumb over the hilt of the knife in his jacket pocket. He could get a proper sum for a coat like that.

"Been walking past here once a week, every week, for the past few weeks. Same time, always alone. Ain't with the school," Bert said with a nod in the direction of the ragged school a few streets away. "She don't belong here, what I can tell."

"And she always goes the same way?" Garrick asked.

Bert gave a sharp nod. "East, then south to the river, then east again."

"And then where?"

"Then off our patch," Bert said, raising his thick, dark eyebrows.

Now it was Garrick's turn to nod. There'd been whispers of something hunting the streets across the eastern border of Garrick's territory. When he'd first heard the chatter, Garrick had dismissed it as a rumor started by the gang on the other side. But when you hear the same thing enough times, it's best not to ignore it.

The woman was now directly across the street from them. Instinctively, the boys pressed themselves to their respective walls. This close, Garrick could see that she had pink cheeks and a round face that looked kind. Nothing like the pale, sharp-featured women who brayed out their windows and chased him and his boys away from their doorsteps with brooms. A lot of nerve to be walking through this patch alone. Nerve or stupidity.

"Booth lady," Garrick pronounced. "'Soup, soap, and salvation.'"

Bert snorted. "Yeah. Don't get too close or she'll put *you* in the bath."

Garrick tugged at the stained kerchief around his neck. He wouldn't have minded a bath, or some soup, either, but it wasn't worth all the Salvationists' "thou shalt nots." He couldn't risk his boys catching religion and sprouting a conscience, not with winter coming on. A nice, fat hen like that probably had a few feathers to pluck, though. Between her coin and her coat, Garrick and his boys could buy their own soup and baths. His stomach growled. They hadn't had a proper meal between them in days. And, well, hello. What was that in her hand?

"She always have that bag with her?" Garrick asked. It was a beat-up old Gladstone, the kind doctors carried. In Garrick's experience, bags like that always had something inside you could sell.

"Every time," Bert said.

Garrick considered his mate. A lot of people underestimated Bert. He was a big bruiser of a kid, looked closer to eighteen than the fourteen Garrick knew he was. All that beef made a good disguise. Most people thought Bert had beef for brains, too, but he was clever. If his tip panned out, Garrick'd give him an extra share of the loot.

"Think she's got medicine in there?" Garrick asked.

Bert turned his clear blue eyes toward Garrick. The right kind of medicine could get a better price than a fine woollen coat. But that wasn't what was in Bert's eyes. Bert was afraid.

"Dunno what she's got in there," Bert said. "But whatever it is, it comes from that building on Shepherd Street. You know the one."

"Huh," Garrick said again, shifting his feet uneasily. That place on Shepherd Street had been empty for as long as he and his boys could remember. Someone had moved in, though, over the past six months. Folk who never showed their faces in the daytime, but at night brought the place to life with lights and shadows and sinister sounds. Nobody'd ever met them that Garrick knew. At the same time, everyone seemed to agree that they weren't the kind of folk you *wanted* to meet.

If Miss Do-Good were a man, Garrick might have approached his next move with caution. But she wasn't a man, and she wasn't a street-savvy East End girl with a fast right hook and a shiv in her boot. She was an intruder slumming for souls, and between her coat, her cash, and whatever was in that Gladstone, five minutes' work could feed Garrick and his boys for a week, Shepherd Street be damned.

The steam whistle of a distant boat cut through his thoughts. Heavy grey clouds were rolling in, bringing with them the faint smell of rotten eggs. There'd be fog that night, thick and rank, but if they did this right, they'd be bedding down in their corner with full bellies for the first time in more than a week.

"Right," Garrick said. "Gather up the boys and meet me by the Old Stairs."

❖

Jin

Dr. Jin Wylie tossed down his pencil and crumpled the sheet of nonsense he'd scrawled. That damned dog next door was barking again. It had barked all through the night while he'd worked, and it was barking now, as the sun was going down on a second day. The sound was constant, almost mechanical. Wylie wished someone would give that poor thing a bone—or perhaps a few drops of laudanum in its drinking water. Perhaps more than a few drops.

No, that would be cruel. Wylie liked dogs. He also appreciated the fact that someone wanted to rehabilitate those that had suffered abuse or lived their lives out on the street. In fact, he'd been meaning to visit the organization in the adjacent building—the Society for the Protection of Creation—to tell them as much, and to offer his services. Much of his own work involved dogs, or at least canids, though he doubted the Society would want to hear about *that*.

But it didn't make it any easier to think with that racket.

It was inevitable, Wylie supposed, that an organization devoted to collecting stray dogs would need somewhere to put them. East London was as good a place as any. If nothing else, you wouldn't get the neighbors complaining. At least not the sorts of neighbors whose money or influence could command the wrath of the law.

If anything, Wylie strove to stay just out of sight of the law, to avoid its long arms and sharp eyes. His work with the Consortium wasn't illegal, exactly, but it probably would have been, had laws existed to regulate such things.

Bark. Bark. Bark. Wylie's head pounded in time with the noise. Perhaps it wasn't a dog at all. Perhaps it was an automaton, he thought cynically. Perhaps the Society was working on a windup dog for people who wanted a pet but couldn't be trusted to care for one. Perhaps, *damn and blast*, he was going to lose his mind.

But before that he'd have to deal with the person knocking oh-so-tentatively at the door.

With a deep sigh, Wylie tossed the ball of paper into the waste bin and stalked across the room, tying his thick, dark hair into a long tail. By the time he reached the door, the throb at his temples had spread over the top of his skull and was pounding behind his eyes. He gave the door a violent jerk.

"What the devil do you need?" he snapped.

The young woman shrank back as if expecting a blow. Miss Kingsley had always reminded Wylie of a china doll: smooth, pale skin, flashing grey eyes, and a head full of white-blond curls pulled back into a style that was a bit too severe for such a young woman. In her terror she now appeared as fragile as china, as well.

"Forgive me, Miss Kingsley," he said, clenching his teeth against the spreading migraine. "It's been a very long night."

Miss Kingsley brought the tea and the mail. She had neither, now, though she was carrying a thick file folder beneath one arm. He sensed she'd been hoping he wouldn't be there. The thought leapt out at him before he could block himself off from it. He watched other thoughts flit across her features as her eyes came to rest on the nest of papers on his desk. It was an act of discipline to let them flutter past without scrutiny.

"I'm terribly sorry, Doctor," she said. "I had a theory I wanted to discuss with you."

"A theory?"

"Clearly this isn't a good time. Forgive me."

Miss Kingsley was educated, but she wasn't a member of the Consortium, and she wasn't paid to construct theories. He had work to do, and that blasted dog was barking again, and he just wanted her to go away.

Pink splotches bloomed on Miss Kingsley's nose and cheeks, as if he'd said the words aloud. It happened sometimes, though he was pretty sure he'd been more discreet this time.

"I should go," she said.

Yes. Yes, you should, he thought. What a bastard he was. He let out a long breath. "But you have something else on your mind," he said instead.

She blinked at him through her spectacles. Her nose wrinkled as the jasmine notes of his cologne rose between them. Her gaze fell on his open collar. He'd removed his tie and undone a few buttons while he worked. Not too much of a liberty, all things considered. But the sight of the corset peeking up through the gap must have been shocking to someone too young to remember when fashionable men wore corsets—or to know that some men still did, when they suffered from debilitating back spasms. He hurriedly buttoned his shirt. She pulled her gaze back up where it belonged. He sensed her gathering her courage once more.

"I—I also thought you might like an update about the new building."

Wylie frowned. He'd told the Consortium numerous times that his work would progress much faster if he had his own dedicated facility. He'd just never thought it would actually happen.

"Go on," he said.

"Well, it seems we've located a property that meets all of your requirements."

"*All* of them?" He'd have been happy if any of the previous prospects had met just one. "Where is it?"

"Not too far. Shadwell."

She rummaged through the papers in her file until she found the relevant one, which she handed to him.

Wylie nodded as he found the salient points: three rooms, alley access, away from main roads, sparsely populated semi-industrial neighborhood, and what's that? Already a working medical facility? His spirits rose, and he found himself grinning despite his grim mood. A cellar would have made it perfect, but this was already more than he'd asked for. Not only that, but Shadwell was close enough to send messengers when needed, yet far enough away that the Consortium would think two or three times before coming out to peer over his shoulder.

"Doctor?"

"This is good," he said with a laugh. He handed the paper back. "It's very good."

Relief suffused her face now. "Shall I tell them that you approve the location?"

"Inform them that it appears very satisfactory indeed. I should like to arrange for a visit at the nearest possible opportunity."

"I'll tell them." Miss Kingsley smiled, perhaps feeling relieved that she wouldn't be forced to go back to her masters to once more convey Wylie's point-by-point dissatisfaction. "Shall I have your tea sent up now, Doctor? Or perhaps a light supper?"

"No, thank you," Wylie said. "I've done as much today as I'm likely to. Besides, I can't think with that da—blasted dog carrying on."

"Dog?" she asked. Wylie listened, but of course the damned thing had stopped.

"Never mind," he said. "Tell Sir Julius that I'll be back tomorrow."

"Very good," she said.

Only after the young woman had started down the hall did Wylie allow himself to appreciate her slender, well-formed figure—the shoulders that narrowed to a tiny waist, which bloomed out again into a modest bell of skirts and bustle. It was a shape to which Wylie aspired, privately, and in places where such things were appreciated. He'd spent the better part of a month pinning, tucking, and darting his own clothing, subtly, to give it the hint of shapeliness. He might have gone overboard with his overcoat, but he liked it.

And so did the people at his club in Holborn.

But Holborn was off that evening. That evening he was off to Chelsea for a very special meeting. He knotted his cravat around his neck, put his jacket back on, and found his magnificent overcoat.

Yes, despite the difficulties with his work that day, despite his disagreements with the Consortium, and despite the constant and horrific noise of that poor beast next door, things would be all right.

Not only did he now have a building, but Dr. Wylie had a date.

CHAPTER TWO

Abby

Bitter cold numbed Nurse Abigail Gordon's face and fingers as she raced the setting sun past the Wapping docks. She'd left Whitechapel later than planned, and the evening shadows were already on her heels. Dark clouds were rolling in, bringing the sulphurous portents of another fog. The cold, black Thames slapped at the embankment as she passed, and the nearby shipworks echoed with ominous crashes and bangs.

Up ahead, a ragged clutch of men watched her approach. Walking faster, she slipped a white cloth band over her wrist and tugged it up her arm, adjusting it so that the red cross was clear. It might make an attacker think twice. It might not. Either way, she had to protect her bag.

She tightened her sweaty fingers around the handle of her Gladstone and drew herself up as tall as her five-foot frame would allow. As the uneven cobblestones passed beneath her feet, her mind registered the Old Stairs on her right, the dark-windowed buildings and warehouses to the left. Except for the men, the street was deserted, but just beyond them lay a passage to a busy marketplace. From there she could take the pennies she'd saved by walking this far and disappear into an omnibus.

As her path brought her closer to the group, she saw that they wouldn't actually be men for a few years yet. Their faces were still smooth, their hard expressions not yet permanent. She guessed their ages to be between twelve and sixteen, which somehow made the implied malice worse. There were four of them, and as she approached, they shifted their glances from her bag, her pockets, her shoes to the pavement, the warehouses, the darkening clouds.

Her heart leapt when one of the youths suddenly stepped out into her path. He was skin and bones, with a threadbare woollen cap that sat askew over lank, brown hair. The filthy kerchief knotted around his neck that had once been white was now grey and spattered with rust-colored stains.

She stepped to the left, to the right. He matched her step for step, then waved his hand and produced a blade from below his tattered cuff.

"What's in the bag, sister?"

"Nothing." She pulled her Gladstone tight against her side. In addition to the phial—the precious phial she'd walked through Whitechapel to retrieve—her scalpel could find a lot of uses in a hand like his.

"Let's have a look, then."

She jerked around as rude fingers evaluated the wool of her coat-sleeve. Abby wasn't that coat's first owner, but it had been expensive once. Heart racing, she turned again, trying to keep all the youths in her sight. On closer inspection, not one of this nasty little pack appeared to have reached his sixteenth year. Sweat broke across her back, and that excellent coat suddenly seemed like a liability—too hot, too heavy, and too constricting to allow a quick escape.

The young men circled, bringing her back to the wall. Behind her the Thames undulated and roiled. If the tide were lower, she could have escaped down the stairs, but that time of day the black water ran high and fast. Abby knew how to swim, but not in the dead cold of November, and not when weighted down by heavy winter clothing.

As the youths closed in, she swung her bag. Three of them instinctively leaned away. The fourth one, though, the one with the knife, caught the bag and pulled her toward him.

"I'll have that," he said.

"No!" She yanked the bag out of his hands. "And," she said, slapping at the nasty little fingers suddenly tugging at her sleeve, invading her pockets, reaching for her hat pin, "you can keep your filthy hands to yourselves!"

Thunder rumbled. A strange energy crackled through the air, and one of the little thieves hissed and jumped back as if burned. The boy with the knife laughed. Abby jerked her head back toward him. Then suddenly the youth flew backward with a surprised grunt, landing on his backside some distance away. His knife skittered across the cobblestones, coming to a rest somewhere in the shadows.

What had just happened? It didn't matter. Abby ran.

Time seemed to slow. Her coat felt like it was made of lead, her bag as if it were filled with bricks. She'd remembered right about the alley, though—a passage between two warehouses. She didn't slow as she turned. Her boots splashed through puddles, spattering her hems with she dared not guess what. Up ahead she could see fading daylight and hear the sound of the marketplace sellers ending their day. Just a few more steps…

It was this last thought that pulled her, chest heaving, feet cramping through to the end of the tunnel—and straight into an unsuspecting pedestrian. She had enough time to register a neat moustache and spectacles, a tidy brown overcoat, and an impeccably tied scarf, when his arms closed unexpectedly around her. She screamed.

"For God's sake, Abby!" the man cried.

"Oh, Gideon!" She threw her arms around her fiancé's neck. Breathing hard, she twisted to look back, but the alley was empty, with no sign of her pursuers.

"Are you all right, Nurse?" Gideon asked, suddenly stepping back. Dr. Gideon Spencer was a man of diligent propriety—for which Abby was grateful. Once they'd married, she would, of course, render unto Caesar. But she was in no hurry to hasten that day.

"Yes, Dr. Spencer." She tugged her coat straight and gave him a shaky smile.

He frowned. "Are you sure?" Concern marred his copper-colored face, and she could swear she saw a few more greys in his moustache and at his temples than she had noticed the day before.

She stole another glance over her shoulder. The contrast between the lonely, vicious stretch of warehouses and the security of the crowded market was so profound, for a moment she wondered if she hadn't imagined the entire incident. The urge to flee drained away, leaving her limbs light and shaky, while a different thought filled her mind. Having been menaced by a gang of boys had been one thing, but the mechanism of her escape was bothering her now—the look on the one boy's face as he'd suddenly flown back, like a puppet pulled roughly by its strings....

"Just a...a wee spot of bother...back near the embankment," she said, drawing a steadying breath. "But it's all over now."

Gideon's expression told her that the discussion was far from finished in his mind. Nonetheless, he offered her his elbow. She gratefully took it, and they began to walk back through the street crowded with stalls, last-minute shoppers, and merchants packing up for the night.

"What are you doing here?" Abby asked. "Were you following me?"

"Certainly not. I was in the area anyway. I needed..." He looked around until his gaze fell on the stall they were passing.

"Ladies' French stockings?" she asked doubtfully.

A pink tinge crept across his dark face. He cleared his throat, straightened his already-straight scarf, and muttered something about Christmas. "Well," he said, changing the subject. "Do you have it, then, after all that?"

"It's right here," she said, patting the Gladstone.

"Good." He kept his gaze straight ahead, his expression neutral, though a tightness in his jawline betrayed his annoyance.

Abby knew that he hated needing the medicine. He *really* hated that he needed her to fetch it for him. It wasn't just the danger to her that bothered him, though that was bad enough. She suspected that most of all he hated the weakness that made her involvement necessary on any level, for it reduced him, the founder of the Cornwall Street Clinic, to the role of patient.

"You know," he said. "I could go myself."

"I'm sure you could," she said automatically. It had become their little ritual.

"But you don't trust me."

"Murderess!" a voice cried. They both stopped and turned. A boy holding a stack of newspapers under one arm held one out for their inspection. "Escaped murderess is still on the loose! Get the full story, only tuppence!"

Gideon reached into his pocket and produced a coin. "Keep the paper, and buy yourself something warm to eat."

"Thank you, sir!" The boy tipped his cap, pocketed the money, and melted back into the crowd.

"That was kind," Abby said.

"Two pence to me, supper to him," Gideon said. Sadness flickered over his face. "I imagine he has to mind what he eats with that rotten molar."

Abby didn't ask how he could tell. As close as they were, they were both entitled to a few secrets.

"I do trust you," she said. "But would you trust me to run the clinic myself for an entire afternoon?" She pulled closer to emphasize that she was joking.

"You could manage."

"But could you? That is, could you trust someone else to run things properly in your absence?"

She stared at the side of his head until he met her eyes. Recognizing her usual gentle teasing, he let out a small, self-deprecating laugh. Then his expression turned serious again.

"That didn't work out so well last time, did it? Not that it was your fault," he added quickly.

She shrugged. "A sudden rush of urgent patients? We've seen worse."

"With inexplicable injuries," he said. "And the same story of a monstrous attacker in the gloom."

"A collective delusion." Abby patted his arm through his brown woollen overcoat.

"Nonetheless." He sighed. "You're right, I suppose. That clinic is my albatross. I'm bound to it, and it to me, for better or worse."

"In sickness and in health?" she asked.

His lips tightened wryly, though she saw that despite his overcoat he'd begun to tremble. He'd gone without his medicine for too long. His eyes met hers over their locked arms, and, ruefully, he untangled himself from her, flexed his fingers a few times, and jammed his hands into his pockets.

"Well then," he said. "That's settled. We should get back to the clinic." He touched a finger to the bridge of his nose to adjust spectacles that did not need adjusting. Then he frowned and cocked his head. "I've a strange premonition we'll be busy tonight."

"Which leads me to ask, again," she said, "What *are* you doing down here, away from the clinic? And don't give me any nonsense about stockings."

He shrugged, a real smile tugging at the edges of his lips for the first time that afternoon. "I had another premonition you might need me."

❖

Gideon

The premonitions were the other side of Gideon's affliction, as was his ability to diagnose his patients with a sniff and a glance. Balancing the gifts with the monster was difficult and tedious, and had almost killed him once. That had been the year Abby had come to London to study at the Florence Nightingale School. She'd found him in a corner of his bedsit, trussed up—at his own request—and incoherent from a self-prescribed cocktail of ill-advised substances. She'd vowed never to allow him to come to such a state again.

She was right. At the same time, precisely controlled, the monster did make him an outstanding physician. A few patients had joked that his diagnostic abilities must be supernatural; others had whispered as much in earnest. If only they knew.

The clinic on Cornwall Street wasn't far, so he and Abby walked back together to save the fare. Amid the bustle of packing-up merchants and last-minute shoppers, the clicks and clatter of closing-up shops, no one paid attention to an East Indian man and an Englishwoman walking arm in arm. Perhaps they would have, if Gideon hadn't personally set their bones, treated their infants' croup, or stitched them up after a round of fisticuffs in the small hours.

People made allowances when you were useful.

The Cornwall Street Clinic was a shabby, unassuming storefront in a row of similar storefronts. Curtains across the bottom half of the front window gave the illusion of privacy, while a plaque near the front door indicated their purpose. The clinic comprised a front room with benches, a stove, a triage desk, and a folding screen in the corner for more personal examinations. A small back closet held bandages and linens. The dispensary was slightly larger, with locking, glass-fronted cabinets of medicines and a door that opened onto the alley behind the building. There was a window as well, but after the last break-in, Gideon had boarded it over.

As they approached, Gideon stopped.

"What is it?" Abby asked, instantly beside him.

Evening had well and truly fallen, and beyond the flickering streetlamp, Cornwall Street disappeared into its black, gaping maw. Out of the darkness, fog crept along the cobblestones, silent and stealthy, its fingers testing the cracks in the walls, the chipped mortar between the bricks.

A crawling sensation rippled up Gideon's forearms, standing the dark hair on end. A feeling of hot pins and needles danced on his fingertips.

"It was…" He cleared his throat and started again. "It was like this last time," he managed to say.

She glanced toward him, eyes narrowing at the sudden thickness in his voice. He gestured toward the fog. She nodded, nostrils flaring as if in response to the threat in the air. Could she smell it like he could?

A London particular had a very specific scent. The usual city smells of sewage, rotting food, unwashed bodies, machine oil, and the murky, unfathomable Thames shrank to insignificance beneath the sulphurous reek of the fog. It came from burning coal, he knew. Home fires and factories belched coal dust into the air, where the right combination of a stale, still atmosphere, moisture, and temperature turned the resultant sulphur dioxide into sulphuric acid. This, in turn, burned the eyes, throat, and lungs, and left its acid touch on buildings, windows, and edifices. It shortened lives and even changed the way people spoke. It had taken Gideon a long time to accustom himself to the breathy London accent, as if the city's denizens were using speech as a means of expelling the poisons from their lungs. Now, though, he understood. Now even he spoke like that when he'd spent too much time out of doors.

He shivered despite his heavy overcoat and scarf. With a worried backward glance, Abby unlocked the clinic door and motioned for him to enter. Manners prevented him from accepting the courtesy, and he gestured her through, stopping to pick up an envelope from the floor.

"What's that?" Abby asked, setting her Gladstone down on the desk.

"Afternoon post." He turned it over, squinted at the logo on the envelope. The glyph blurred. He removed his glasses and tucked them into the breast pocket of his jacket. "From the Association of Poor Clinics?" At least that's what it looked like through his changing vision.

The Association had sent an inspector round recently. The man had tried very hard to find something to criticize but, in the end, had grudgingly surrendered a report of "satisfactory."

"What do they have to say for themselves?" Abby asked.

Gideon set the envelope down on the table and rubbed his eyes. The smells of the clinic were sharpening, as well, and his head was starting to throb. "I can't think about that right now."

"I'll have a look. You take this." She handed him a rag-wrapped lump. As his fingers closed around it, the crawling beneath his skin began to recede. He sighed with relief.

"Give me ten minutes."

"Take all the time you need. We have no patients, and this place could use a good tidy-up. What?" she asked.

Slipping the phial into his coat pocket, he took her hand and raised it to his lips. Her skin was warm, with the comforting smell of the familiar. Beneath it, her blood coursed calmly and evenly. From almost any other man, the gesture might have been provocative, presumptuous, or even lewd. But her expression told him she understood the gesture as he meant it: a deep and chaste show of appreciation.

Too chaste for someone who would soon share his name and his bed? He pushed the thought away. As a physician, he understood the mechanics of marital intimacy, though he had a difficult time imagining it, no less conjuring enthusiasm for the idea. Still, they had an understanding. How much, Gideon wondered, did one owe to an understanding? Abby cared deeply for him, and he for her, it was true. But what kind of husband would he actually make in the end?

A gentle, warm pressure on his fingers brought him back to the present. Abby was still holding his hand. His palm had gone moist. Slipping out of her grasp, he discreetly wiped his fingers on his trousers. The clinic would absolutely fail without Abby. And probably, so would he. Yet...

"You're too good for me," he said in response to her questioning look.

She paused for a moment, skewering him with those ice-blue eyes. Then she smiled. "Yes, I am."

She turned, and he ran for the back room with his phial.

They rarely cut things so close. The last time had been the day of the inspection. Gideon had managed to hold himself together throughout the process, but by the time the inspector had left, Gideon's voice had grown too deep and rough to even qualify as human. He'd run straight home to barricade himself in his flat.

And then the patients had come. The cases had been both urgent and strange, and Abby had been alone.

He heard a scratching sound, like someone pulling a wire brush across the wall outside. Normally he might not have noticed it at all, but with the creature's enhanced hearing, the sound drove a chill down his spine and made the fine hairs along the back of his neck stand on end. He peered at the planks covering the window, but the sound didn't come again. Shaking his head, he let out a long breath.

Clutching the phial tightly in one hand, Gideon unwrapped the rags from around it and set them aside. The liquid inside was the color of dark algae. As his skin warmed the glass, the color grew lighter, pulsing, until it glowed a brilliant green.

Outside, a wind swept through the alley—first a whistle, then a violent howl that shook the boards and rattled the window frame. And then it went still—a sudden, resounding absence of sound. Gideon's hands gave a violent shake, and the phial flew from his grasp, shattering against the wall.

"Damn and blast!" he cried. The precious liquid ran down the wall, chartreuse turning dull, then muddy against the faded paint.

He glanced back toward the examination room. If Abby found out, she'd be out the door and back in Whitechapel before the fog had even cleared. The room throbbed in time with his pounding head. Again the familiar ache as the bones of his forearms tried to stretch, the dreadful tingling on his fingertips as the demon attempted to claw its way out. Drawing a shuddering breath, Gideon reached for a rag and dabbed at the wall with trembling fingers. Then he carefully gathered the glass and set it, together with the rag, in the bin.

Shaking, he lowered himself onto the stool and took several long, deliberate breaths, noting the wooden stool beneath him, the shelves of carefully sourced and organized medicines, his case notes and Abby's standing reference-ready. He could get through the night. Just one night. He'd done it before. Yes. All he had to do was take himself in hand and push himself through the long moments, one by one.

"Gideon?" Abby's voice shattered the tenuous calm. He began to respond, but his voice was a guttural snarl.

With a rueful glance toward the door, he threw open the back exit and ran out into the fog.

CHAPTER THREE

Eli

"Serves you right, attacking a lady," Eli said. The sun had well and truly gone, the smell of fog was on the air, and they'd really have to scramble to find somewhere to sit out the worst of it.

"She weren't no lady," Garrick snarled. He glanced at the palm of his hand, which had gotten a nasty scratch when he'd gone ass over teakettle across the cobblestones. The Booth lady had scarpered after that, and well she should have, though they'd all been too flummoxed to chase her just then.

"A woman, then. Nothing good's going to come from that."

Garrick said, "Something good would've come out of that bag if we'd got it off her."

"But we didn't, did we? I'm telling you, we should stick to wallets and watches."

A shadow passed over Garrick's face, and he met Eli's eyes. His expression suggested he knew Eli was right but wasn't about to admit it in front of the others.

They'd all seen it happen, how the Booth lady had thrown Garrick halfway to the other side of the street just by looking at him. It had shaken them all, from big, tough Bert, to Garrick with his sharp knife and fierce expression, to scrappy little Clyde who was holding himself together surprisingly well, all things considered. Eli saw it in their faces, even if they were still too scared to talk about it. Their staring contest continued for two seconds more, and then Garrick spat and wiped his hand on his trousers.

"Shut up and keep walking."

Eli did shut up. The boys always did what Garrick said. Garrick's quick thinking and sharp tongue had made him the leader, and for the most part that worked fine. But Garrick wasn't perfect, and this time he'd stepped in it. Eli had never held with attacking women, and you never knew when one of them charity types might be able to help you. Better off lifting wallets from drunks or slumming toffs who thought their dosh and connections meant something on these streets.

There was also the feeling that this business with the Booth lady wasn't over. Eli didn't know quite what that meant, exactly, but he felt in his bones that it was true. Garrick kept saying she'd kicked him, saying it over and over like a person did when he wanted to convince himself but wasn't quite there yet. But they'd all seen Garrick fly back like an invisible hand had slapped him, and as far as Eli was concerned, that hand had been the hand of God himself.

Eli glanced at Clyde, who guiltily swallowed whatever had been in his mouth. Through the side of Clyde's thin coat, Eli could make out a lump. Half a bread loaf? They were supposed to share any food they found. Eli was hungry. They all were. He considered ratting Clyde out to the boys, but everyone was on edge, and Clyde was so much smaller. Eli didn't hold with three-on-one beatings either.

The fog was coming in properly, now. They were wading through it, thigh-deep, its rotten-egg smell burning Eli's nose and making his eyes water. They'd left the Old Stairs right quick after the Booth lady'd run off and Garrick had picked himself up. Bert had suggested wandering north to find a drunk to roll on the way back to the corner under the tenement stairs where they usually slept. It had seemed like a good idea at the time, but it had got dark quick, and now there was the fog. More than anything Eli just wanted to find somewhere to sit still and out of the way until morning.

"Fog's rising," Clyde said.

Bert snorted. "Yeah. It must be up to your neck by now." It was, in fact, near the waistband of Clyde's trousers and would soon be that high on Eli, as tall as he was.

"If it gets any higher, you'll have to carry me," Clyde shot back.

"Not if the Hanwell Murderess gets you first."

Eli shivered. You couldn't throw a rock in some parts of town without hitting a murderer. But there was something even worse about a woman murderer. And even worse than that, an escaped lunatic woman murderer.

"Leave him alone," Eli told Bert.

Clyde had to be around thirteen, Eli reckoned, but he was still as puny as a girl, and his voice showed no sign of dropping. Eli hoped the situation would right itself. He and the boys kept Clyde out of mischief, and Clyde's nimble fingers were always finding something they could sell, but life was uncertain, and there was no guarantee that they would always be there to look out for each other.

"Where are we, anyway?" Eli asked. They'd got turned around at some point, and Eli reckoned they were wandering east. He hoped Garrick knew where they were going, because if they wandered over the eastern border of their territory, the gang who controlled the streets on the other side wouldn't take fog as an excuse for their trespass. And then there was the Thing.

"Sure stinks tonight," Clyde said.

"It always stinks," Garrick said.

"Not like..." Eli put a hand on Clyde's shoulder, and the younger boy's voice trailed off.

They had turned into an alley—and a bank of fog that went up as high as anyone could see. They turned back, but the fog was all around them now, swirling and so thick Eli couldn't see his own feet. Clyde's little hand grasped his, and Eli instinctively closed his fingers around it.

It was quiet, thickly quiet like a pillow over the face. The kind of quiet that's tense with waiting.

Something rattled over the cobblestones. Clyde's fingers tightened around Eli's. Bert let out a noise halfway between a gasp and a squeal.

"Idiot." Garrick sneered from somewhere nearby. "It's just a rat."

"It's not a rat," Bert said.

Whatever it was rattled across the stones again. Eli's pulse began to race. He heard another noise, soft and low, like a moan.

"It's the wind," Garrick said, but he didn't sound convinced. All the same Eli did feel wind. It came in from below, near their feet. He could hear it picking up dust and rocks, feel the debris hitting his legs through his trousers. That low moan came again, raising a shiver up Eli's back.

"*That* ain't the wind," said Bert, and nobody corrected him.

Instinctively, the boys pulled together in a group, standing back-to-back. Eli had taught them that after he'd heard it in a Bible story. His name came from the Bible, the woman telling the stories had said. A priest in the house of the Lord. Eli didn't know nothing about that, but he liked those old stories, and he liked that his name was in such an important book. He also liked the other stories she'd told him, after the other boys had grown tired of lessons and slowly drifted away. Stories of monsters and heroic rabbis and—

A wet, slapping sound jerked Eli from his thoughts. It was like someone smacking wet clothes against the cobblestones, or like heavy, wet footsteps slopping over the pavement toward them. The wind was swirling around them, pelting his face and hands with little bits of dirt and rock. Everything smelled like rotting fish. He closed his eyes and pulled his shirt over his nose. Clyde's hand pulled away from his. Eli reached for it again, but Clyde was gone. They were all gone, and Eli was stumbling around blindly, waving his arms, trying to find them in the swirling, howling wind and the flying dirt and muck.

A terrible animal sound tore through the wind, and Eli did force his eyes open a crack as his back hit a wall. Two green eyes glowed through the swirling, raging gloom, and above them, strange characters written in green fire. He shut his eyes tight.

Where were the others? He heard footsteps and muffled cries, but every time Eli opened his eyes, all he saw was the fog. He wrapped his arms around his head and crouched against the wall, hoping it would all be over soon.

"Eli! Eli!" Clyde was calling him. He opened his eyes, and the wind was gone, the movement was gone, and the fog was receding. "Eli, come quick!"

On the other side of the alley, Bert was squatting next to Garrick. Garrick was making horrible noises, and his face was swollen up like a rotting tomato.

"He can't breathe!" Clyde cried.

"What happened?" Eli asked, springing to his feet.

Clyde started to babble some sort of nonsense. Eli cut him off. "Never mind. Tell me later. Get him on your back," Eli said to Bert. "I'm pretty sure there's a clinic around here. We'll get help."

CHAPTER FOUR

Abby

The back door slammed.

"Gideon?" Abby called. Tucking her dust rag into the pocket of her apron, she hurried toward the dispensary.

The little room was empty. The lamp still burned in its corner, and the swirling dust hinted at recent and hasty movement. A sharp, chemical tang hung in the air. She recognized it, felt the pins and needles on her tongue. Gideon's medicine tasted vile, and the sensation had made her shiver, but she'd put a bit on her tongue every time, to make certain she'd received the same formula.

His spectacles sat on the shelf next to their reference books. The waste bin lay on its side. She tipped it up and glanced inside. Broken glass peppered with muddy green droplets.

Whatever had happened, he'd cleaned up the mess the best he could before fleeing. She wished he'd told her, allowed her to help him figure out what to do. But fled he had, and she could not pursue him until the fog lifted. How far would he get between now and then? Even after the air had cleared, where should she even begin?

The back door shuddered against its hinges.

Abby froze and listened but heard nothing more. She hoped it was the wind. Though if there'd been any wind at all, the fog wouldn't have been able to bank up like it had outside the front window. She glanced at the lock. They'd replaced it after the last break-in, and it was solid. Still, Abby couldn't help but wonder how well it would hold up if the burglars came back with more determination or better tools. Her curiosity returning, she drew back the bolt, cracked the door open, and peeked out.

A foul, fishy-smelling fog had settled over the alley, as well. It burned her eyes, her throat. Something rattled along the cobblestones not far away. She darted back inside and slammed the door, gasping as whatever it was brushed up against the boards covering the window as it passed. Dear God, Gideon was out there in that. Either that or…She'd never seen Gideon's feral state, though she'd come close a few times. It was a level of intimacy they'd not yet reached, and he guarded that part of himself like many women guarded their chastity.

Pounding at the front door scattered her thoughts.

"We need help out here!"

Abby ran back to the front room and threw open the door. Four young men stood on the doorstep. Her heart stopped. As recognition dawned, she felt their hands in her pockets, heard their jeers, and saw the glint of the knife in the day's dying light. But the one with the knife was slumped between two of the others, his eyes wide, face turning dark as he struggled for breath.

She yelped as the door suddenly slammed itself shut between them.

"The Fiend, miss! It's right behind us!"

Fiend?

The thing in the alley. The rattling lock.

Briefly she considered throwing the bolt and leaving them to the night. Then her training prevailed. She fumbled with the doorknob, but the blasted thing was stuck fast.

"Push!" she cried.

She twisted the doorknob and pulled with all her might, as the young men pushed and kicked. Finally the door gave way, and she staggered backward as they stumbled inside.

"Put him down there," she said, pointing toward the folding cot near the back wall.

As she secured the door again, she wondered, too late, if it was a trick. Had they followed her here? Had they come to finish what they'd started by the river?

The one was making a horrible gulping sound as he clutched at his stained kerchief, his lips a silent scream around a dark mass that filled his mouth and pushed out his cheeks. Whether they'd followed her or not, this was no trick. He needed help.

"What happened?" she demanded as she knelt beside the cot.

With no time to be precious, she pushed two fingers into his mouth and scooped. Black, filthy clots of matter fell onto his threadbare coat, the cot, the floor. Whatever it was, it reeked of rancid fish. It was strangely granular, as well, like fine sand. At last the youth coughed out a walnut-sized lump and heaved in a great breath. Sighing relief, Abby wiped her fingers on her apron and rose.

"Well?" she asked.

The young men stared for a moment, then all started to speak at once, their words tumbling over each other as they described swirling clouds of dirt and sand, glowing green eyes in the fog, a man-shaped attacker that wasn't a man.

Her breath caught at the repetition of the word "fiend"—she'd heard it before—the last time Gideon had disappeared and she'd been left to tend to a different group with strange and inexplicable injuries. She shook her head. An accident most likely, or even a dare gone wrong, mixed with a heavy dose of superstition. Abby held up a hand and they fell silent.

"I want the truth," she said, as their leader wheezed out painful breaths. "One at a time."

The youths glanced at one another. After an exchange of looks, nods, and frowns, one of them, a beanpole of a fellow whom Abby remembered had been eyeing her hat pin, cleared his throat.

"We was down by the Old Stairs, see, by the wall," he said. He scratched at the greasy, dark curls that stuck out at all angles from beneath a woollen cap. His gaze traveled over her face, and she watched recognition light in his eyes.

"Miss...." He said, his eyes going wide. "I...we...We was just makin' conversation, like. We...we didn't know you was a nurse and all."

She said, "If you had, you'd probably have slit my throat and rifled through my bag for medicines."

"We never would, miss! We was just havin' a bit of fun!"

"Like the fun a pack of wolves has with a sheep?"

"A sheep don't kick like you do," croaked the young man on the cot.

The words had cost him; they would continue to for several days while his throat healed. Good, Abby thought. Then, *kicked?* Is that what he thought had happened? They probably thought she'd slammed the door in their faces as well. She chose not to disabuse them, though she would definitely give the matter some thought when she had a free moment.

"What's your name?" she asked.

"That's Garrick, miss," the curly-haired youth said. "And that's Bert." He indicated a broad-chested young man with an upturned nose that might have been cute when he was younger, but which now gave him a pugnacious appearance. "That there's Clyde." He nodded toward the youngest member of the group, a slip of a lad with fair hair and pinched features that hadn't lost the androgynous cast of childhood. "And I'm Eli."

She looked the motley bunch up and down, her gaze finally returning to rest on Eli. Interesting. He was as filthy as one might expect from an urchin, but not more so—not like the others. And he wasn't scratched or bruised like the others, either.

"So, Eli," she said. "You were harassing passers-by for fun, and your mate received a well-deserved kicking for his trouble. Then what happened?"

"Then the fog came. You saw it, miss, right? We had to go through it to get here."

"All the way back there? By the embankment?" Abby asked. It must have been a vast fog. How far had it stretched?

"And up the Old Stairs, too, at the same time," Clyde added in a high-pitched, preadolescent voice.

"And there were shadows," said Bert.

There was a horrible sound like a sick cat evacuating its stomach. Garrick spat another clump of filth into his hand, glanced at it warily, then wiped it onto his mud-caked trousers. When he spoke, his words sounded like they'd been scraped from between the cobblestones. "Wind."

"Oh yeah," Eli said. "The wind was howling, really howling. I ain't never heard it like that before. There was sand in the air. And a big, swirling cloud."

"Wind?" Abby asked, for everyone knew the fogs were caused by still, stagnant air.

"And then there was the Thing," Clyde said.

"Fiend." Bert corrected him.

Abby looked from him to Eli, who appeared to be taking the role of leader during his mate's indisposition. She scrutinized them for any sign of lying: a furtive glance at the floor or ceiling or one another, fingers worrying at the edge of a coat, but the young men simply stared back at her, as if hoping, she thought, that she might believe them.

"I've heard that word before," she said.

Some weeks earlier, after Gideon had gone missing, another ragged group had taken shelter in the clinic during a fog: a young woman—Nell Evans—and her two…accomplices, Abby had surmised, though she hadn't had the time to ponder the question further. Evans, like Garrick, had been the focus of the incident, though unlike Garrick, she hadn't stumbled in with a mouth full of dirt. It had been her right hand—her fingers, mangled, twisted, and crushed. Abby had splinted the fingers, braced the hand, washed and disinfected what she could. Still, she doubted Miss Evans would ever regain full function of her hand again. Like Evans, one of the accomplices had been covered in scratches and dirt. Like Eli, the other had not.

"Tell me more," she said.

Outside, something brushed against the window—a sound like fingernails dragging across the glass. The youths fell silent as it passed, and for a moment, it seemed the only sound inside the clinic was the rapid beating of her own heart.

"What the devil was that?" Bert said.

Abby shook her head. Whatever it was, it had been in the alley before, when she was in the back room. Now it was passing by the front of the clinic. What did it want? The thought that it wasn't trying to force its way inside wasn't nearly as comforting as it should have been.

"I'm sure it's nothing," Abby said. The lie trembled in her voice. "Right. So, now that your friend isn't in any imminent danger, the wise person would send you on your way, I suppose."

Quiet fell over the little group. Turning them out was the sensible thing to do. Garrick would have a sore throat for a few days. His belly might suffer if any of that filth had gone down. A small price to pay for avoiding whatever trouble they might think to visit upon her, or the clinic, now that the immediate danger had passed. But they weren't looking so dangerous now. And the little one, Clyde, was it? He looked close to tears.

"Well," she said a bit more gently. "I suppose I shouldn't send even you lot out into that. So, you," she said to Bert. "Draw the curtains and lay the bolster down across the door crack." She turned to Clyde. "You can put an extra piece of coal on the fire and lay some of those blankets on the floor in front of it. And you, Eli," she said, regarding the curly-haired youth with a stern eye. "After you settle your friend Garrick in his bed, you can come here and tell me why it is you think the Fiend left its mark on your friends but doesn't seem to have touched you at all."

CHAPTER FIVE

Nat

The magnificent Jin Wylie stood a little under six feet tall. Jin was broad-shouldered, with a narrow waist that Nathaniel knew from intimate experience did not need the corset that defined it so dramatically beneath his bespoke white silk shirt. Over the shirt, Jin wore a body-hugging long suit coat and tight trousers tucked into a pair of high black boots that laced from toe to knee. The coat had once been a man's cut, though someone had altered it to appear subtly otherwise. The boots, on the other hand, with their pointed toes and raised heels, had been handcrafted by a world-famous maker of breathtakingly expensive women's footwear favored by certain friends of Nathaniel's sister.

Strictly based on anatomy, Nat supposed Jin was a man. But there was so much more to these things than anatomy. Every time they met, Nat discovered a new facet to his companion, and each facet combined with the others into a delicious puzzle of contradiction and ambiguity. This ambiguity, more than anything else, kept a flame burning in the back of Nat's mind and the depths of his groin, that would have winked out after one or two tumbles in the sheets, no matter how skilled a lover Jin might have been. Parts and definitions and categories were of decidedly less interest than an enigma. And Nat had met no more delicious enigma than Jin.

Just how much older he was than Nat was impossible to tell. His long, heavy black hair had a sprinkling of silver, and his nose, which, framed by high, hollow cheekbones, would have been *perfect,* had been broken more than once, and quite long ago. He must have taken quite a bit of time over those eyebrows, Nat thought. Definitely the conceit of a younger man. And his cologne— bergamot and jasmine—was the scent of someone who had already made his way in the world.

"When will I see you again?" Nat asked, his hands playing with that thick, smooth spill of hair.

"Soon, I promise."

"But *when?*"

Jin's mouth tightened against a smile, and he gently tugged Nat's collar into place. Only then, in the dim light of the lamp on the table behind them, did Nat see what appeared to be *wrinkles* around Jin's dark eyes.

"Is everything all right?" Nat asked, tracing one of the wrinkles with a fingertip. Jin jerked his head away, and Nat suddenly remembered that they didn't actually know one another all that well. "Sorry," he said.

"Just a bit tired. I've been working a lot, recently."

"What do you do?" Nat asked, smoothing down Jin's cravat. "I've been meaning to ask."

Jin's delicate hand closed around his and moved it away, a gentle reinforcement of the deliberate distance they'd agreed to maintain.

"It would bore you to death, my dear. I couldn't have that on my conscience."

Nat narrowed his eyes. As if by way of compensation, Jin pressed a little peck against his lips. "I'll be in touch," he said.

"I'll be waiting."

Nat watched Jin's silk-wrapped form rustle up the stairs toward the street. A carpet of fog had silently unrolled itself along the streets while they had been playing, notes of sulphur dancing on the still evening air. The fog was knee-deep and rising, unfurling exploratory tendrils upward. Nat shivered.

"It's dreadful out there," Nat called. "Are you sure—"

At the top of the stairs, Jin turned, lips tightening in a smirk. "You worry too much." Then, as quick as a cat, he was gone. Nat watched as the fog swallowed him up—corset, top hat, silks and all—until nothing was left but the clack of those wooden heels along the pavement. Shutting the door, Nathaniel turned around and sank back against it.

The spark that had animated his laboratory was gone, snuffed out, vanished into the fog. Now all that remained were the remains of an afternoon squandered in unsuccessful experiments—that, and an unholy mess.

At least he had the makings of an acceptable sandwich in the kitchen upstairs.

He crossed the room, then paused at the bottom of the servants' stairs, turning to survey the wreckage of his lab. He'd begun the takeover of the downstairs kitchen years before—a few books on Mrs. Finch's table, then a flask or two on the counter, always removed before they proved a danger to food preparation. Still, he continued to transfer his equipment from his study into the old kitchen until eventually Mrs. Finch relocated her operations upstairs.

Mrs. Finch indulged him. Even Nat knew it was true. He was absolutely spoiled—not just by the housekeeper, but by his parents, who had taken it unreasonably well when he'd been expelled from university for reasons he still didn't quite understand. Wasn't higher education meant to foster thought? Experimentation? Exploration? Shouldn't a genius be free from the straitjacket of common morality and everyday expectations?

In retrospect, he supposed he might have made more of an effort. Attended classes, revised for exams. *Sat* for exams. Yawn. Still, it wasn't his fault that those fools refused to make allowances for genius. His parents, at least, made allowances—possibly too many, even by his own admission. Things might have turned out differently if they'd held his nose to the grindstone. On the other hand, wasn't his sister the busiest little bee, even without the interfering hand of parental guidance? No, it all came down to nature. He was willing to allow that *some* of his troubles were of his own making. By and large, though, it was to be expected, considering the raw material he had to work with.

And speaking of materials…

He looked upon his lab and despaired. It were as if a library had exploded and taken a chemist's back room with it. It always seemed to happen when his research had hit a dead end. Did the chaos cause the work to stall? Or was it only when his feverish rush of ideas stuttered to a halt that he noticed the degree to which his carefully laid notes and plans had descended into anarchy? He'd hoped that a good romp would clear the old head, but once Jin had left, all pretense of order had left as well, and now his mind was a morass of second thoughts and self-recrimination.

It was definitely time to tidy up. No, scratch that. It was time for a proper cleaning.

Just not yet. That sandwich was calling, and possibly the lamb chop Mrs. Finch had said she'd set aside for him. Yes, that would settle things nicely.

Turning off the lamp, which, from its perch atop a stack of dusty volumes on botany, electromagnetism, and Kabbalah, presided over a pile of scribbled notes and diagrams—*scintillam vitae*—how preposterously flamboyant—he shut the door on the remains of his ambition.

And he opened, halfheartedly, the spring-loaded door to his secret lift. Adapting the dumb waiter had been a summer project when he was sixteen. He hadn't used it since the novelty had worn off, but that night it seemed fitting.

What would the servants think, he wondered, as he folded himself into the little box and leveraged himself up with its series of ropes and pulleys. Rather what would they have thought, had more than one or two remained?

Eisenstadt House had *had* a proper complement of servants once, not just Mrs. Finch to cook and the current rotation of pale, pinched-faced girls who came in to clean every now and then. What was the current one called? Cleo? Cleta? Cleta the Cleaning Girl. No, that wasn't it. The point was that there had been proper servants, once, before his parents had started selling off everything they owned to fund their round-the-world, monster-chasing jaunts. They were in Romania at present. Such a cliché. Ah, well. Quixotic quests and enthusiasms were in the blood, it seemed. He just wished they paid better.

The thing about science, though, was that when it paid, it *really* paid. It was galling how much money some of these charlatans at the Academy of Occult Sciences were already raking in from their fraudulent ghost-detecting machinery and poorly written monographs stuffed with huge words but bereft of actual content. He might have taken a more charitable view of their creative approach to science, had they deigned to admit him to their number. Anti-Semites. He would show them all. *Scintillam vitae*!

His stomach growled, reminding him of his promise to it, now several hours gone.

Right. A sandwich. Fresh bread, he promised the organ. Fresh bread, passable meat, and perhaps a glass of claret to wash it all down.

At last he reached the ground floor of Eisenstadt House. He secured the lift, popped the panel, and unfurled his long legs into the hallway.

It was a shame that to reach his feast, Nat would have to tiptoe past the room where his sister Meg was entertaining the basilisks she called friends. It was some sort of political group, ostensibly. Socialistic do-gooders. Bored young women with too much money and too little to do, who wanted to impress people. Dreadful—and misguided, too. That bunch couldn't bring about a picnic, no less generalized social justice. But tilting at windmills appeared to be a genetic predilection.

The parlor door was firmly shut, but as Nat passed, a shriek split the air. What the devil was going on in there? Cries and shouts, and…oh, dear. Something crashed to the ground. Could it be that the scheduled discussion of working conditions for farm animals had taken a violent turn? He knocked on the door.

The room immediately fell silent.

"Hello in there," Nat called. "Are you ladies quite all right? No one needs a blast of smelling salts or anything? A terminal case of the vapors, what?"

He opened the door to an appalling sight. They were all there, the Flowers of Chelsea. Or, rather, of Chelsea-adjacent. Lily, Daisy, Iris, Rose, Bernadette, and, of course, his sister Meg. Not one of their homes actually lay within the district's blooming boundaries, no matter how much each of them might have secretly desired it, but a girl could pretend, he supposed.

They were all dressed in men's pajamas.

"Well," he said, as six sets of eyes bored into him. "Well. Sorry to interrupt your…fancy-dress party, is it?"

"What it is," said Bernadette in a tone that would make the harshest headmistress's blood run cold, "is a demonstration of the Eastern fighting arts."

Nat blinked. The most vigorous activity in which he'd ever witnessed his sister participate had been a brisk walk while holding a sign supporting voting rights for chipmunks or some such. It was quite a departure from music lessons and slapping out a still life from time to time.

"Well, please, continue, then," he said with a magnanimous gesture.

Bernadette Kingsley—oh, that had been a mistake—regarded him coldly. Everything about her was cold, in fact, from the icy grey of her eyes to the snowy color of her curls, to the gaslight glint off the metal frames of her spectacles. She hadn't always been cold. In fact, he recalled one rather delightful night a month or so ago when her blood had run hot. His had, as well, and it had been quite a lot of fun. But fun, it turned out, was the very least of what she had expected.

"Come now, love. Loves," he said, expanding his gaze to include them all. "Give us a show."

"Women do not exist for your entertainment, *Mr. Eisenstadt,*" Bernadette said.

The other ladies were exchanging glances and murmurs, and Nat was beginning to feel like the guest of honor at a cannibal picnic.

His sister was twirling a fierce-looking hat pin, looking much like the chief cannibal herself.

Bernadette drew herself up to her full, barefoot height. "In fact, we have lives of our own, if you can imagine it. Interests beyond hair and dresses and dancing. Some of us even conduct scientific research, as you well know."

He did know. But how? Ah, yes. Snatches of conversation from that jolly, boozy, ill-fated night. He had, actually, listened for a bit. Some grand, unifying cosmic theory about nature and animals and the interconnectivity of something she called Spirit. And then more interesting things had…come up.

When he refocused, she was still talking.

"The problem is, *Nathaniel*," she said, uttering his name as if it were a curse, "that we're not separate from nature. I've proved it, you see. Everything and everyone is equal in the grand scheme of things. We all have a place and a purpose. Even you, I suppose."

"Yes, well, that's…delightful? But enough about that. Who is going to play us a song?" He glanced meaningfully at the piano sitting, silent and lonely, in one corner. To Nat's utter surprise, no one rushed to take her place at the bench.

"Go to hell, Nat," Bernadette said. The passion had drained from her voice, and she was the snow queen once more.

"Now, that's really—" he said.

"To hell." She actually sounded a bit sad. Nat was confused. "Forgive me, Meg," she said to his sister. "It was a long day, and I suddenly feel nauseous."

He watched Bernadette slip on her shoes, not bothering to tie them. Then she swept her coat off the coat rack near the front door and jammed her arms into the sleeves. "Wait," he called in a moment of inspiration. "You forgot your—"

The slam of the door cut off his words. Feeling the tiniest pang of—dear God, was that *conscience*?—he carefully laid her silk scarf back over a coat hook.

"Now look what you've done." Meg fumed, steaming past him on her way to intercept her friend.

"Don't forget your coat," Nat called helpfully. "The fog is really quite grim tonight." He turned back to his audience. The remaining Flowers of Chelsea Adjacent were blinking at him as if expecting that *he* would now entertain them. "So, ladies," he said, "about that song."

He was unsurprised when the parlor door slammed in his face.

With a sigh, Nat made his way to the kitchen, where he found that the seeded loaf that Mrs. Finch had brought yesterday was gone. What bread remained was the heel of an ancient baguette, which had been destined to become crumbs to coat the lamb chop upon which he was to dine that night—also missing. He found only an inedible rind of cheese, but neither meat nor wine.

What the devil? Had his parents shorted Mrs. Finch on her pay that month, and she was taking back her own from the larder? More likely it had been that new girl, Clara or Cleo or whatever her name had been. That girl had the whiff of the street about her and looked like she could use some meat on her bones. Quite a bit of meat. More than a mere lamb chop, in fact. He would have to get Meg to talk to the agency.

But for now he had his sad-looking heel of bread.

"Spiffing," he muttered, taking a vicious bite. "Ouch!"

That tooth had been bothering him for a month, but he'd been afraid to go to the dentist. It would have hurt to pull it out, but even worse, losing a molar would have caused one of his cheeks to become just that much more hollow than the other. Asymmetry was not a fashionable look. Tossing the bread aside, he opted for a half bottle of cooking sherry, instead. He'd make it up to Mrs. Finch later.

Bruised in gum and in spirit, he made his way back to the lab. Taking a long swig of the sherry, he set the bottle down to take another look at his notes on the last experiment. *Scintillam vitae, scintillam vitae.*

But his notes were gone.

❖

Meg

How dare he? Meg fumed. *How very dare he?*

The sound of Bernadette's slamming door rang in the hallway; her friends' whispers and titters followed her like the attic-scrabbling of little mice. Meg stormed down the servants' stairs to beard her cad of a brother in his den.

He'd always been a character, had Nat, but since leaving university, he'd become much worse than that. When she threw open the door to his lair, a warm fug greeted her—a reek both chemical and organic: solvents, alcohols both potable and otherwise, neglected laundry, and...oof. There it was. The olfactory remnants of an evening spent with some or another playmate. Meg did not want to know more.

And there, down below, like a giant rat, stood Nathaniel Herschel Eisenstadt, tearing through the haystacks of papers on the kitchen table, as if life itself, or perhaps his sanity, were there somewhere waiting to be uncovered.

Apparently hearing her footsteps, he looked up, frazzle-haired and glassy-eyed.

"What the devil possessed you?" Meg demanded.

He blinked at her through the glow of the lamp balanced precariously atop a stack of thick, leather-bound volumes. The gentle kerosene light made him look much younger, though he was the elder of the two of them. In that light, he looked almost innocent.

"They're gone," he said. "My notes are gone."

She blinked back. Then she said, "Ask me if I care. You were inexcusably rude to my friend for no reason. You ruined a very educational evening."

"And I'm telling you, my notes are gone." He shuffled some more papers, then began pacing. "It was my most important work to date. *Scintillam vitae*. In Latin, that means—"

"The spark of life," she said. "Humbug. Like all your other projects. You owe Bernadette an apology."

He stared. "An apology? Never! She took those notes!"

"Are you out of your—" She stopped. Nat looked appalling. His thick, dark curls—which had gone too long without a trim—were even more disheveled than usual. His large, dark eyes were red-rimmed and frantic. Dark stubble sprouted across his chin and neck. His gangly frame was vibrating with nervous energy, and he needed a wash.

"What the devil have you poisoned yourself with, now?" she asked, drawing closer. It wouldn't have been the first time Nat had experimented upon himself. It wouldn't be the first time he'd suffered for it, either. She sniffed, feeling her lip curl with distaste. "Smells like a whorehouse down here—not," she said preemptively, "that I have any idea what such a place might smell like." A ghost of a smile crossed Nat's plump lips. Clearly, she'd predicted his line of thought exactly. "Seriously, though," she said, "I don't think any of my friends shall ever speak to me again." They both glanced up at the angry clatter of expensively shod feet along the hallway above them. The front door slammed, as if to underscore her point. "You see?"

"You're better off without them," Nat murmured, once more elbows deep in paper—loose leaves covered in arcane sketches and his chicken-scratch scrawl.

His hyper-focus was worrying. Probably chemical. He needed strong coffee, and fast. She cleared a space from what used to be Mrs. Finch's kitchen counter and glanced around. Right. Beaker, clamp, Bunsen burner, water. She rigged the contraption together, poured the last of Nat's expensive, hand-roasted beans into the grinder, and gave the handle a few satisfyingly vicious turns. Then she tipped the grounds into the water and clamped the beaker above the flame, while her brother continued to root around his palace of paper.

After the mixture had boiled to a nice, black sludge, she tipped it into a sieve and let it drain into the only mug that hadn't developed fuzzy, green *scintillam vitae* of its own. This, she placed in front of her brother, while she set about organizing his haystacks into tidy piles.

"Thanks, sis," Nat said, meeting her eyes for the first time that evening. Sighing, he lowered himself onto the edge of his stool and let his head drop into his hands.

"You've lost weight," she told him.

"My notes for *scintillam vitae* were here when Jin left. *Right* here, on top."

"Jin?" She hadn't heard that name before. But Nat tore through his roster of playmates so quickly, few of them ever had names.

"Jin's not the issue. Bernadette took those notes. I know it. She hates me. Everyone hates me."

"I doubt that's true," Meg lied.

"What would you call it?" He sighed. "I came upstairs, made the mistake of trying to be friendly, had two doors slammed in my face, then went to make a sandwich. *Not*, by the way, that there was either bread or meat or edible cheese, or my lamb chop, either, for that matter. I blame that girl."

"Bernadette?" Meg asked, now thoroughly confused. Bernadette was a vegetarian.

"No, that other one. Clementine…Cleophilus…Clostridium…Cloaca…the one who comes in to clean house sometimes. She stole my supper. You should contact the agency."

"Seems to me you should do that," Meg said. She shook her head. "But your *notes*, Nat? What makes you think they were stolen instead of…lost in this chaos, and…and what would Bernadette want with any of it?"

He started to pace.

"Revenge. You saw it. Tell me you saw it."

"Everybody saw it, Nat."

"And I have no idea why." He peeked up at her from beneath his heavy-lidded eyes. Meg imagined that, had he been bathed, shaven, and dressed in his club-clothes, there were those who would have found the gesture irresistible. It looked pathetic now, though, especially accompanied by the self-conscious smile that followed. "Fine," he admitted. "I do know why, and so do you. But really, must the girl be so very *vengeful*?"

"I'd count yourself lucky she didn't set the entire place on fire. It would have been easy," she said, glancing from paper stacks to lamp to the bundles of drying herbs hanging from the ceiling. "Theoretically speaking. But we both saw her leave. How do you think she managed—"

"Isn't it obvious?" Nat cried, his voice rising. "She waited until I embarked upon my abortive sandwich-finding mission, then doubled back, sneaked into my lab, and took them."

"So she came back through the trade entrance? You didn't lock it?" Meg asked. Nat hung his head. "I have to ask again, how would she know what to take? Did you ever speak to her about your experiments?"

He looked off to the side. "It's hard to talk with your mouth full."

"Nat!" She didn't want to know. She really didn't. But she couldn't help herself. "When?" she asked.

"Last month, at your poetry evening," he said. "You have to admit she is pretty."

Yes. Meg did have to admit that. Nat wasn't the only one who had a weakness for wide eyes and deceptively sweet features. "Especially when viewed through a decanter of expensive wine," Meg said with a sigh. Really, how could she, of all people, blame him? "Pretty, and dreadfully clever."

Wonder crossed his features, then something like glee. "So you do know," he said.

She felt a small smile tugging at the edges of her mouth. "From personal experience, I'm afraid."

Nat gasped, placing his hands against his cheeks in mock horror. "Sister, *dear*, I never would have guessed. All right, I would have. It's practically expected in your circles." Then an uncomfortable expression crossed his face as certain implications sprang up in his mind. "So you...and I..." He shuddered, and Meg was pretty certain it wasn't an act. "It's...a bit wrong, don't you think?"

Meg snorted. "You do have a conscience in there somewhere. All the same, we must never speak of this again."

"Agreed."

They shook on it. Quiet descended over the laboratory. Then Meg said, "I still don't think Bernadette stole your notes, but I suppose it's possible. But you also mentioned Claudia."

"Who?"

"The little maid from the Kensington Agency. Has she ever been down here?"

"A few times."

Meg looked around the dark, crowded laboratory dubiously. Polished skulls of who knew which species grinned down at her from the nails upon which they hung. Samples of tissue and organ glowed in the lamplight from jars tucked away among Nat's books. Pity any poor girl who'd had to venture down here. Meg made a note to give little Claudia a bit extra in her next envelope. And speaking of.

She grasped her brother's chin and forced his red-rimmed eyes to meet hers. "Claudia," she said. "Business or pleasure?"

"Steady. On." He peeled her fingers away and, as if noticing his rumpled shirt for the first time, gave a few vain tugs as if to straighten it. "Cleaning only, I swear." She arched her eyebrow again. "Sis, the girl is…a…a *girl*. I only play with grown-ups," he said primly.

That much, at least, seemed to be true. "Did you discuss your work with her?" Meg asked.

He scoffed. "With the cleaning girl? Certainly not."

"But she does read. I've been teaching her. Is it possible she might have taken your notes, thinking, what, she might sell them? To whom? No. I'm not convinced." said Meg. "Seriously, though, what about your Jin? How well do you know…him? Her? Which is it?"

"Does it matter?" Nat asked.

Meg shrugged. "Not to me. But really, how much do you know about…them?"

Nat drew in a dramatic breath. "Jin is above suspicion."

"Why?" she demanded.

"Well… I've known…him…for quite a while."

"How long? A month? Two?"

"Give or take," he said with a little shrug.

"And that's long enough to let him into your sanctum sanctorum with all of your precious notes and equipment? Those chemicals must have addled your brain. What the devil *have* you been sipping at, anyway?"

"It's none of your business." He sighed. "Unfortunately, the only way to get to my...chambre de plaisir..."

She held up a hand. "Please don't."

"Is through the lab."

"The point is," she said, "you've known this person a month, maybe two. You come together only to...come together. What do you really know about him? Do you have any mutual friends?"

He thought about it. "No."

"How did you meet?"

His mouth crimped in a tight smile. "The usual way."

"In a club in Holborn," she said. This time his shrug was downright Gallic. "Right. Well, may I ask you to consider the idea that being amusing in bed doesn't necessarily mean that a person is honest or incapable of criminal behavior."

"Do you also know this from personal experience?" he asked.

She crossed her arms over her chest. "That's none of your business. If there really was a theft, as opposed to an act of catastrophic disorganization, we need to figure out who perpetrated it. Listen, brother dear, I'll make you a deal."

"I'm all ears," he said, cupping his spidery fingers at the sides of his head.

"I'll deal with Bernadette, if you promise to take a good, hard look at your..."

"Jin."

"At your Jin. And whichever one of us sees Claudia first can conduct that particular interrogation. But be nice. She's twelve if she's a day, and she has a hard life."

"How do you know that?" Nat asked.

"Well, she tidies up after you, for one thing." He shrugged again, not denying the charge. "But also, a lot of those agencies are downright predatory. Who knows how much they pay her from what we give them? Who knows where she lives—or how? Do you even think about her life, or Mrs. Finch's for that matter, once they leave this house? Where do they go? Where do they stay?"

"I think it's none of our business," Nat replied. "And if it is, it's more up your alley—agitating the workers and all—than mine. But I will try to find out more about Jin."

Meg nodded. "That's fair enough."

They shook hands for the second time that evening. And then Meg turned to go back upstairs to see if she could find anything in the larder for her own supper.

CHAPTER SIX

Abby

Morning broke with weak light pressing through grey clouds and faint sulphurous traces of the night's fog hanging in the air. The fog itself had cleared, though, and the city was as quiet as a hangover. Outside the clinic's front window, Cornwall Street was deserted.

It had been a long night—one of the longest Abby had ever spent. She hadn't found it within herself to turn the gang of youths out into the fog, but neither had she trusted them not to strip the clinic of everything of value while she slept. So she hadn't slept. Instead, she'd tidied and paced and checked and double-checked the windows and doors, and then she'd sat down to puzzle out her next move.

Gideon still hadn't returned. Either he'd found his way back to his rooms, or he was wandering the city somewhere, possibly injured and most probably lost and confused, not to mention half-blind without his spectacles. She would have to close the clinic and find him. And then she'd need to go back to Whitechapel and throw herself on the mercy of the men who provided his medicine.

The problem was, they hadn't struck her as men of mercy.

A crooked, winding path of whispers and rumors had first led her to their door—a metal-reinforced door to a room in an otherwise unremarkable two-story building near Dorset Street. Unremarkable except for the rough-looking men lurking nonchalantly at the perimeters and rather less nonchalantly inside.

She'd dealt with two different men in that room, as far as she could tell, though it had been difficult to discern. They dressed, spoke, and even sat in a very similar manner. The room was always dimly lit, the windows obscured by thick curtains, and the men themselves wore identical hats and covered their faces from the eyes down. Their clothing was unremarkable, and they were always seated, which meant that she couldn't tell how tall they were or divine more than the basics about their respective builds.

But that didn't mean they hadn't revealed themselves in other ways. Their speech, for example, was more Westminster than Whitechapel. The timbre of their voices and the confidence of their tone reinforced this impression. One had been quite a bit older than the other. Father and son, perhaps? Employer and protégé? But both had moved and reached and gestured with gloved hands in a vigorous way that spoke of good health. Likely deprivation had never touched them.

Their words marked them as educated men—if not a medical education, then at least a scientific one. But the fact that they carried out their business in a tumbling-down building near Dorset Street made it clear that their work fell outside the bounds of their profession—and possibly outside the law itself.

But she had been desperate.

She was desperate today.

On the other side of the clinic, the boys were sleeping near the stove in a pile like puppies. They didn't look nearly so menacing, now, with their hands and faces clean, and sleep having relaxed the sharp edges from their features. Strange to think they'd have happily robbed her not twelve hours before. She yawned. As if this were the signal the boys had been waiting for, the pile suddenly twitched. Limbs stretched. Another yawn proceeded from somewhere beneath the blankets, and the one called Eli pulled himself into a sitting position. Blinking away sleep, he felt for his cap and screwed it back over his dark curls.

"Good morning," Abby said a bit more curtly than she might have, had she had a moment's sleep herself.

She and Eli had spoken late into the night while the others had dozed. He hadn't been able to offer any insights into why the Fiend, as they called that strange presence in the fog, had focused its efforts on Garrick. Nor had he a theory about why he himself had escaped injury. As Eli had spoken, his tongue loosened by a warm mug of tea and the heat from the stove, Abby had drawn parallels to Nell Evans's story two weeks before. There had been fog, a swirling mass of dirt and sand, a malevolent green-eyed figure, and an attack. The attack had centered on Miss Evans—as it had on Garrick—though the other members of Miss Evans's group had suffered minor injuries as well, with the exception of one. Unfortunately, that one had slipped away before she could speak to him properly.

The problem would require further thought. But that would require time she didn't have right then. The other young men were beginning to stir. Soon all four of them were standing, stretching, shaking themselves awake, and glancing at her with the tentative, guilty expression of dogs who had snatched something from the table but weren't certain if anyone had noticed.

"Sleep well?" Abby asked after the little group had rejoined the living.

A chorus of grunts and nods, and one soft, "Yes, miss."

"Good," she said, folding her arms across her chest. "In that case, there's the matter of the bill."

"The bill, miss?" croaked Garrick.

A night of pacing the floors had stripped away a bit of Abby's compassion and not a small part of her patience, but it had also sharpened her vision for the day. Finding Gideon was her first business, of course. But something else was stalking the night, and it had brought her two lots of patients, now. Speaking to Nell Evans was almost as important. If her instincts were correct, this ragged little group was in a better position to do that than she was. But she also knew that any lingering feelings of goodwill would fade as quickly as the heat from the clinic's stove once the young men disappeared back onto the streets. So she had to, as the vicar would say, be as wise as a serpent and as innocent as a dove.

"Emergency medical care and a night's lodging—not to mention the fact that I had to sit up all night to make sure you lot didn't rob me blind. Now, by my account, that makes—"

"But this is a free clinic, miss," Bert said.

"There's also the matter of harassment," Abby said. "Really, I should turn you all over to the police."

"You wouldn't!" cried Eli.

"Wouldn't I? It'd be for your own good, as well as the good of decent Londoners everywhere. You'd have a bed in a workhouse and regular meals. You'd be out of the cold and off the street. Safe from fog and fiends and creatures of the night…"

Really, the more she thought about it, the more she wondered if that wouldn't be better than sending them back out onto the streets to chase down a young woman who probably hadn't even given her real name. Still, Miss Evans's injuries would make her memorable enough.

"Sure, and locked in at night with guards what beat you when no one's looking…or worse," Garrick rasped. He straightened his thin, dirt-encrusted coat and gave his filthy kerchief a tug. "Like Bert said, this is a free clinic. Besides, you didn't do anything my boys couldn't have done."

"Before you suffocated?" Abby asked.

Garrick rounded on her, and the fire in his eyes made her take a step back. "You knew we couldn't pay when you let us in. No one told you to give us food or let us sleep here. We're sorry about… about at the river, but we're going, now. Come on, boys."

"Wait!" Abby cried as Bert unlatched the bolt.

Just then footsteps scraped by in front of the clinic, and the tall, unmistakable hump of a bobby's hat appeared in the window over the top of the curtain.

"There's our bobby, right on time," she said. "He takes a dim view indeed of assaults on innocent women. Now, are you going to help me?"

The little group wavered, eyes darting between the window and their leader, who crossed his arms tightly and scowled.

"Right," Abby said. She pushed past them and unlatched the door. "Good morning, Constable Dawson."

The constable, a thin young man who nonetheless looked quite capable of holding his own with a gang of ruffians, stopped and turned.

"Good morning, Nurse Gordon."

Abby was gratified to see three of the boys shrink back from the doorway. Even Garrick appeared to deflate a bit. Dawson had always struck her as a decent sort, but he was stern beyond his years and watched over the shops and businesses on his beat with a keen eye and not a whit of tolerance for nonsense.

"Is everything all right?" Dawson had started to walk back toward them, hand on the handle of his baton.

"We'll help! We'll help!" little Clyde squeaked before Garrick silenced him with a glare. Eli opened his mouth to speak, but before he could, the constable was on the doorstep.

"What's all this, then?" he asked, slipping a foot through the doorway. He smiled at her, but his eyes were cataloguing the scene, memorizing the boys' faces, his mind no doubt running through the lists of petty criminals he'd encountered in the area, checking to see if any of them was a match. "Starting your own ragged school, Nurse Gordon?"

"A few of my helpers," Abby said. "Meet Bert, Eli, Clyde, and Garrick." The leader of the group flinched as she set her hands on his shoulders for emphasis. "We were discussing a job they might do for me."

"Is that so?" Dawson asked. He folded his arms over his chest and pinned Garrick with a hard look.

"Yes," Abby said, thinking quickly. "I'm looking for one of my former patients, a Miss Nell Evans. She came through the clinic two weeks ago, her right hand having been injured in some sort of accident." Miss Evans had actually said that the Fiend had grasped her hand in a swirling, crushing cloud of sand and grit, but Dawson was one of the few men who seemed to treat women as inherently rational creatures, and she didn't want to disabuse him of the notion. "I asked her to stop round so I could check on her healing, but I haven't heard from her, and I don't know where to look. I thought if anyone could help me find her, these clever young men could. Besides, they owe me for their supper."

Dawson nodded. "It sounds like a fair trade to me. What do you say, boys?"

Abby watched with satisfaction as they squirmed beneath the constable's gimlet eye. Garrick muttered something that sounded like *some free clinic* before Dawson's gaze fell on him and he straightened.

"Just find her?" Garrick asked, his voice sharp with suspicion.

"Then send someone back to tell me where *I* can find her. She's a thin little thing, probably nineteen or twenty, dark hair and eyes, pale skin, and her right hand and forearm are set in plaster. Nell Evans, probably lives nearby."

"We can do that," Bert said before Garrick could object.

"See that you do," Dawson said. "Garrick, Bert, Eli and Clyde. Now move along."

Abby watched as the boys crept out into the daylight, throwing furtive glances over their shoulders. "Thank you, Constable," she said.

"Did you really let them stay the night in the clinic?" he asked.

"They had nowhere else to go."

"A lot of people have nowhere else to go. That was a very dangerous thing to do."

"They came just as the fog was rolling in. I couldn't send them out into it."

He considered her carefully. "Was the doctor there, as well?"

Briefly she thought to confess everything and ask for Dawson's assistance finding Gideon. But the last thing Gideon needed in his probable condition was to have the police on his trail.

"Yes, of course," she lied. When he glanced over her shoulder into the clinic, she added, "He stepped out for the morning newspaper. He should be back soon."

"I see. Please give him my regards. Good day, Nurse."

"Good day, constable."

She shut the door and listened to the constable's footsteps recede into the sounds of morning traffic. Then she reached for her coat.

She had to find Gideon before someone else did. She paused with her hand on the doorknob. It would look suspicious if she rushed out the moment the constable's back was turned. She'd let herself out the back. Locking the front door, she turned, reaching into her pocket for her gloves. Her fingers found an envelope instead. The letter from the Association of Poor Clinics.

Earlier, when the inspector had grudgingly rendered a grade of "satisfactory" before leaving the premises, he had left them with a certificate attesting to the fact. Abby couldn't quite picture the Association wasting paper or postage on confirmatory communication, so what did they want? She knew she should open it and get it over with, but something about the letter troubled her at a deeper level. Had the clinic's inspector changed his mind? Was there, God forbid, some fee they'd failed to pay? Something always seemed to be falling apart, running out, or coming due. Under normal circumstances she'd find a way through it. But with Gideon gone God knew where, and doing God only knew what, it was too much. Her nerves were standing on end, and she couldn't pin down her thoughts to move forward. There was nothing for it. She had to find him. And the letter would have to wait. She shoved the envelope back into her coat pocket and drew a deep, steadying breath.

Outside, the fog had cleared away, replaced by weak grey sunlight. The alley behind the clinic looked the same as it always did: an unpaved walkway between high brick walls that cast cold, deep shadows. Soot dusted the bricks and the neglected back windows of the nearby shops and businesses, and bits of rubbish cluttered the cracks and corners. As she slowly walked toward the street, nervous energy drained away, and her senses attuned to the smaller things: bits of broken glass, leaves blown in from who knew where by the whistling winds, and there, yes, there, along the back wall of the clinic, where she'd heard something scratch along the bricks, the glass, and the wood of the door, were signs that something had done just that.

Four thin, uneven, parallel lines ran through the soot and grime about three feet above the ground, as if someone had dragged their fingernails across the back of the building. No, not quite fingernails—not unless those nails were narrower than average, as thick as an animal's, and blunt. Not unless the owner of the nails had been pressing hard enough to scratch through the grime and into the brick and glass and wood itself.

What had passed by the night before, as she'd stood by the clinic's back door? What, and not who—she was sure of that, now. Gideon had been long gone by that time. Even in his feral state, he wouldn't have lingered in the alley trying to frighten her. He'd have been off running wherever the wolf took him. And if she knew him, he'd run as far away from her as he could get.

She scanned the path ahead of her. She wasn't certain what she should be looking for, but she'd know it when she found it. And then she did. There, in a patch of mud that hadn't quite dried up, was a footprint. It was larger than that of a man, even a large man. She saw a rounded heel—the heel of a foot, not a shoe—and the suggestion of four extremely long, clawed toes. What on earth? It was a track, but definitely not a wolf track. In fact, not the track of any animal she knew.

But what really baffled her was the mud.

Why was there mud? It rained often enough but hadn't recently. At least not recently enough that there would be mud puddles in the alley. Where had it come from, then?

Frowning, she crouched and took a pinch of the mud between her finger and thumb. Nurse Abigail Gordon was no expert when it came to minerals, but the fine, silty material that housed the footprint felt different from the ground between the buildings that she'd walked a thousand times. With the index finger of her other hand, she scraped up a bit of the surrounding dry dirt. Then she spat onto her fingertip to moisten it. The fishy, rotten scent of the Thames rose to meet her.

The river was more than a mile away. What on earth was its mud doing in the alley behind her clinic?

Gideon would be fascinated, if she managed to find him, that was.

And what then? Deal with the footprints, deal with the clinic's inspector, then back to the way things had been before? She'd no complaints about their comfortable arrangement. At the same time, it wasn't a *usual* arrangement. It wasn't completely *normal*. People, here and there, had begun to remark on it, and that attention, in turn, made her question.

She loved Gideon and he loved her. But the few times she'd allowed herself to think about it, to truly explore the depth and nature of her feelings, that love, as strong as it was, felt more like the bond of siblings or, at the very least, of close platonic friends.

It wasn't unusual. Many marriages seemed to be based on similar grounds: a common background, mutual respect, and chaste affection, all natural and sound bases for a shared life. At the same time, she couldn't help noticing, growing up, how many of her friends had been preoccupied with male attention, with romance, and with speculations about the nature of married love. They'd all assured Abby that she would feel the same way one day, but that day had never come.

One or two people recently had suggested that work occupied the natural place where romantic thoughts might have flourished, with the attendant but unspoken suggestion that she might spend less time patching up indigent strangers and more time thinking about affairs of the heart. But she and Gideon had fallen into step so naturally, it seemed silly to question their arrangement when it worked so well.

Yet how well could it be working when neither of them seemed much interested in progressing to the next logical stage? Shouldn't she at least want to move things forward? Shouldn't he? Did he? It troubled her to realize that not only had they never discussed the issue past the awkward acknowledgement of what seemed inevitable, but that she really had no idea how the man felt about that inevitability at all.

But did it matter? If they were both happy spending their days in one another's pockets at the clinic, and their nights in single rooms in different rooming houses, why was it anybody else's business?

Of course, at times she'd wished for someone to curl up with in the night. But she'd never been able to picture that person beyond the vaguest of images: a warm presence stretched out beside her;

soft, sweet breath on the back of her neck; a tangle of smooth arms and legs. Never a face or any other information that might give her a clue as to whom her heart sought in the night.

The only thing of which she'd been certain was that it wasn't him. Even if he weren't battling a monster.

She spotted more footprints up ahead, so she shook off unwanted thoughts and hurried to the next one. Much of the footprint was still distinct, but less mud surrounded it, and it was quickly drying. The footprints, each one drier and less clear than the last, led out of the alley, turned left down the street, then went left again, until they came to a stop near the clinic's front steps. She found a bit of dried mud on the steps, but four sets of adolescent shoes had obliterated it.

As she looked up the pavement past the clinic, she saw no further footprints. It was as if whatever the creature had been, it had materialized in the alley behind the clinic, walked around to the front of it, then melted back into mud once it reached the front steps. What was it? Where had it come from, and where had it gone? Would it be back?

Her heart pounded. Escaped murderesses aside, it had never occurred to her that more than one creature might be stalking the London night. She'd thought Gideon's affliction to be unique. But why should it have been? The fact that someone was manufacturing medication to suppress it proved that this was very much not the case. How many more were wandering about with Gideon's same burden? Or indeed with different burdens, judging from the footprints? Abby might never look at a stranger the same way again.

The thought was even more discomfiting than an unexpected letter from the Association of Poor Clinics. At least she was, at last, ready to face *that*.

With a small sigh, she took the envelope out of her pocket, slipped the letter out, and unfolded it. The first thing she noticed was the letterhead. The glyph in the upper left-and corner was similar to that of the Association of Poor Clinics—similar enough that it had been easy to mistake when she'd first seen it on the envelope. It reminded her of a caduceus in a wreath of pointed leaves and included an unfamiliar inscription in Latin. The address was in

St. James's, the solicitor's office. Salutations followed, and then a barrage of words she'd heard before but wasn't quite certain of their meaning. *Compulsory purchase. Fair compensation.* References to the Lands Clauses Consolidation Act.

Good God. For some unfathomable reason, someone wanted the clinic, or at least its building, for themselves. They hadn't bothered to approach Gideon about it but had gone straight to force of law. Why? She read through the tangle of unfamiliar terminology, looking for a name—a person, an organization, or any kind of clue—but she found nothing, save for reference to a Consortium with a capital "C." How pretentious. Pretentious or not, though, the threat of legal action was real.

Blood raced to her head, and she blinked to dispel a sudden wave of dizziness. She and Gideon had put everything they had into that clinic. The letter hadn't specified what was meant by "fair compensation," but she'd seen enough to know that when it came to the wealthy snatching resources, "fair" seldom was. Even with whatever compensation this Consortium was offering, she doubted she and Gideon would have enough money to start over in a new location. Could they fight this? Or would a solicitor only drain their meager funds more quickly? Dizziness threatened again, but she took a deep breath and steadied herself.

Now, more than ever, she needed to find Gideon.

CHAPTER SEVEN

Bernadette

"Shall I take this, miss?"

"Yes, thank you, Ivy," Bernadette said.

Before the housemaid could whisk away her breakfast plate, however, Bernadette snatched a crust of toast and held it under the table, careful to keep the buttered side away from the pressed linen tablecloth. The maid frowned at the sound of the spaniel's snapping jaws.

"You know your parents don't like it when you do that," Ivy said.

"I'm too old to be ruled by the approval of my parents," Bernadette replied, fondling the dog's silky ears. Her parents might have added that she was also too old to be ignoring the business of finding a suitable husband and starting a household of her own. A good job that they preferred to breakfast in their own chamber.

The maid's mouth twitched in a knowing smile. "I reckon that's true, miss. Shall I clear all this away and help you with your hair?"

Bernadette sighed. From a practical standpoint, she understood that it was better to employ a small complement of servants with multiple skills than an unnecessarily large staff of specialists, but part of her would always envy those who could afford a separate lady's maid. Still, Ivy was a wonder with curlers and comb, and Bernadette's lack of sleep showed in every crinkle and crease. She sighed again. Fancy hair and clothing would be a liability on the East End.

"No, thank you, Ivy. I'll see to it myself."

The young woman smiled. "Going to do your voluntary work today, then?"

"Yes, that's right."

"Shame there ain't much call for lady scientists. They're missing out on a lot of talent, if you ask me, miss."

"Thank you, Ivy. In a different world, I imagine you and I might have had quite different positions in life."

Bernadette had allowed, even encouraged, a bit of informality between the two of them. Their informality hadn't, of course, extended to Bernadette telling Ivy the truth about where she went most days. As far as Bernadette's family knew, Bernadette performed voluntary work with the Society for the Protection of Creation, a newly formed animal charity. Bernadette wasn't sure which part of her actual employment would have shocked people more—the fact that it dealt with the occult, that she spent her days surrounded by men, or that she was paid quite decently to do the things her parents paid Ivy to do.

But that wouldn't be for long. She pushed back from the table and went to fetch her coat. Ivy thought the coat too severe, like Bernadette's plain work dresses. But the clothing told her colleagues at Consortium House that she wasn't simply there as decoration.

She suspected that Sir Julius had chosen to hire from the women's college because the students' gender and class would have necessitated a certain level of secrecy about their daily activities. But why he'd sought out Bernadette in particular—that had come down to her thesis. Specifically, Bernadette Kingsley had postulated a unifying force that animated all of life—human, animal, and even plant. It wasn't an original idea, but to Bernadette's extensive knowledge, she was the first to put it to experimental test. To attempt to measure and quantify *it*—Spirit—the soul.

Sir Julius had promised her that when the time was right, she would be able to continue her research at Consortium House. But he hadn't set a specific timetable. In retrospect, it had been a mistake not to insist upon it. But Bernadette had been so elated that the organization had even had an interest, it simply hadn't occurred to her to ask.

But months had passed, now, and she was becoming a bit fed up with fetching people's tea and luncheon.

The path to the train station took her past Nat and Meg's house. Normally, she might have glanced through the front window to see if Meg was about. But that morning embarrassment made her hurry past the place on the other side of the street.

Taking Nathaniel Eisenstadt to bed had been another mistake. She'd known it at the time, even through the haze of wine and the wonderful, heady realization that he'd actually been listening to her ideas. In fact, he'd been entertaining ideas of his own that had complemented her own in interesting ways. She'd marveled that someone with whom she'd resonated so strongly on both the intellectual and the physical planes had been hiding in plain sight all this time. And when he invited her below stairs, she hadn't even minded that he'd led her straight to the bedroom, bypassing the laboratory.

These things had made it all the more painful in the days afterward when he'd pretended to have been too drunk to remember anything. By the time she reached Kensington Station, she was fuming all over again. She fumed all the way to Whitechapel. When she reached Consortium House, however, she forced herself to take a deep breath before letting herself in through the back door.

Yes, she thought. This was where she belonged.

Consortium House was quiet that morning. Sir Julius was probably already ensconced in his attic offices, she thought as she ascended the stairs, the woollen carpeting swallowing the sound of her footsteps. At the head of the staircase, she turned right and headed for the utility closet. She selected a duster, a few cloths, and a box to gather any rubbish she might find. She liked to finish tidying the offices before Dr. Wylie and Mr. Hathaway began their day's work. It made them happy, and it gave her a chance to peek at their research. She wasn't ashamed of it. If she was to be a useful part of the organization, it behooved her to have an idea of what her colleagues were getting up to.

"Good morning, Miss Kingsley."

Bernadette turned quickly, nearly dropping her box of supplies. "Oh, good morning, Mr. Hathaway. You surprised me."

Annoyingly, the idea seemed to please him. She stepped aside, keeping the arm full of supplies between them, and shut the door.

Hathaway glanced at his watch. "You're early this morning."

"All the better to prepare for the day."

"Quite so. We do like to see that sort of initiative. Nothing like coming into a nice, clean office."

"Yes, sir."

She tried to keep the disappointment out of her voice. They'd had a few encouraging conversations, into which she'd casually dropped ideas she'd gleaned from Dr. Wylie's notes. She'd thought to demonstrate her knowledge of the Consortium's business and had hoped the carefully chosen ideas might lead to a discussion of her own research, or possibly a position in the study group he'd been assembling.

He'd appreciated the ideas at the time, but the condescension now seeping through his words made her glad she'd held back her ambitions and spared herself the embarrassment.

Grinning, Mr. Hathaway gave a little salute, turned on his heel, and continued along his way. Bernadette raised her chin and continued in the other direction, toward Dr. Wylie's office.

Perhaps, she reflected, Dr. Wylie would be a better one to approach. He was older, after all, and might not feel so keen a need to put her in her place. He also struck her as someone of unorthodox personal tastes. She'd never discuss the subject with him, of course, but simply knowing that they might share these secret proclivities made her feel a bit of kinship with the man.

Outside Dr. Wylie's office, she stepped past the tray with Dr. Wylie's supper dishes and knocked on the door. After a silent moment she let herself in.

Dr. Wylie didn't live in his office, but it wasn't far off. He kept several sets of spare clothing in a chest in the corner, and he'd set up a wash basin and a dividing screen. Many were the mornings she'd come in to find him already up to his elbows in scribbled notes, his fingers and forearms flecked with ink. More often than not, lamplight from his window would light her way in the alley when she left for the day.

From the papers she'd glanced over as she'd transferred them from bin to fireplace, she gathered that his work involved lycanthropy—a subject outside of her own expertise, of course, but surely, at some level, compatible with her own research. A few times the words had been on her tongue, her mouth open to broach the subject. But the truth was, Dr. Wylie was so dashed intimidating.

She started by laying a fire in the fireplace. If nothing else, the Consortium didn't skimp on small comforts for its research staff. There was always plenty of coal. Then she emptied the wash basin out the window—disgusting but necessary—wiped it clean, and set it back in place. She pinched a damp towel from the hanging rack and deposited it outside the office door next to the dishes, sparing a thought of gratitude that her responsibility for these objects stopped there.

Returning, she made her way around the room, fluffing a pillow here, folding down a carpet corner there. And by that time, the fire was crackling and warm and ready to receive. She brought the wicker bin from beneath Dr. Wylie's desk, carefully unfolded each of the discarded papers, glanced over it, and fed it to the fire. Rubbish, rubbish, a grocery list.

And then she stopped.

Scintillam vitae.

She blinked and held the paper closer, but there had been no mistake. Somehow, Dr. Wylie had stumbled upon—no. That wasn't right. The man did not stumble. Somehow he had availed himself of Nat's research. Her pulse raced. She glanced over her shoulder, then set the waste bin on the floor and quickly shut the door.

Dr. Wylie's desk was generally a mess, but she'd no doubt that he kept that mess in a meticulous order of his own devising and would notice any disruption. She carefully leafed through pages of his looping script until she found it.

"I knew it," she muttered as Nat's spiky scrawl stared back at her. Three pages of *scintillam* blinking *vitae*. Before she knew it, she'd folded the pages into her skirt pocket. Dr. Wylie wouldn't dare question her about it directly. He probably wouldn't question her at all.

What would she do with the information?

At one time she might have taken it to Mr. Hathaway. But the sour taste of his condescension was still with her. Perhaps she'd keep it back as a last resort. Perhaps Dr. Wylie himself might be receptive to her ideas. And if he wasn't, she could always tell him that she knew where his own ideas had come from.

CHAPTER EIGHT

Jin

Dr. Wylie arrived at Consortium House just before noon. That was later than usual, much later, but he was filled with a new energy and purpose that would more than make up for it. A sound fuck, a vigorous scrub, and a solid night's sleep in his own bed had done him a world of good. Eisenstadt had done him a world of good.

He stopped at the back door, keys poised just before the keyhole of the first lock, as a lorry clattered past the alley behind him. At what point, he wondered, had his arrangement with Eisenstadt become personal? When he'd met the young man at that club in Holborn, he'd thought he'd be good for a bit of fun. A way to blow off steam. And he was. But Eisenstadt was good for quite a lot of things, it turned out.

The complex system of locks and bolts gave way, and the door opened into a dark foyer. Straight ahead, a corridor led to a door that opened onto the unused front rooms. Those rooms, Wylie understood, were being held in reserve for when the Consortium expanded its operations. Their lack of present use added to the veneer of abandonment that Sir Julius was attempting to cultivate. In addition to boarded-up windows, the street-facing facade had a forbidding-looking door and a staircase that needed a good sweeping.

Still, the Consortium was taking the abandoned-building approach a bit too far, in Wylie's opinion. It was, he thought, in danger of attracting, rather than deflecting, attention. While it was true that respectable people hurried past the building without a second glance, Wylie reckoned it would only be a matter of time before enterprising squatters eyed it up for a nest. And considering the nature of the Consortium's work—at least the work with which Wylie was involved—that wouldn't end well for anyone.

Wylie's office was on the next floor up, as was Hathaway's. Sir Julius, to whom both Dr. Wylie and Hathaway reported, kept a private office on the top floor. Those rooms were well appointed, luxurious, even, compared to Wylie's monk-like office at Hanwell Asylum. Wylie was grateful. After what had happened at Hanwell, he was lucky to have a position at all.

Wylie shut the door behind him and mounted the stairs. He felt remarkably loose-limbed and light. Eisenstadt's fingers had the uncanny ability to find every last one of the knots buried deep in his muscles. Last night, as Wylie lay on soft and surprisingly clean sheets, having been fucked into a state of mindless oblivion, those fingers had worked over his shoulders, neck, and back until they had reduced him to a puddle. And it had done wonders for his back. The soreness that he felt now was in a completely different location and was the kind that brought to mind pleasant memories. As for the spinal pain that sat upon him like a heavy cloak every moment of every day, it was much diminished. It was as if the muscles that surrounded the area didn't know what to do, having been relieved of their burden of constant resistance. The combination made Wylie almost giddy.

Or was the giddiness from something else? That was a thought Wylie did not have the luxury to entertain, not that day, and not in general.

Especially with that godforsaken dog still carrying on.

"Doctor," said a voice behind him.

Wylie turned. "Sir Julius."

"I'm glad I caught you. Do you have a moment?"

"Of course."

Sir Julius was around sixty years of age. Tall and vigorous, he had barely lined skin that glowed with health, and his eyes glittered with intelligence. Wylie's father had introduced them when Wylie was an awkward, precocious teen grappling with the unexpected development of new and frightening abilities. Wylie only realized later that their quiet chats in his father's study had actually been lessons in how to control those abilities.

"I trust you're settling in well?"

"Yes, sir. It's quite a change having the resources to undertake my work properly."

"You were being wasted at Hanwell," Sir Julius said.

Wylie blinked. "Wasted, sir?"

His post at Hanwell Asylum had been his first after finishing medical school. He'd enjoyed the work and had quickly formed a rapport with some of the most intractable patients. Had it not been for one critical miscalculation, he would, he was certain, still be there.

"Sometimes these things can't be helped," Sir Julius said with unnerving perspicacity.

"I suppose," Wylie said.

"Still, one might say it's for the best."

"Perhaps."

Sir Julius's expression turned sharp. "You've not forgotten all that the Consortium has done for you. After Miss Chase and all."

"No, sir," Wylie said quickly. Though in truth Wylie had wondered at the timing of it. When he thought about it in the dark hours, the incident, his dismissal, and the Consortium's need had lined up rather neatly. But to think Sir Julius had engineered it somehow? It was a stretch even for Wylie's fertile imagination, if for no other reason than universities were filled with bright sparks like his colleague Hathaway, who would jump at the chance for a well-appointed office and a fat monthly envelope, and who had not yet blotted their copy books.

More importantly, if Wylie's work had taught him anything, it was how easily he himself might have ended up at a place like Hanwell, had it not been for Sir Julius. And had not the Consortium offered him a congenial refuge after the incident, there was no telling what might have become of him.

"I only hope that the Consortium's trust will prove well placed," Wylie added.

"I'm certain it will. Do you have everything you need? Aside from a specimen, of course. We're still working on that."

"Yes. That would move things out of the realm of theory, at least," Wylie said.

Sir Julius frowned. "You don't believe that lycanthropes exist?"

To the contrary, Wylie suspected he'd met one. Miss Chase had consigned herself to care at Hanwell before Wylie had arrived, believing that she had a monster inside her. Wylie had never seen it, but his work with her convinced him that more than madness had been at play. He'd been certain that a breakthrough had been imminent, when the woman had escaped from the asylum. A tribunal had found him culpable, and he couldn't disagree. Things had moved quickly following his dismissal, though, and he'd not had time to dwell. And that was, as Sir Julius would say, also for the best.

"The Consortium has asked me to investigate the theoretical aspects of the phenomenon, and I'm doing so to the best of my ability," Wylie said.

Sir Julius laughed and clapped him on the shoulder. "That's the spirit. What we want to know is how does it *work*? What's the nature of the transformation? Is it voluntary? More to the point, can it be controlled—not only by the affected individual, but by others remotely? You work on the theory, and we'll work on getting you that specimen."

"You sound quite certain that such a thing is possible," Wylie said.

"Oh, we are certain."

Wylie felt a prickling sensation across the back of his neck. The Consortium were powerful men. Men who made world-changing decisions behind the closed doors of rooms that reeked of cigars and brandy. The reality was the very opposite of comforting.

"Ah, there you are, Doctor. Sir Julius," a voice said behind him.

"Algie," Sir Julius said.

Wylie suppressed a sigh. Algernon Hathaway, a spindly Oxford man in an over-starched shirt and tortoiseshell spectacles, had taken against Wylie from the outset. That's-Mr.-Hathaway-to-You was quite a bit younger, perhaps in his mid-twenties, which was why, Wylie supposed, he always seemed so eager to assume authority.

"You're late," Hathaway said.

"My contract didn't specify working hours," Wylie retorted.

"Nevertheless—"

"I left yesterday evening after working twenty-four hours straight. Not that it's any of your—"

"Gentlemen." Sir Julius interrupted them. "Do you have business with Dr. Wylie, Algie?"

Hathaway looked Wylie up and down appraisingly. Wylie attempted to peer into his thoughts, but Hathaway, like the other members of the Consortium, was a firmly closed book.

"I do, actually," Hathaway said.

"Then I'll leave you to it, but for God's sake, be civil. Not a lot of men of Dr. Wylie's caliber are willing to work for a few pennies and the glory of it. Good day, Doctor."

"Good day, sir," Wylie said, pursing his lips against a laugh. Despite his ambivalence about the organization itself, the "few pennies" the Consortium had slipped him each week were more than sufficient for any man, and double what he'd made at Hanwell.

"I came for a progress report," Hathaway said as they watched Sir Julius disappear down the hall.

"You came too late. I reported my progress to Sir Julius."

"Sir Julius isn't addressing the academy later this week. I am."

The Academy of Occult Sciences was Hathaway's pet project. From what Wylie had surmised, it was a club for university students with an interest in the subject and, perhaps, Wylie suspected, skills or ideas for lucrative inventions that the Consortium might nurture and exploit.

"I regret that I have nothing to report at this point."

"But you've been with us for nearly a month," Hathaway said.

"That's barely enough time to set up operations, much less report results."

"And yet you've more than set up operations. You've made yourself quite at home, if reports from the kitchen and Miss Kingsley are to be believed. One might even think you'd taken up residence here. Quite frankly, the Consortium is wondering when we might see some return on our investment."

Wylie straightened. He'd expected oversight, to be sure. He should have guessed that the staff would be spying on him. But when exactly, he wondered, had Hathaway expanded his purview to include other people's expenses?

"Without a specimen, anything I might have to say would be pure speculation," Wylie said.

"Even speculation would be an improvement at this point. I need something, Doctor. That is, if you expect the Consortium to continue funding your research."

Funding was the least of Wylie's concerns. His service hadn't been coerced, exactly, but it remained the single option open to him after all other doors had slammed shut. Any sympathy Wylie might have had for Hathaway's position dropped dead. Hathaway wasn't his supervisor, and he should have known better than to make such a threat.

Somewhere in the distance that dog was beginning to bark again. Wylie pinched the bridge of his nose.

"This would all be much easier and much faster if the Consortium would allow me an assistant."

Wylie couldn't bring himself to say if *you* would allow me. He braced for a curt response and was surprised when, instead, Hathaway frowned and asked, "Have you someone in mind?"

It was another surprise to realize that he did.

It hadn't been a conscious thought, but when Hathaway mentioned it, Wylie realized that his subconscious had been turning the idea over for some time. Nathaniel Eisenstadt would make an excellent assistant, and not only because he was pleasant company and an easy sight for overworked eyes. Eisenstadt was clever and quick, and he had an impressive breadth of scientific knowledge for an autodidact—a fact that had quickly become evident when Wylie had snooped through the notes that littered the center table in that cyclone of a laboratory of his.

"I do, actually."

"And it would help you to make faster progress?"

"It would," Wylie said.

"Then tell me his name. I'll have him vetted."

Wylie wondered at Hathaway's sudden attitude shift. He braved another futile attempt to probe the man's thoughts and came up once more against a wall of resistance.

"Nathaniel Eisenstadt," Wylie replied.

An ugly expression flashed over Hathaway's face. "Under no circumstance."

"You know Mr. Eisenstadt?"

Wylie wracked his brains but couldn't come up with any reason their paths might have crossed. Hathaway didn't frequent the Holborn clubs, and Eisenstadt's family didn't move in the same circles as the members of the Consortium. Besides, when Eisenstadt wasn't in the clubs or in Wylie's arms, he was in his basement laboratory—at least Wylie hoped as much.

Hathaway tugged at his lapels. "I know of him. I'm surprised I need to tell you that someone like that is wholly unsuited for work with the Consortium."

Wylie frowned. Could Hathaway possibly know that Wylie was of a similar ilk? Or that he and Eisenstadt knew one another in an other-than-professional capacity?

"Right," Wylie said, straightening. "Well…"

"But I do have some good news for you, Doctor."

"Oh?"

"We've arranged for you to visit the site for your new facility. Just to make sure it actually meets your expectations." His tone suggested he still hadn't forgiven Wylie for pushing so hard for such a thing, then turning down every single site the Consortium had suggested.

"Where is it, exactly?" Wylie asked.

"On Cornwall Street in Shadwell. Tucked away in an alley and already kitted out for medical work. A driver is out front waiting for you now."

"Thank you," Wylie said.

He turned on his heel and doubled back down the stairs toward the rear door, still shaking his head. Every time he thought he had Hathaway sussed out, the man managed to do something completely unexpected.

When Wylie emerged once more from the rear door of Consortium House, a vehicle was waiting on the street at the end of the alley: a slick, black two-seater with the Consortium's seal in miniature below the handle of the door. It was a handsome seal that featured the staff of Hermes, a crown of laurel leaves, and the motto *Prudentes Sicut Serpentes*. Every time he read it, his mind wanted to add the rest of the saying—*simplices sicut columbae*—though he knew that as serpent-wise as the Consortium members undoubtedly were, he'd yet to meet one that was as innocent as a dove.

"Where to, Doctor?" the driver asked.

Wylie looked up toward the top of the vehicle, where the man was seated. "Cornwall Street. Shadwell."

"Very good, sir."

Before he stepped onto the running board, Wylie took a moment to glide a hand over the horse's sleek black neck. He liked horses almost as much as he liked dogs, and he liked both better than the majority of people. Inside, the smell of leather turned his thoughts back to Eisenstadt—specifically to some of the man's bedroom implements. He shook his head at his foolishness. This had to stop, especially if he were to insist the Consortium hire the man as his assistant to spite Hathaway.

What *were* Hathaway's objections, anyway?

The driver shifted in his seat above Wylie's head, whistled, and flicked the reins. The hansom began to roll, slowly at first, then picked up speed as it merged into the flow of traffic.

Wylie had always treated his need for physical companionship like any other physical need, pushing it aside until it became unbearable, then seeking quick relief. Anything more than that had been dangerous—not simply because the sort of companionship that Wylie preferred was inconveniently illegal, but because the abilities that allowed him to read other people's thoughts meant that the emotional demands of intimacy could easily overwhelm his own.

He couldn't allow that to happen again.

Though sometimes he wondered if there weren't someone out there who was worth the risk. Someone whose presence would invigorate rather than drain. Eisenstadt invigorated. He was an unreasonably generous lover and surprisingly undemanding company—as amusing as he was clever. And, Wylie suspected, he might also be kind, given the chance. Wylie didn't know if giving him that chance would be prudent, but he was starting to care less about prudence.

More to the point, Eisenstadt was really on to something with his research. *Scintillam vitae.* The spark of life. They'd never discussed it. Eisenstadt's mouth ran over in general, but his work was the one subject upon which he refused to speak. Yet he left his notes lying about as if he were *hoping* someone might discover them.

Wylie had taken that as an invitation, and he was glad he had.

The idea of a current—or a spark, as Eisenstadt liked to describe it, that animated all living things—it wasn't just interesting. It had proved useful. In fact, it had nudged Wylie's own research ahead. That was part of the reason he wanted to bring him on as an assistant. Not only because it could greatly accelerate his own work, but part of him felt guilty about having taken advantage.

But all of that could wait for now. Now he was going to see the site of his new laboratory, and he couldn't wait.

Eventually the cobblestones became smoother and more regular beneath the wheels of the hansom. The cab swayed gently instead of jerking, now. Wylie looked out. They were still in Whitechapel, but at the less dodgy end. Still, Shadwell would be respectable by comparison.

How had the Consortium come by the place in Shadwell, anyway?

Wylie had been keeping an eye on the East London property listings and had seen nothing for sale in Shadwell recently. Of course he knew by now that the Consortium worked in ways that it was often best not to question. Still, one would think that if a dedicated scientific facility existed in that part of town, he'd have already known about it.

The grey morning light filtered through thick clouds. Last night's fog had been brutal. Even as he'd climbed the tradesman's steps from Eisenstadt's basement lair, white tendrils curling up around the tops of his tall boots, he'd known it was foolhardy to venture out into it. If one didn't lose his way, there were always criminals who used the fog to their advantage, lurking there, waiting to turn their attentions upon an unsuspecting person. And it was terrible for the lungs—worse, Wylie suspected, the more one was exposed to it. He coughed discreetly into his kidskin glove, expelling the last sulphurous traces.

Perhaps he should have allowed Eisenstadt to talk him into staying. Wylie had been tempted—sorely tempted—but in the end his self-protective caution won out, as it always did. And that was, it occurred to him, a sad and limiting thing.

The driver gave the reins a quick jerk, and the horse pulled abruptly out of the flow of traffic. Wylie braced himself against the side of the hansom as the vehicle careered around a corner. Outside the carriage window, warehouses flanked the street on either side. His nose twitched at the coppery, organic reek that hung in the air. Rust-colored water puddled around the cobblestones. Abattoirs.

And then the sound came again: a barking dog. Not the same dog, of course. The timbre was different, and the tone was agitated rather than resigned. Yet the sound hit that same spot at the base of Wylie's skull, throbbed over his scalp, and formed a sharp point at the bridge of his nose.

"Driver!" Wylie pounded on the roof of the hansom.

The hansom jerked to a halt in front of a pair of buildings.

Cautiously, Wylie cracked open the door. The front windows of the surrounding buildings were filth-blackened, but the air rang with the clanks and cries of their damnable industry. The smell of blood hung heavily in the cool, still air, and the echoes of suffering seethed at the edges of Wylie's senses.

Slaughterhouse workers, Wylie had learned, had one of the highest rates of insanity of any profession.

Wylie himself was a vegetarian.

The dog-sounds came again. Whimpering. Injured. Scared.

Wylie jumped out of the hansom. The driver frowned down from his perch.

"Wait here," Wylie said.

What the devil was he doing? Anything might have been waiting for him in that alley—at the very least an injured animal with which he was ill equipped to deal. If only he'd thought to bring his medical bag.

He jogged toward the alley, rust-colored muck splashing his expensive boots. The shadows deepened and Wylie slowed. The sound was louder now: a growl rippling across the bricks and boards, raising a fine mist of soot. He stopped. Searched the darkness for a glint of eye or the hint of something crouching in the gloom, or hiding behind the pile of rubbish someone had carelessly covered with a length of canvas.

Wylie cried out when a hand shot out from the pile and grasped his ankle.

"Pain," a voice croaked.

"You're in pain?" Wylie's heart beat a rapid tattoo against his ribs, but training was taking over. It wasn't a pile of rubbish at all, but a man, aged about thirty, Wylie noted as he drew back the cloth, with a neat haircut and moustache that suggested he didn't belong in this part of London. The arm that was still connected to Wylie's ankle through an iron-strong grip was the color of cherrywood, and the man's bare feet peeking out from beneath the cloth were cut and bruised.

"Doctor?" the driver called. "Should I send for the police?"

Probably, Wylie thought. A naked, injured man left out like so much trash. At the same time, there was a lycanthrope in this alley. Wylie was certain of it. The growling he'd heard had been less of a sound than a feeling—a sharp pinch behind his eyes, a throbbing at the base of his skull.

Very similar, in fact, to the barking that had tormented him back at Shepherd Street.

Dear God.

"Your back," the man rasped. He let go of Wylie's ankle, his expression turning incredulous. "It's *terrible*. How do you tolerate it?"

"Doctor!" The driver called.

"No!" Wylie shouted back. "No police!" To the man now pulling himself up to a sit and rubbing at his eyes, he said, "How could you possibly know that?"

"The smell," the man said, rubbing a hand over his face, "is overwhelming."

The smell of the *alley* was overwhelming. Blood, excrement, soot, rotting wood. But even with all his training, Wylie had never smelt a backache. The growl came again, vibrating against Wylie's cerebellum with a dizzying intensity.

"I'll be sure to bathe when I return home," Wylie said. He glanced anxiously up and down the alley, but the creature, whatever it was, preferred to remain hidden. "Right now, I need you to stand up, if you can. We must leave immediately. I have a vehicle waiting."

Wylie extended his hand. The man blinked at it, then up at Wylie. His face gave a twitch, and Wylie felt a sensation that could only be described as snuffling at his wrist, at the back of his neck, and then, alarmingly, at his crotch.

"My God," Wylie whispered as recognition prickled up his spine.

"What is it?"

Wylie had been wrong. The Consortium had been wrong. They'd thought that lycanthropy was a discrete state. That at any given time, a person was either wolf or man. But it appeared that the two states could exist simultaneously. There was no lycanthrope lurking in the shadows, and this man wasn't the victim of an attack. The man and the creature were one in the same.

The new building could wait. Wylie had to get an interview.

"Let me help you," Wylie said.

The man gripped Wylie's hand with both of his and slowly pulled himself to his feet. He was clean for all he'd been lying in the muck. Or at least his dark skin lacked the ground-in dirt that came with a life on the street. His fingertips, though, were bloodied and bruised, and the tips of his nails were shredded. Wylie stole a glance at his naked form before he hurried to cover himself with the filthy canvas. Straight, well-formed limbs. Powerful, if compact musculature. He was well fed and looked after himself.

The man's dark eyes met Wylie's, and Wylie felt a familiar jolt. Yes, this man was objectively attractive, and he would be even more so cleaned up and packaged in fine clothing. A brown wool suit, perhaps, to set off his coppery skin, dark hair, and moustache. Wylie didn't have to probe his thoughts to see that the man felt the attraction as well. But it would be criminal to take advantage of him in this situation. And then there was Eisenstadt.

Slowly Wylie stepped away. As an afterthought he took off his fine coat and offered it. The man's shoulders were too broad for the garment, his waist too thick. But his bloodied fingers buttoned the bottom buttons to create a type of modesty.

"That's better," Wylie said, schooling the tremor from his voice. "See? All you need is to be warm and clean, just like any creature."

"Creature?"

He knows what he is, Wylie thought. Which answered another question.

"We're all creatures, are we not?" Wylie said. "My name is Wylie." He extended a hand.

"Spencer. Doctor." Dr. Spencer squeezed his hand.

Fascinating. The possibility of an educated medical opinion on the subject quickened his pulse. Between Eisenstadt's research and a medical man's first-hand experience…

"Well, Dr. Spencer, I think we'd best make our escape. Two men in an alley, one of them dressed in only an overcoat, is bound to attract the wrong sort of attention. Don't you think?" The man nodded. "Good."

What were the chances, Wylie wondered as they hurried toward the vehicle? And what of the lycanthrope in the basement of the building next to Consortium House? Had the Consortium been hiding it there all along? If so, why would they charge him with finding a specimen? Or perhaps the Society for the Protection of Creation had unwittingly taken in a lycanthrope, mistaking it for a dog in distress. Wylie saw his week's work setting itself out for him.

The question remained, though, how to broach the subject.

"I know what ails you," Wylie said as they reached the carriage.

"That would surprise me," Dr. Spencer replied.

The driver made to hop down from his perch to open the door, but Wylie gestured for him to remain in place. Instead, Wylie opened the door himself. Dr. Spencer looked longingly into the vehicle but remained where he was. Gently, Wylie probed his thoughts. What he found made him bite back a smile.

"Believe me, Doctor," he murmured. "The floor of this vehicle has seen much worse than the tattered soles of lycanthropic feet. Now step inside. Please. A wash, fresh clothes, and a hot mug of beef tea are just a short ride away."

CHAPTER NINE

Meg

Meg stepped off the train at Aldgate East Station. It had been a devil of a morning. She'd washed her face, pulled back her hair, put on her most sensible dress, and made her way to Bernadette's house as early as was reasonable, only to find that Bernadette had already decamped for a day of charitable work.

The organization sponsoring said work, Meg had been told, was located at 18 Shepherd Street. It had seemed odd to Meg that Bernadette's charity should lie in Mayfair. Bernadette had never shown much patience for the sitting-around-drinking-tea-and-talking-about-it sort of charity. As long as Meg had known her, she'd preferred to roll up her sleeves and dirty her hands. After two hours of walking up and down the stately streets of red-brick, terraced homes, wandering briefly through Burlington Arcade with its gleaming windows and fierce-looking beadles, and wondering whether she was losing her mind, Meg finally found a newsstand, and there, amongst headlines still screaming about the Hanwell Murderess, a London street guide. And then she realized that she should have been listening to her instinct all along.

There was a second Shepherd Street in London. In fact, there was also a third. But the second one lay in a dusty back corner of Whitechapel, which, as far as Bernadette was concerned, would be the perfect place to undertake voluntary work. Now that Meg had arrived in the correct part of town, the job would be finding the place.

Outside the station, Whitechapel High Street bustled with foot and horse traffic. Pedestrians flowed around her out of the station, then trickled out in all directions, stopping now and then to examine goods for sale at the temporary stalls and tables that dotted the pavement. The street rumbled with the vibrations from an underground train, and, as the muted sun passed behind a thick swath of clouds, a cold, sharp breeze cut through the heavy smell of horse urine and closely packed humanity.

Meg suddenly felt very, very small. In her world of libraries, lectures, and salons, Meg Eisenstadt was more than capable of holding her own. But there, alone in what might as well have been a different country, and with only a vague idea of where she was meant to go, she found her carapace of confidence disintegrating. She was painfully aware of her fine coat, expensive shoes, and her hat. Standing in her room back at Eisenstadt House, they'd seemed a reasonable choice. Now, however, she feared they stood out stood out like plumage amid the sea of rough wool and stained bombazine. She was utterly, completely, out of her element.

She pulled the edges of her coat tighter, adjusted her scarf, and fingered her pocket street guide through the front panel of her coat.

"You waitin' for someone, love?"

Meg whirled at the gravely male voice coming from someone standing much too near. He was a sharp-faced individual with stained teeth and a close, pointy beard straight out of a children's cautionary tale. Meg gasped in surprise and took a step back. He smirked.

"All alone, then? Young lady like yourself ought to be careful." He made a show of glancing to either side of them before stepping even closer.

"Thank you for your concern." She straightened. "I'll be on my way."

"Not so fast, love. Anything can happen in this part of town, if you don't know where you're going."

"I'll be careful, I'm sure." The cold, haughty tone she took had proved more than adequate for dissuading unwanted conversation from overly eager young gentlemen, but this specimen seemed impervious. Meg's heart began to beat faster when he took another step toward her.

"Careful ain't enough, love. "Why, do you know, a young woman much like yourself disappeared right off that corner, right there." He gestured toward Whitechapel High Street. "Mindin' her own business, she was, and snatched—" he snapped dirty fingers just inches from her nose—"just like that. Now, if you like, I could…"

Why was he talking to her? What did he want? On the safe, manicured streets of Chelsea-adjacent, this conversation would have attracted several offers of assistance by now. More likely still, it would never have happened in the first place. She glanced at the crowd around her. People walked by, averting their eyes as they passed. Meg might have been arranging an assignation for all they knew, yet not an eyebrow rose in response. It was a strange kind of freedom. Meg was ever so interested in freedom. At the same time, she couldn't help now seeing the other side of that particular coin. Absolute freedom meant no help if one needed it. Oh, why hadn't she paid better attention during Bernadette's self-defense lesson?

"Actually," she said.

The man glanced up suddenly, training a look over Meg's shoulder. Footsteps slapped up behind them, and Meg turned to see a young woman running up to them.

"Louisa!" the woman cried. She was pretty. Tidy and efficient-looking, but also vibrant, with flashing eyes and pleasing curves beneath her deliberately plain clothing. She had a little Cupid's bow of a mouth that must have looked quite naughty when it wasn't reading from the Bible. Meg's second thought was to wonder who on earth Louisa was.

"Louisa!" The woman was catching her breath.

"Forgive me, Miss," Meg said. "I believe you've mistaken me for—"

"*Cousin* Louisa, it's been absolute *ages.*"

"Er…"

The man was looking from one of them to the other. He hadn't gone away as Meg had hoped, but the arrival appeared to have unbalanced him.

"What absolute *serendipity*," the woman went on. "Imagine running into you here, of all places. I say, is this a friend of yours?" she said, narrowing her eyes at the man. Then she frowned. "I can't imagine your parents would approve."

The woman took her by the hand. Meg was too surprised to resist. The woman wore no gloves, though her hands were as clean as the rest of her. Through the silk of her own gloves, Meg felt strong, capable fingers, along with a warmth that seemed to pulse, like a heartbeat, to Meg's soul. Meg looked into the woman's clear, blue eyes, and all of Whitechapel seemed to fall still around them.

"Going somewhere, love?"

Meg cried out as a different, ruder hand fell on her elbow. She jerked her arm away, but the hand, with its ragged nails and dirty creases, held fast.

"I don't believe we've been introduced," the woman said, giving that hand a slap.

It was such an odd thing to do—daring and dangerous, and the woman realized it as well. When Meg locked eyes with her, she saw the expression of someone who had recognized they'd just poked a bear. The man drew a sharp breath, perhaps to issue a rejoinder, and then suddenly the woman's fingers were closing around hers, and they were sprinting through the crowd, hand in hand. They didn't stop running until they were several streets away, at which point nervous laughter overcame them, and they stood there giddy with their daring escape and giggling like a pair of naughty children.

"Thank you," Meg said once she'd caught her breath. "I should have extricated myself from that conversation a lot sooner, but I wasn't quite sure how."

"He was using your politeness against you," the woman said. "It's a common tactic. You're fortunate. You were very close to being snatched. See? There he goes with his confederate."

A shiver crept up Meg's spine. Everyone had read the stories, of course. And one always wondered how the victim could have failed to see what was plain from someone watching outside the situation. As she watched the two men slink away into an alley, Meg felt the blood drain from her face.

"But you're quite safe now, of course," the woman said, patting Meg's shoulder.

"How did you know what he was going to do?"

"I saw him and his associate emerge from the alley. I watched him position himself outside the entrance to the station. Then you wandered out, looking all alone and lost. That probably isn't your fanciest dress, but if you observe carefully, as such people do, you can see how it's still not quite right for this part of town."

"Oh." Meg felt completely ridiculous and also rather impressed with Bernadette, who had obviously been navigating this side of town on her own for some time, now.

"I'm Abigail Gordon," the other woman said, extending her bare hand. Meg quickly took it. Again that sensation of connection pulsed through the fabric of her glove, through the muscles of her hand, and into her very bones. The women locked eyes again. Miss Gordon felt it, too. Meg could see it in her clear, wide-open eyes. But she was also certain that Miss Gordon was some sort of missionary, which meant that the coded words and glances one used to test the romantic potential of a new connection at university probably wouldn't translate, and that if they did, they wouldn't be appreciated.

"Meg Eisenstadt." Meg reluctantly broke the grip.

"Miss Eisendtadt, if it isn't too forward, might I ask where you're going? If you like, I could accompany you part of the way, in case that horrible man decides to follow."

"I should like that very much. I'm going to meet a friend of mine. She works on Shepherd Street."

Miss Gordon's sweet face took on a serious expression. "Shepherd Street? What on Earth does your friend do there?" Perhaps reading the question in Meg's eyes, she continued. "That is to say, there are two buildings on Shepherd Street which aren't completely boarded up, and neither looks like anywhere a well-bred young woman ought to be spending her time."

Meg bristled at the term *well-bred*, but Miss Gordon clearly knew the area, and the reservations in the other woman's expression were giving Meg reservations, as well.

"Do you know the area?" Meg asked.

"Reasonably well. As a matter of fact, I'm headed in that direction myself. If you like, it would be safer for both of us to go together."

"I should like it very much."

"Then it's settled."

Miss Gordon glanced back toward the station. Meg followed her gaze, relieved to see no sign of the men. She turned back to find Miss Gordon regarding her with interest. They exchanged a smile. Well, Meg thought. However the morning eventually shook out, she would enjoy sharing part of it with such a charming companion.

CHAPTER TEN

Gideon

With a crack of the reins, Mr. Wylie's two-seater began to roll. Gideon watched the warehouses pass by outside, felt the relief as the soup of abattoir smells began to fade, making room for the scents of new leather, jasmine, and bergamot. Industrial sprawl gradually gave way to tenements and the occasional shop. They were going in the wrong direction for the clinic, but Gideon didn't care. The thought of the promised beef tea and a good washup crowded out any inconvenient pangs of caution.

It was wonderful stuff, beef tea—the nutrition and energy of an entire steer distilled and compressed into a single jar. It had been a battlefield invention. Now it was one of the most powerful tools in a medical man's arsenal, which made him wonder how Mr. Wylie had come by it. For as far as Gideon knew, beef tea was not generally available outside the profession.

He glanced at his companion. Mr. Wylie was staring straight ahead, sitting with the ramrod posture of someone who had spent years looking for a position that would relieve a bad back, or at least not exacerbate it. A young man to have such a problem, but it happened. The smell of his pain—sharp, bitter—had faded somewhat. Now Gideon could sense anticipation. Or was it nervousness? A bit of both?

Something had passed between them in that alley: a rush of sensation when Gideon's fingers had met Wylie's ankle. Perhaps Mr. Wylie, in his silence, was responding to this. It had been a bit like an electrical shock he'd received in a friend's laboratory once, though it wasn't strictly physical. What was physical was the sensation of being drawn toward the other man. Animal magnetism—was that what Mesmer had called it? Something in Wylie's blood that called to something in Gideon's own.

The thought was disturbing, and Gideon shook it off as a vestige of the departing wolf.

Eventually the vehicle turned down another alley and pulled up to the rear entrance of a long, brown brick building. The main structure no doubt housed several entities, whether businesses or residences he couldn't tell from this angle. The atmosphere suggested abandonment. At the same time, the building's construction appeared sound, and the door and the lock upon it looked solid and new.

It was midmorning by Gideon's estimate, yet shadows were gathering in the corners and crevices. Thick clouds had obscured the sun and cast a cold pall over it all. Somewhere nearby a dog was barking, rhythmically, almost monotonously, as if it had been barking for a very long time and didn't expect an answer. The wolf would have been able to give him more information, but the wolf was all but gone.

"Where are we?" Gideon asked as the vehicle pulled to a stop.

"Consortium House," Wylie said.

"What's that?"

Instead of answering, Wylie gave a small smile, opened the door, and slipped out. Gideon followed him to one of the doors that opened onto the alley.

He tapped his bruised toes while Wylie unlocked the door. He really should go back to the clinic. Abby had no doubt found the remains of the broken phial by now. She'd be out of her mind with worry. At the same time, he felt compelled by the promise of beef tea, the possibility of a fresh set of clothing, and that tantalizing jolt of attraction that even now still sizzled across his nerves.

Inside, the building looked anything but abandoned. The entryway was swept and clear. Gas sconces shed a warm light on a polished staircase laid with a dark-red patterned runner. Wylie alighted on the stairs, and after a moment of hesitation, Gideon followed, taking care to mind the stiff wool against the cuts and tears in his soles.

At the top of the stairs, the carpet spread out in both directions, rising into walls of honey-colored wood. Small lamps illuminated a row of paintings with pools of yellowish light. As they passed, Gideon attempted to examine the paintings, but his eyes refused to focus on the images long enough to interpret them. His mind, however, had regained its full sharpness, and a new foreboding was setting in. Consortium House looked like some sort of gentlemen's club. But what kind of gentlemen's club set up in Whitechapel?

Sweat broke out across Gideon's scalp, his pulse pounding in the still air.

Gideon jumped at the delicate hand on his shoulder. "I really do want to help, Doctor. I promise, I intend you no harm."

"What do you want from me, then?"

Realization sparked in Wylie's eyes, then pity.

"Doctor," he said. "It's Doctor Wylie." He offered his hand, and Gideon, not knowing what else to do, gave it a perfunctory shake. "I apologize for not having said as much earlier. The truth is, I've never come across…across someone like you before. There's so much I want to ask you."

Gideon searched Wylie's face. He drew in a deep breath, searching for olfactory traces of malice or deceit. Such things, like certain illnesses, usually left strong traces that Gideon could detect even without the wolf. However, all Gideon could smell was jasmine, bergamot, and, interestingly, beef tea.

"All right?" Wylie asked.

Gideon nodded.

They continued down the corridor to a door. Wylie produced another key and led them into what appeared to be a small library. A desk in one corner was stacked with piles of papers and books. A leather-upholstered sofa and a pair of chairs sat at the perimeters of a Chinese rug. A wood fire crackled away in a large fireplace, and Gideon shivered with pleasure at the warmth that suddenly surrounded them. A wooden screen stood to one side of the fireplace, and behind it, Gideon could make out a spindly wooden stand that held a basin, a pitcher, and a clean towel.

"My work often keeps me here at all hours," Dr. Wylie said. "I'm sure you understand."

Gideon nodded. He'd spent more than one night on the clinic's folding army bed. But this was no clinic. He reevaluated his earlier judgment. Not a gentlemen's club, either, but perhaps a private sanatorium. Luxurious inside to justify the price, but tucked out of public view to minimize familial embarrassment.

Gideon glanced around warily. That dog was still barking. It was in the building next door, probably in the basement. It was a sad sound tinged with resignation, but the wolf was well and truly gone, now, and Gideon couldn't interpret beyond that without it.

Wylie crossed to the bell pull that hung beside the fireplace and gave it a yank. A young woman appeared in the doorway so quickly Gideon wondered if she hadn't been lurking somewhere nearby this entire time. She had the face of a porcelain doll: pale, flawless skin; wide, grey eyes behind metal-rimmed spectacles; and white-blond hair that fell in ringlets around her face.

"You rang, Doctor?"

"Yes, Miss Kingsley. Please bring a pot of beef tea and a tray with luncheon for two."

Gideon felt a prickle at the back of his neck. The young woman was staring unabashedly past Wylie, curiously, intelligently dissecting him. He caught sight of himself in the glass front of a bookcase and, mortified at the degraded, bashed-up, all-but-naked stranger he saw there, made a useless attempt to pull Wylie's coat tighter across his bare chest.

"Miss Kingsley," Wylie snapped. "I require luncheon for my patient."

Dear God, it was an asylum. Dr. Wylie definitely had that air about him—the quietly commanding, preternaturally patient alienist. Gideon wondered how far he'd get if he ran.

"Yes. Yes, of course, Doctor," the young woman stammered. "I'm sorry. I didn't mean…forgive me."

Wylie shut the door and turned to Gideon, his expression softening. "I'm so sorry, Doctor. Good help is hard to find."

"My God, what must she have thought of…of all this?"

"It's not her place to think anything of it. Please don't trouble yourself. What she thinks she saw will go no further. Now," he said, his voice softening as well. The lines around Wylie's eyes tightened, and Gideon sensed the spasm in his lower back, even as Wylie's muscles tightened against it.

"How long has it been like that?" Gideon asked.

"What?"

"Is it congenital or the result of an injury?"

Wylie closed his eyes for a moment, as if attempting to master the pain. Then he let out a long breath. "There's a basin and a washcloth behind the screen. Would you care to freshen up while I find you some clothes?"

Gideon nodded, embarrassed. He'd overstepped. It was a professional hazard. At the same time, he'd be damned if he would be reduced to the role of patient. He should leave immediately. At the same time, the smell of Wylie's carbolic soap was tickling his senses, and by God he needed a wash. Grateful for the excuse for a few minutes alone, Gideon found the basin, filled it from the thankfully full pitcher, and set about cleaning himself up. The soap stung the cuts on his fingertips and the soles of his feet. Still, it comforted him to feel the disinfectant working. He heard a muffled *flump* as Wylie hung a shirt and trousers over the top of the screen.

"You told her I was your patient," Gideon said, reaching for the trousers.

"Consultant would be more precise, I suppose, only I can't imagine my employers would appreciate my bringing someone else into the organization without so much as a by-your-leave. The work we do is rather sensitive."

"And what work is that?"

As Wylie paused, perhaps planning his next deflection, Gideon noticed that the dog next door had gone quiet. A pair of shoes had appeared nearby on the floor, along with a clean pair of socks. Gideon put them both on as well.

"Please, come sit with me. We've a lot to discuss."

The shirt was silk, and though it wasn't new, it was clean and well cared for. The shoulders fit well around Gideon's own, but the torso fit closer. A strange cut, but not uncomfortable. It smelled of jasmine and bergamot, and he felt a small shiver of pleasure at the thought of wrapping himself in something that had once wrapped itself around Wylie. But a different thought dispelled the pleasure. Wylie was making a study of lycanthropy, and it seemed that Gideon was to be part of that study. An odd word, lycanthrope, better suited to legends and penny dreadfuls than to such an ordinary individual as himself.

As he emerged from behind the screen, Wylie gestured for Gideon to join him on the sofa.

"So," Gideon said nervously. He perched on the edge of the cushion.

"So." Wylie positioned a pen above a stack of paper. "You're a physician by day."

"And a beast by night," Gideon said with a little laugh.

"Every night?"

"No." Gideon fell serious. "No. In fact, it only happens when I've gone too long without my medicine."

Wylie narrowed his eyes. They were large, inky-black, and beautiful. "There's a medicine?"

"My nurse brings it from Whitechapel."

"What sort of medicine?" Wylie asked. "Who produces it?"

"I don't know." Gideon frowned. He should have that information. "She brings it to me, I take it, and it suppresses the condition admirably."

The pen stopped mid-sentence. "That's a lot of trust to put in another person."

"We should trust one another. We're engaged to be married, after all."

"Oh." Wylie's eyebrows rose in a pair of elegant arches.

Heat rushed to Gideon's face as he realized how hollow the words sounded, even to him. Remembering the sensation that had passed between them in the alley, well, it was proof enough that it hadn't been one-sided after all.

Gideon cleared his throat. "What sort of doctor did you say you were?"

"I'm an alienist."

"Ah. Am I mad, then?" He laughed nervously.

"I couldn't possibly know that, having spoken with you so briefly. I don't believe that lycanthropy is imaginary or a type of madness. But I would like to ask you a few questions, with your permission. Please know that you're free to leave at any time."

Gideon nodded. "I suppose I do owe you that, for the sake of the clothing. Goodness knows how I'd have made my way back to Shadwell in the condition I was in."

Wylie looked up sharply. "Shadwell?"

"My clinic is in Shadwell, on Cornwall Street."

Wylie had gone absolutely still. Somewhere in the background, that dog began to bark again.

"Does that mean something to you, Dr. Wylie?" Gideon watched Wylie school his features once again. It reminded him of someone shutting, then locking a gate. The dog continued to bark. Gideon strained to listen, but by this time, the wolf had departed completely, and Gideon perceived it as no more than an irritating noise.

"A bit annoying, isn't it? The dog, I mean," Gideon said.

"You hear it, too?" Wylie asked.

"Excuse me?"

Wylie blinked. Gideon could sense him suppressing something, though it wasn't another spasm. "Do you know any others like yourself?" he asked. When Gideon remained silent, he continued. "One wonders in cases such as yours, how one…part of your life affects the other. How much wolf is in the man, and how much man is in the wolf, if you take my meaning. It is a wolf, isn't it?"

"Yes," Gideon said.

"And wolves live in packs. One theory has it that lycanthropes may also live in packs."

"Not that I know of," Gideon said. Wylie nodded. Gideon watched his pen dart across the paper once more, making neat loops and dips. "Are there people who…become…other things?"

Wylie shrugged again. "We don't know."

"What *do* you know?"

Wylie let out a long breath and paused, perhaps to consider his words. "I once had a patient who believed she had a monster inside her." Gideon couldn't put a finger on why, but the words seemed to pain him. "She couldn't control the transformations—or so she said. No one had ever witnessed them."

"But you believed her?" Gideon said.

"I was skeptical at first, of course. I'd worked with other patients with complex delusions. But none of those delusions appeared to sharpen the senses to the point that the patient could repeat conversations that had taken place on the other side of a noisy, crowded building complex or describe the perfume my dinner companion had worn the night before. There were other things as well, but…"

"Do you still see—?"

"No."

Tension thrummed in the air between them. Gideon's pulse quickened. The more the other man tried to hide, the more Gideon felt compelled to pursue. But to what end? The ghost of jasmine rose from the collar of the borrowed silk shirt, along with a different scent. No, not a scent, exactly, but a *sensation* that danced on a primitive part of Gideon's brain. A presence simultaneously male and female, which elicited an unmistakable atavistic response in other parts of Gideon's anatomy that neither Abby nor any other woman ever had.

How had he never felt it before? So pure, simple, and all-consuming. Was this what his friends had felt as, one by one, they had developed an obsession for female company? Gideon had never understood that. He figured he'd understand in time, that marriage would eventually teach him.

But now he understood that marriage wouldn't help one bit.

Wylie was watching him closely, his own expression guarded. Gideon had the mortifying suspicion that Wylie was reading his thoughts as easily as one reads the newspaper.

In the building next door, the dog's barking exploded into a furious frenzy.

Wylie stood quickly. "Excuse me," he said, stepping toward the door. "Someone has got to do something about that godforsaken animal."

❖

Jin

This wasn't how the interview was meant to go.

It was his own fault, Wylie told himself. He reached the end of the hallway, turned around, and stalked back the way he'd come. Dr. Spencer had seemed so helpless that Wylie hadn't guarded his thoughts. Bit by bit he'd been drawn into the currents of the man's emotions, and those emotions had overwhelmed his own before he'd known where he was. Damn and blast it.

To wit, there was an *actual* lycanthrope in his office, with a heretofore unrecognized attraction to men, and an attraction to Wylie in specific. On top of that, the attraction was not entirely one-sided.

Wylie didn't have time for another personal distraction, and he didn't even want to think about the potential for disaster in pursuing such distractions with a subject. If that weren't enough, the man owned the building on Cornwall Street and appeared to be unaware that the Consortium had promised it to Wylie for his new facility.

That spot in his lower back began to throb.

"Dr. Wylie?" A voice said.

Wylie turned. "Miss Kingsley."

She hadn't been there when he'd fled his office, and he was certain he'd have seen her emerge from the stairs. Had she been hiding nearby? Hathaway's earlier comment was a nasty little whisper in his ear. *If reports from the kitchen and Miss Kingsley are to be believed...*

"Were you spying?" he demanded.

"Spying?" She frowned. "Certainly not. I came to…" She peered closer, narrowing her eyes behind her silver-rimmed spectacles. "Is everything all right, Doctor?"

"No, as a matter of fact, it is not." A light sweat had broken across his face, and that damned dog was still barking. He pulled his sticky hair back from his forehead. "Did you need something?"

She blinked again. "Not precisely. I thought…An idea occurred to me…about your…guest, and I thought…"

"You have a lot of thoughts and ideas for someone who brings me my tea," Wylie snapped.

Her delicate features went hard, and she raised her chin. "I do, actually, sir."

Was that so? Another time he might have been in a mood to indulge the intellectual conceits of glorified housemaids, but at the moment, he'd a bit too much on his plate.

"What is it that you do, here, again, Miss Kingsley?"

"Scientific support staff, but—"

"Do you have a scientific education?"

"I have a first-class degree in biology from Girton, actually. I've been making a study of—"

"*You* have been making a study?"

The words had come out more sharply than he'd intended. Her thin lower lip trembled. A very small, quiet voice at the back of his mind whispered he was being unreasonable, but his nerves were alight with fight-or-flight fire, his back was killing him, and his head was throbbing in time to the monotonous barking of that damned beast next door.

"Sir?" Miss Kingsley asked.

"It's that godforsaken dog. It never stops barking. Don't you hear it?"

"I don't hear anything," she said.

"What do you mean? Dr. Spencer heard it, even through the door."

"I don't know, sir. But I can tell you, there is no barking dog."

She met his glare and squared her thin shoulders. He reached out a tendril of thought, but she'd veiled her mind, as, no doubt, Sir Julius had taught her to do. Did she really not hear it? Or had the barking been going on so long it had become part of the background for her? Or perhaps something worse was transpiring.

"So you say," he said.

"Sir?"

"You work very closely with Hathaway, don't you?"

"I…I support all of the key staff, sir."

"But Hathaway in particular."

Her eyes blinked furiously behind her spectacles. Nervousness? Or deception?

"Perhaps it's a joke between you," he said.

"I…"

"Or something more sinister. He's had it in for me from the beginning, Hathaway. Perhaps the two of you are conspiring."

It made sense. Oh, yes, it made perfect sense, now. The disgraced alienist who lost his position and then lost his mind. And in the end, who would the Consortium believe? Hathaway, who had been one of them all along? Or Wylie, who was lucky to have a job at all?

Miss Kingsley shook her head and took a step back. A flush was creeping up the pale skin of her neck, and she was clutching her hands tightly in front of her. When she spoke again, he could hear her holding back the tremor from her voice.

"I can see that this is a bad time."

"Can you?"

"Whatever I did, I apologize. Good day, Doctor."

She turned on her heel and fled.

Cool relief flooded over him, but it was short-lived. She'd go straight to Sir Julius, now. Or at least to Hathaway. And it would be his own fault.

"Miss Kingsley, wait!" he called. But she was racing down the stairs, her footsteps light yet noticeable.

Wylie glanced at his office door. If he went after her, would Dr. Spencer leave? He wanted to lock the door. But he'd told

Dr. Spencer that he was free to go. If he locked the man in, he'd never get another word out of him. Though that wouldn't matter at all if the Consortium threw him out on his ear. To hell with it.

"Miss Kingsley!" he called as he ran for the stairs. He took the steps two at a time, checked the back entrance—still double-locked—then ran into the empty front rooms. He registered shafts of muted light through boarded-up windows, bare floors, and a few sticks of furniture, but no sign of life.

He burst out the front door into watery grey daylight and a deserted street flanked by padlocked doors and darkened windows. Well, almost deserted. Miss Kingsley's prim, tweed-swaddled figure was mounting the stairs of Number 18. He was wavering on the precipice of decision—to follow her inside or return to his guest—when a voice called out behind him. A familiar voice, bursting with pleasant surprise.

"I say, Jin Wylie!"

CHAPTER ELEVEN

Garrick

In the end, Clyde had led them to Nell Evans. Being small and spry, Clyde could appear suddenly and easily disappear into the shadows before anyone noticed. Being young and even younger-looking, his presence rarely caused concern. And being able to pass as both male and female—he presented himself as male, generally speaking, but even Garrick didn't know for certain what was actually beneath his clothing—he had been able to take on the types of housework that allowed him both a small amount of money when he wanted it, and also access to wealthy homes. Clyde had never, to Garrick's knowledge, combined his considerable fingersmithing skills with his cleaning skills, but regular proximity had taught him how to speak and act around respectable folk.

And in the end that was how they'd found Nell Evans.

"Who the devil are you, again?" Evans asked.

Evans was, as the nurse had said, a woman in her early twenties, with a thin build, lank dark hair, and the pasty skin that a lot of people in East London had. One of her arms was in plaster, held tightly to her chest with a knotted scarf. Distorted fingers stuck out of the plaster: twisted and dry-looking, almost like sticks.

Evans didn't stand up, and Garrick was pretty sure she wasn't going to. She was sitting on a step outside of a boarded-up shop. Next to her was a box. In the box were two babies dreaming laudanum dreams.

Clyde said, "The name's Claudia. I'm with Kensington."

The Kensington Domestic Agency—that was where Clyde, now in a dress with a washed face and mob cap, had finally found the information that had led them to Evans. Garrick had waited outside while he—she—had gone in to charm the information out of the girl working behind the counter. It had actually been the fourth agency they'd tried that morning. Garrick had to admit, he never would have thought to ask, but Claudia—Clyde—had said that it was a common way for a common girl to make a little money, and some girls worked for more than one agency.

"Never heard of 'em," said Evans.

"Funny. They heard of you. Let you go, didn't they?"

"After years of solid work, too." Evans scowled.

"Spotty work, more like," Claudia said. "At least that's according to your records."

"And who are you to be looking at my records?" Evans eyed Claudia up and down. "Too young to be a manager, and them's the only one with that information. Last time I checked, Kensington didn't have no one behind the counter named *Claudia*."

Claudia shrugged. "Either way, they gave you the sack two weeks ago on account of that arm, and now you're a baby farmer."

Evans snarled. The term wasn't a compliment.

"It's honest work, innit? Keep the little mites safe while their mums are working in the factories. Besides, what else am I gonna do with my arm and all?"

"Yeah. What happened with that?" Claudia asked.

One of the babies fussed drunkenly, and Evans reached over with her good hand to smooth its hair away from its face.

"*Why* am I talking to you, again?"

Garrick's lips twitched. He could just picture Nell Evans in that nurse's clinic, giving the nurse lip and trouble as the nurse tried to patch her up and get her story.

"That nurse in the Cornwall Street Clinic, Nurse Gordon, she sent me. She said you was meant to stop by so she could check your plaster, but you never showed."

"How do you know about *that*?"

"I done some cleaning for her, didn't I?"

"And she discusses her patients with the cleaning girl?"

"She knew we both worked for Kensington, innit? She thought maybe we knew each other and—"

Evans's expression went hard. "I never said nothing about that to her."

Claudia's expression wobbled so slightly, Garrick was pretty sure only he had seen it. "Well...she's worried about your arm and wants you to stop by when you can."

Evans's expression went cynical. "And that's all you came to say? Tell her thanks for her concern. I'll try to come by when my hands ain't so full." She gestured toward the box. "Or my hand, that is."

"Actually, that ain't all," Garrick said. The other two looked at him as if he'd just appeared. He'd agreed to let Claudia lead on this one, and it had been the right decision, but Garrick wasn't about to let Nell Evans get rid of them that easily. "We want to know about the Fiend."

Claudia frowned at him, probably wondering where that had come from. But even as he'd been choking, Garrick had noticed how the nurse's eyes had gone wide when the boys had mentioned their fight with the creature, how the color had drained from her face when one of them had used that word. *Fiend.* The nurse had heard that word before. Garrick was willing to bet *his* right arm on it—or at least a finger. And then in the morning she had been desperate to find Nell Evans. Garrick would have bet his *left* arm on the two of those things being connected. He'd never known a nurse to go out and check up on patients.

Nell Evans stared. Garrick hazarded a glance at her eyes, and it was like she was looking right into his soul. "So you seen it too, then," Evans said.

Garrick nodded. "Last night."

Evans gave him another long, hard stare, then began to speak.

It had happened exactly two weeks before. Nell Evans had been down near the clinic with her boys. They weren't a tight-knit gang like Garrick and his own, but they ran messages for her, and she looked out for them. At least that's how she told it.

"So you was already near the clinic when it happened," Garrick said.

"That's right."

"What time?"

"Around eight o'clock in the evening."

"There was a fog that night, wasn't there?" Claudia asked.

Evans nodded gravely. "Like you never seen before."

"Like last night?" Claudia asked.

"Well, maybe you did see it then. It was just like last night, come to think of it. Anyway, we was walking down that alley near Rook Street when the fog came in."

"Looking for custom?" Claudia asked.

It was a fair question, Garrick thought. Claudia wasn't judging, and neither was he. Plenty of women made a living that way, or part of a living. But the look that Evans gave Claudia was pure poison.

"No, not that it matters. And not that I'd tell you nohow. I don't have to make my living on my back. I got skills." She flicked her eyes toward her ruined arm. "Or I did have, anyhow."

Claudia raised an eyebrow and glanced at her fingernails. Garrick would have bet money she'd picked up the gesture from some rich lady. "Ain't no pockets to pick on Rook Street," she said.

"No, but there's locks to pick, and treasure behind them, if you know what to look for."

Silence fell then, and the two women stared at each other. Garrick was fascinated. He watched the wheels turning behind Claudia's eyes. Clyde's eyes. He was so damned convincing when he put on a dress that even Garrick found himself following along. A dangerous current sizzled through the air. Claudia put a finger to her lips and nodded.

"You was breaking into the Cornwall Street Clinic."

"What if I was?" Evans blustered. "Some of them medicines could bring a right pretty penny! Set me up for a week!"

Garrick felt torn. Not twenty-four hours earlier, he'd thought exactly the same thing. Yet after that night he felt a strange protectiveness over the nurse and the clinic. But before Garrick could think more on that, Claudia was off and running.

"Did you get in?"

"No, I bloody well did not. The fog was right thick by then. I could hardly see my fingers or my picks. Then there was a sound like something rattling along the cobblestones, and one of my boys cried out."

"Who was with you?" Claudia asked. She was leaning in close, now, and pulling the story right out of Evans. By God, she'd make a cracking detective if she weren't a—damn and blast! He'd never keep it straight.

"There was two of them. Jim and little Raffi," Evans said.

"*Raffi?*" Claudia asked, wrinkling her nose. Garrick tensed as Evans leaned back. The spell was breaking.

"Raphael. It's a Jewish name. What's the problem?"

"No problem," Claudia said quickly. "Your lookouts, yeah?"

"Yeah," Evans said, eyeing them warily, now.

"So what happened then?"

"It were Raffi who made the noise. So I turn and I see the fog swirling. It was so strange. It doesn't do that, does it? The fog. Usually just sits there on top of the city, poisoning everything until it decides to drift away. And that's when I notice that there's something *in* there."

Garrick hugged his arms to his chest, remembering their own encounter. He'd never forget the eyes. Glowing, green eyes that flashed through the swirling wind and fog. Arms that reached out to grab him, and the swirling fog that surrounded him. He'd tried to scream, and that had been when the sand and mud and muck had gone in.

"It picked me up," Evans said. "Picked me up and twisted my arm behind me. But it kept on twisting. I felt the bones snap. I *heard* the bones snap. And those *eyes*. I'd take afternoon tea with the Hanwell Murderess every day and twice on Sunday before I'd look into them eyes again."

"And your boys?" Claudia asked.

"That were the strangest thing. Jim were all scratched up and bruised, like that thing had picked him up and given him a good shake before tossing him across the alley. But Raff…"

"Didn't have a scratch on him," Garrick said.

Evans whipped her head around to stare at him. "How did you know?"

How did Garrick know? Because the same thing had happened the night before with them. A swirling cloud, a beast with green eyes, and an attack that focused on the leader of the group. Him. Garrick. Clyde and Bert had taken their lumps, as well, but nothing like what had happened to Garrick.

But Eli, like Raff, had escaped without a scratch.

"So what the devil do you think it was?" Garrick demanded as they walked away, leaving Nell Evans sitting on the steps with her crop of infants.

"I think it *was* the devil," Claudia said.

"Be serious."

"I am. It weren't nothing natural. It weren't a man, or an animal. It was—"

"A fiend," Garrick said.

"And a fiend is a demon, like. It's in the Bible."

"Is not," said Garrick. And Garrick knew. The Booth ladies had taught him to read the Bible, and he never saw anything like that. Claudia glanced at him and raised an eyebrow. "And when are you going to take off that ridiculous dress?" Garrick grumbled.

"Worked a treat, though, didn't it? I'm telling you, the right clothes will get you places."

"I don't want to go anywhere looking like that," Garrick said.

Claudia shot him another look but took off the mob cap and stuffed it into a pocket of the dress. They stopped into an alley, and she shrugged off the rest of the outfit, right down to the trousers and shirt beneath it. She rolled the dress up neatly, tucked it under one arm, turned around, and then lo and behold, Clyde was back, as if he'd never been away.

"I'll never get used to that," Garrick said.

Clyde grinned. "And that's why you need me. That and the fact that I could pick the nose right off your face and be away before you was any the wiser."

"Don't even think about picking my nose," Garrick said, returning the grin.

"So, what are we going to tell that nurse?" Clyde asked.

"Tell her we found Nell Evans and told her to come in to have her arm looked at, just like she told us to," Garrick answered.

Clyde nodded. Something about the sly cant of his head told Garrick that he had more to say about this.

"What?" Garrick demanded.

"I think we should also ask that nurse if she believes in coincidence."

"What the blazes is coincidence?" Garrick said.

Clyde stopped and pinned Garrick with his icy-light gaze. "You can't tell me you ain't seeing the common denominator."

"Now I *really* don't know what you're on about." He was picking up some fancy words cleaning rich people's homes. Garrick wondered if he'd been cleaning anyone's library recently.

"Don't you think it's funny," Clyde asked in a tone that made it clear that Clyde did not find it funny at all, "that two different groups of thieves tried to help themselves to the bounty of the Cornwall Street Clinic, on two different nights, two weeks apart, and they both end up being attacked by some green-eyed devil in the fog?

Garrick opened his mouth but then snapped it shut again. It was funny, but not in a laughing way. The previous night's events rushed back to him all at once. The look that nurse had given him right before he'd gone flying back. She'd had the same expression before the clinic door had slammed shut in their faces.

Clyde was staring at him, again, and as Garrick turned, Clyde began to nod.

"Bert says she goes to that place on Shepherd Street every week," Garrick said. "That place is the devil's very own."

Clyde said, "Don't know about the Devil."

"Oh?"

"Doctors, maybe. Or chemists. Only I was in the area the other day…"

Garrick knew that a lot of Clyde's stories about being *in the area* often ended in petty theft.

"...when I thought I'd poke my nose in and see what them devils is really up to."

"And?"

Clyde frowned. "They got it all locked up tight, but someone didn't draw the curtains tight enough. They got a lab in there. Tubes and flasks and chemicals."

"So medicines, then," Garrick said.

"Maybe...."

"What else could it be?"

"I dunno. But whatever it is, they don't want people to see it."

Garrick nodded. "You think the nurse is one of them, then?"

"Dunno," Clyde said. "You say Bert sees her there once a week? Sounds like somefin' of a transactional nature."

"You what?"

"Deals," Clyde said.

"What kind of deals?"

Clyde shrugged. "Deals for medicine? Free clinic probably doesn't have two farthings to rub together."

"Maybe," Garrick said. "Only if she's getting medicine from them, what's she givin' them in return?"

Clyde stood up straight and squared his puny shoulders. "Couldn't tell you, but there's more to that nurse than what you see, and I aim to find out what it is. Before we go back to the clinic with her information like good little boys, I say we pay a visit to that building on Shepherd Street."

CHAPTER TWELVE

Abby

It was a bit of a hike to Shepherd Street. Abby was grateful for that. She was also grateful for the fact that Miss Eisenstadt—Meg, for they'd found themselves on first-name terms from the moment they'd reluctantly let go their hands—was a chatty sort of person. Abby needed time to think and process. She wasn't normally shy, and generally speaking she had little trouble finding topics of conversation of interest to herself and whoever she happened to be with. But something had happened there, in front of the train station, when she and Meg had touched hands. The entire world had fallen away around them, and a current had jolted through Abby, as if she'd been one of Galvani's electrified frogs. Yes, it had been just like that. For, like Galvani's dead frogs, which had been brought twitching back to apparent life by the application of animal electricity, something inside of Abby had come to life, which had lain dead, or at least dormant, until then.

As they strode through Whitechapel, through the steep-walled canyons of tenements and shops, weaving around the handcarts and pamphleteers and piles of horse dung, Abby had a realization that shook her to the core. The rush of emotion, that electrifying connection that she'd experienced when she and Meg Eisenstadt had touched, was that feeling to which she'd always thought herself immune. Abby wasn't naive. She fathomed that sometimes women felt romantic attraction for other women, and she didn't judge that attraction. She'd simply never considered it, as she'd never felt any sort of romantic attraction for *anyone*.

This was the sort she should have had for Gideon.

How would he feel about that? Abby wasn't even certain how she felt.

Gideon had always been proper to a fault. For many years, she'd thought it was because he was simply a respectful sort of man. And he was. At the same time, in retrospect, it struck her as strange that he'd never attempted to steal a kiss, or even hold her hand. They'd known one another longer than many married couples, after all. And they'd made their promises, so of course any display of affection would be seen as a momentary lapse of decorum rather than an assault.

Could it be that he, too, was ambivalent about the prospect of their marriage, despite the deep and abiding affection they shared? Did she dare hope as much? Dared she hope that he would greet the idea with relief?

"Don't you think so, Abigail?" Meg said.

Abby blinked. "I'm sorry, what?"

There it was again—the vertigo-inducing rush of blood to her head when she met Meg's bright eyes. Her face burning, she turned her gaze back to the street ahead.

Meg thankfully laughed. "Never mind. I say, I have been going on. You never told me where you were bound when you stopped to come to my rescue."

"Yes, well." Abby's cheeks warmed again as she found herself the object of Miss Eisenstadt's undivided, wide-eyed attention. "Gideon, that is, Dr. Gideon Spencer—we run a clinic together—" Abby wondered briefly why she hadn't said that he was her fiancé. "He requires a special medication…for our stores. I'm going to pick it up."

"And this medication comes from Whitechapel?" Meg's face wrinkled with disbelief. She had a spray of freckles across the bridge of her nose and cheeks.

"Yes, well…"

"Is there a specialty chemist there?" Meg asked. "I suppose the East End is full of all sorts of things. Bernadette never mentioned a chemist on Shepherd Street, though, of course—"

"It's not so much a chemist's shop as a house. Or offices, I suppose," Abby said. "A funny sort of place, really. Tumbling-down looking on the outside, but inside it seems quite posh. I've often wondered—"

"And this Dr. Spencer of yours sent *you* to fetch it? From a falling-down building in one of the most dangerous parts of town?"

"Well…actually…the thing is…." Abby wasn't one to stammer, but the combination of Meg's penetrating gaze, tumbling words, and Abby's own giddily lurching stomach was making both thought and speech uncharacteristically difficult.

"Really, Abigail, I have to wonder if this man has any regard for you, or for your safety, at all."

"Of course he does!" Abby cried. "I should hope so, considering we're to be married."

The air around them suddenly became heavy. Meg turned her face toward the path ahead, and Abby realized that she hadn't imagined their connection. Meg's reaction proved that she'd felt it as well, and now Abby would have given her left arm to have taken the comment back.

"I see," Meg said. The careful way she pasted on a smile made Abby regret her words all the more.

"The thing is," Abby said, "the medicine isn't actually for our stores. It's for Gideon. He suffers from…from a rare but debilitating condition. I first heard about an experimental medication about a month ago. I, too, was dubious, when I saw the building. But—"

"But you would do anything to ease your beloved's pain," Meg said quietly.

"Yes," Abby said, equally subdued. "There is no recognized treatment, you see, and he suffers so."

"I see," said Meg.

"I tried it myself," Abby said. Meg swung her head back toward Meg, an astounded look on her face that Abby found strangely gratifying. "To make certain that it was harmless and, of course, to attempt to determine the formula. It was, but I did not," she said.

"But the medication works," Meg said, her expression now one of interest.

"It does. I know it's wrong. I'd never recommend that a patient do such a thing. But—"

"But you would do anything to ease his pain," she said again.

Abby nodded.

They walked along for a bit in silence. Abby wracked her brains to come up with some acceptable topic for conversation, something interesting that Meg had said about herself. She really had been listening, at least at some level, but all she could remember were pieces and fragments of the other woman's prattle. A gathering of some women's charitable organization. Meg's brother, who sounded like a maddening combination of selfishness and charm. Some sort of falling-out. She was about to comment again on the weather, when Meg suddenly said, "You know, my brother might be able to help you out with a formulation."

"Your brother is a chemist?"

"Of sorts," Meg said. "He read chemistry at university. Of course he was expelled during his second year, but not for academic reasons. He really is quite clever. He just…has difficulty applying himself, I suppose," she said. "That, and he certainly does test a person sometimes."

"I did get that impression," Abby said. Meg's mouth twitched, and Abby felt a rush of relief, of a possible return of the golden moment they had experienced before Abby had unfortunately mentioned her betrothal.

"Mm. The combination, I'm afraid, didn't do him any favors in the eyes of the university. But he truly is quite brilliant."

"Is he working on anything interesting at present?" Abby asked.

Meg looked thoughtful. "Something he calls *scintillam vitae*. The 'spark of life.' The idea is that all of life is animated by the same substance. He's trying to recreate that substance chemically."

Abby frowned. "I'm not sure about *that*. Though to be fair, there is *something* there. One could even call it a spark. It's there at birth. You can see it in the eyes. I've also seen it wink out at the moment of death."

"Have you?" Meg asked. "What about animals? My friend Bernadette is most interested in proving that humans and animals are animated by the same vital force. She and my brother spent an entire evening talking about it some weeks ago."

Abby paused. "Yes, come to think of it, I did see it once, on these very streets. A cart had tipped over with the horse trapped under it. They had to put the horse down. It was watching me the entire time, and I saw the spark leave its eye."

"Yes, that's exactly it," Meg said. "Bernadette had a similar experience. She hasn't touched flesh since."

"No," Abby said. "If one isn't used to seeing life and death on a daily basis, I can understand how something like that could be quite disturbing. Is your brother also a vegetarian?"

Meg shook her head. "Bernadette believes that human life and animal life are of equal importance. Nat, on the other hand...I suppose you could say that he finds humans and animals to be equally insignificant. Plus, he does love a nice bit of lamb," she said with a chuckle.

"But they've fallen out over it?" Abby asked. It seemed strange to her that Meg would go to all the trouble of pursuing her friend to the worst part of London over a philosophical argument. But then again, Meg clearly came from a different world.

"I'm afraid it's a bit more serious than that," Meg said. "There was a romantic...entanglement of sorts. I know it's none of my business, but Bernadette is a friend of longstanding, and Nat really was quite rude to her. I doubt he'll apologize on his own, but I'd like to salvage my friendship with her, regardless of his actions."

"You're a good friend, putting yourself in danger to seek her out."

"She's been a good friend to me."

She turned to Abby, and something in her expression told Abby there had been more to the friendship than simple camaraderie. Abby's heart begin to race. Romantic friendships between women were increasingly common as one ascended the social ladder, especially among the university set. Sometimes they took on physical dimensions as well. Despite the chill, Abby began to perspire. She would not be at all averse to exploring those dimensions with Meg, she realized. In fact, she was certain she would enjoy it.

But the romantic entanglement Meg was endeavoring to resolve...had it involved the three of them? Meg and Bernadette and...Meg's brother? That, Abby feared, was a step too far. She let out a long breath. It was none of her business, at least not at present. If a friendship eventually developed between her and Meg—and this thought set her heart to racing again—then Meg could reveal her past in her own time.

As they had been walking, their surroundings had been subtly changing. Busy shops, crowded pavements, and traffic-clogged streets had gradually given way to boarded-up windows and crumbling stairs. Shepherd Street was not far away. How would she proceed once she'd arrived? Her previous visits had involved complicated processes of messages and appointments. Would anyone be there to receive her?

"It's not far now," Abby said. "What's the address of your friend's organization?"

"Number 18," Meg said.

"How convenient. I'm for Number 16, which should be next door."

Meg smiled. "Will you wait for me? I've so enjoyed talking to you. Perhaps we could walk back to the station together after we're both finished."

"I'd like that," Abby said. "Oh!" A sudden pain stabbed at the back of her skull.

"What is it?" Meg asked.

Abby blinked at the spots that had appeared before her eyes. The street seemed to swim around them. She squeezed her eyes shut and took a deep breath. Shepherd Street was just a few streets away, but Abby suddenly wondered if she'd be able to complete the journey at all. Then the pain sharpened, focused, and changed. Abby realized that wasn't pain at all, anymore, but a sound, poking a throbbing tendril at the back of her mind.

"Abigail?"

"Did you say that your friend works at an animal sanctuary?" Abby asked. "Because that has to be the saddest-sounding dog I've ever heard."

CHAPTER THIRTEEN

Nat

"I say, Jin Wylie!"

The words were out of Nat's mouth before he realized it. He was thrilled, of course, but his magnificent Jin was the last person he'd have expected to run into in this part of town, or anywhere outside of Holborn, his bedroom, or, quite frankly, a bank of rising fog.

The man just ahead of him on the pavement stopped. Nat's heart skipped a beat as the terrible thought occurred to him that it might not, in fact, be his magnificent Jin, but someone else entirely, and that he had just called out to a stranger. But then the broad shoulders turned, the weak sun highlighted the silver strands in the mass of smooth, black hair tastefully tucked beneath the silk shirt collar, and Jin began to walk toward him.

But his heart juddered to a stop when Jin's expression told all the world that he wasn't nearly as happy for a chance encounter.

"Mr. Eisenstadt?" The stiffness in his voice made Nat wish he'd never been born, no less called out. "What on Earth are you doing here?"

Nat had been on his way to the building at 16 Shepherd Street, which he had, through careful deductions and deciphering of clues, determined to be the meeting place of the Academy of Occult

Sciences. When he'd heard about the group the previous year at university, the cloak-and-sword aspect of it all had intrigued him. They had seemed intrigued by his ideas, as well. That is, until that one fateful week had brought both his expulsion and the subsequent and speedy withdrawal of interest from that toffee-nosed little prat Hathaway.

That morning, refreshed from having spent the evening with his magnificent Jin, Nat had reconstructed what he could remember of his notes from *scintillam vitae* and set off to beard Hathaway in his filthy den to demand that the man reconsider. It was ridiculous that the academy would deny him admission, given his work and his discoveries. He could more than afford the annual dues, and even though his had been a second-rate university, he could hold his own with any of the leadership on either occultism *or* science.

"As it happens, I have business here," Nat said, shifting his bundle of papers to his other arm.

"*You* have business *here?* " He glanced up the front steps of the very building to which Nat had been walking. "At Consor—at this address?"

Nat had to admit that the building didn't *look* like an occultists' lair. It looked, in fact, as if it might collapse in upon itself at any moment. But he'd checked and rechecked his calculations. It could not possibly be anywhere else.

"That's what I said." Nat didn't know what he should have expected then, but it was not yet another person questioning his abilities and qualifications. Jin's obsidian eyes were raking him up and down, and not at all in a thrilling way.

"In this building? Number 16? You?"

"Yes, me," Nat snapped. "Does this…does it *surprise* you that I might have business somewhere? Do you think…" Nat stopped himself. He had been about to say something to the effect of *Do you think I cease to exist once you pull on your trousers and leave?* But even though discretion wasn't his strong suit, Nat did have *some* sense. Unlike Jin, who, for some reason, was wandering about in the cold in his shirt sleeves.

A woman had stopped at the top of the stairs of the building next door. Something was familiar about her upright posture and her deliberately plain clothing. She was also minus her coat, and she was staring.

"Oh, dear God," Nat said as he recognized her. She recognized him as well, it seemed, for now Bernadette blasted Kingsley was storming down the steps, steaming toward them like an ironclad warship. Good God. What were the chances? What were the actual chances?

"What in blooming blazes are you doing here?" she demanded without preamble.

Her eyes were hard and wide, her hair appeared to be even more tightly wound than usual, and her usually pale skin had gone a most unattractive shade of puce. Despite her lack of outerwear, spleen seemed to be keeping her plenty warm, as she shared out her glare between him and Jin. As for the magnificent Jin, he appeared annoyed and terrified in equal measure.

Nat cleared his throat. "Do you two know each other?" he asked with admirable sangfroid.

Jin and Bernadette exchanged a glance.

"Miss Kingsley and I work together," Jin said.

This he had not expected. "At the zoo?"

"Zoo?" Bernadette said. "Do you mean the Society for—"

"Yes, yes, that," Nat said impatiently.

Jin said, "You might say that. Might I ask how you and Miss Kingsley are acquainted?"

Nat ventured a glance at Bernadette and wished he had not. Her entire face was a dare. Nat looked away.

"Miss Kingsley is a friend of my sister," he said primly. "Delightful to see you again, Miss Kingsley."

Bernadette gave a satisfied little nod, and a bit of the fight relaxed from her expression. For just a moment, Nat remembered how once that pugnacious spirit had drawn him like a moth. He tucked the thought back under his hat before it got him into trouble, then picked an imaginary bit of lint from his cuff.

"Yes, well," Nat said. "As it happens, I've come to meet with Mr. Algernon Hathaway of the Academy of Occult Sciences."

"Hathaway," Jin said, as if he'd never heard syllables combined that way before.

"Of the Academy of Occult Sciences," Nat repeated. "It's regarding my latest research." Jin's jaw dropped nearly to the tip of his handmade pointed boots. "You know him as well," Nat said.

Jin nodded. "I do."

Nat laughed. The absurdity of it all. "I suppose you're also with the academy. And you, too, *Miss Kingsley*." He laughed again. The sound was a bit alarming. "I suppose everyone and their barking dog is a member except me. Oh, what a grand conspiracy—" Another thought occurred to him. "Well, which one of you was it?"

"What—" Jin said.

"Which one of you stole the notes from my laboratory table? *Scintillam vitae*. You've both spent time in my lab. You've both spent time in my—never mind that. Was it all a game to you? Either of you?"

He found grim satisfaction in the color rising from Jin's collar, though it was chilly comfort. What the devil could it mean, though, that Bernadette, too, was looking a bit green?

"Oh, my stars and garters," Nat said. A sinking feeling was filling his insides, and he feared it might swallow him from within. "You were in it together. You." He pointed at Jin, then at Bernadette. "And you. And that little prick, Hathaway. How did I not see it? Yes, of course. It's poetic justice."

His laugh was sounding quite unbalanced now, which was appropriate, given how Nat felt. Unbalanced and giddy and swaying on a precipice above an abyss of dread. He'd thought to have a bit of fun with each of them, then move on when it became tedious, just as always. Only they'd had *their* bit of fun, then maneuvered him right into their trap and played him like an oboe with a cracked reed. And Hathaway. *Sodding* Hathaway.

"Mr. Eisenstadt. *Nathaniel*." Now Jin's thieving hand was on his forearm.

"Don't *Nathaniel* me." He jerked his arm away. "And don't *you* pretend to be so upset," he said, returning Bernadette's expression glare for glare. "As if you've anything at all to be upset about. *I* am the injured party, here."

It wasn't, perhaps, the most cutting response, or the most clever. But it did allow him to stalk off with a shred of his original dignity, leaving the duplicitous Bernadette fleeing into the very building he'd meant to storm that morning, and the magnificent, malevolent Jin standing on the pavement and staring after him.

CHAPTER FOURTEEN

Bernadette

Bernadette slammed the front door of Number 16 behind her and slumped against it. It wasn't like her to run from a fight. That response had been childish and weak. But the horror if it all! Clearly Dr. Wylie no longer thought of her as part of the scenery. Now, it appeared, she was a central figure in some imagined conspiracy involving Mr. Hathaway. And Nat reckoned that she and Dr. Wylie were conspiring against *him*. On top of that, it was obvious that Dr. Wylie and Nat knew one another uncomfortably well. How the devil had it all gone so catastrophically awry?

Exhale.

Red haze melted away from her vision as Consortium House wrapped her in its cool, dignified embrace. Calmly—panic helped nothing—she laid out her options.

Dr. Wylie would never listen to her ideas now. He'd painted her and Mr. Hathaway into the same traitorous corner, and anything she might say would be seen through that lens. Overcoming Mr. Hathaway's prejudices now seemed silly by comparison. In fact, if the two men were as bitterly opposed as Dr. Wylie seemed to think, then she had two additional pieces of information that she could craft to her advantage. First, that Dr. Wylie had lifted some of his ideas from Nat, and, also, that he had a werewolf in his office.

Oh, yes. Even as Dr. Wylie had chased her from the room, she'd seen his guest for what he was. Dr. Wylie's notes had been quite explicit. How fortunate he'd been too lazy to put them in the fire himself. He probably hadn't thought she'd read them. Probably hadn't even considered that she could read. Another idea occurred to her, then. She'd overheard Sir Julius saying that he was seeking a specimen. Well, now they had one. If Mr. Hathaway didn't give her satisfaction, she could always take matters quite literally upstairs.

She straightened her chignon, tugged her collar into place, and walked calmly toward the staircase. So Dr. Wylie considered her an enemy? She wouldn't stoop to behaving like one. At least not right away. No, she'd hold back the most damning information for now. Simply having it would give her the confidence to speak to Mr. Hathaway as a colleague. She'd present her ideas, ask him about his own, and then ask to join his study group.

And if Dr. Wylie put himself in her way, well, she would handle him.

She reached the top of the stairs and paused. To the left, she could hear Dr. Wylie's doggy pacing across the parquet floors. To the right, someone was speaking behind the closed door of the meeting room at the end of the hallway. Listening to their modulated tones and careful cadence, she amended her evaluation. Someone was giving a speech.

Perhaps she, too, would give a speech to the Consortium's membership one day. What would Dr. Wylie have to say about that?

It was Mr. Hathaway speaking, she realized, as she drew closer to the door. What immense luck. She didn't want to disturb him, of course. And yet, the brass doorknob was daring her to touch it.

"Who's there?" Mr. Hathaway suddenly called.

Panicked, Bernadette turned. But before she'd gone a step, the door opened.

"Miss Kingsley."

His hair was a mess of spikes and cowlicks, as if he'd been running a hand through it. He'd taken off his jacket and was standing there in his waistcoat and shirt sleeves, clutching a piece of paper in one hand. She glanced around the room. He was alone.

"I hope I didn't interrupt you, sir," she said.

"Not at all. I was just going over my notes for a presentation. Come in."

She'd never been inside the meeting room before, not properly. It looked much as one might expect. The wood-paneled walls were hung with expensive paintings. The heavy curtains were drawn back, and tall windows allowed the room to be bathed in muted light. A large, rectangular hardwood table took center place, along with eight leather-upholstered chairs spaced evenly around it. A large world map hung on one wall. Beneath their feet lay a Persian rug of such ornate design that, briefly, Bernadette worried she might lose herself in it.

"Miss Kingsley?"

"I…"

She'd come up the stairs with a head of steam, fueled by righteous indignation and prepared to burn another man's career to the ground. Now the steam had dissipated, and she felt the cold creep of doubt. She might not have been conspiring against Dr. Wylie, but if she turned over more of his research to Mr. Hathaway, wouldn't the effect be the same? Was she prepared to make an enemy for real?

And then there was the wolf.

Dr. Wylie's lycanthrope had been a sad and bedraggled thing, even in his human form. Bernadette had limited sympathy for humans. For the most part, they brought their troubles upon themselves. But that one had still had the shimmer of wolf about him. Hadn't the entire point of her research been recognizing the divine animating spark in animal life? She should be aiming to elevate that life, not sacrifice it to further her own ambition.

"I…heard voices and thought…well…" She straightened. Sighed. She would have to consider her plan more carefully. "I wondered if you might like some tea, sir."

He frowned. "Tea?" Narrowing his eyes, he stepped closer, and Bernadette had the distinct impression that he was searching her thoughts. She hurried to veil them as Lord Julius had trained her to do. "Forgive me, Miss Kingsley. You do make an excellent cup of Darjeeling, of course, but that can't be the reason you're here."

He took another step forward, and she stepped back into the table. His nostrils flared, and Bernadette suddenly realized what a mistake she'd made. One heard of men who took liberties, who considered young women in their workplace to be fair game, especially if those young women comported themselves in a way that could be construed as taking the initiative. He advanced until she could smell the tobacco smoke in his clothing.

"I mean no offense, of course," he said. "All I meant was that anyone can see that you're a young woman of education and refinement. And you don't strike me as someone's bored niece or daughter. What are you really doing with the Consortium, Miss Kingsley?"

Something predatory flickered behind his eyes. She shrank back with a muffled cry as he took a long, noisy sniff.

"Come now," he said, his voice barely above a whisper. "There's no need to be frightened. I won't bite."

Bernadette stepped to one side, pushing one of the chairs off its balance. He caught it easily and set it back in its place.

"Or is that what you're afraid of?" he said.

His expression now resembled that of a hound on a scent. Her pulse pounded. At the same time, something primitive in the back of her mind reassessed. The threat wasn't sexual. If she had to put words to it, as absurd as it sounded, her fear was that he might actually eat her.

"Are you afraid of me, Miss Kingsley?" he murmured.

"Should I be?"

"Perhaps." He met her eyes, and something dangerous glinted in the depths. "I see you skulking around these halls, listening at keyholes..." Something in her expression elicited a dark chuckle. "Please. Did you think I thought that those were all *your* ideas? Passing off Dr. Wylie's work as your own. Mm-mm. Bad form."

"They weren't all his ideas," she blurted before she could stop herself.

An unpleasant smile crept across his face. That intrusive prickle crawled over her scalp, and he leaned close, taking another sniff. With a cry she pushed him away and lunged for the door. Mr. Hathaway caught her wrists in a surprisingly strong grip.

"What do you *want*?" she cried.

He didn't answer. Instead, he pushed her back against the table. He loosened his grip on one of her wrists, then ran a hand gently down her forearm and over her hip. His grin widened as his hand found her skirt pocket.

"I think I've found what I want." Ever so gently he teased Nat's notes out of the pocket. As his eyes darted across the lines of jagged scrawl, she felt him flipping through her thoughts as if through a library card catalogue. Then he stepped back, his smile knife-edged and triumphant.

"Well done, Miss Kingsley. Your meddling has proved an advantage once again. I shall spare you for the moment. Now, take me to the specimen."

Chapter Fifteen

Clyde

It was past noon when Clyde and Garrick found the other two lurking in a crowded market square, looking for something to nick. It took a bit longer to convince them that they wouldn't go hungry, nor would the devil cart them off if they had a poke around that place on Shepherd Street instead. That was because Clyde himself wasn't convinced. It was all Garrick's idea, and that alone should have made anyone think twice.

Clyde had said one thing—one!—about the nurse, the Fiend, and the old, abandoned building, and Garrick was off like a horse with the bit in its teeth. The other two had their doubts, sure, but at the end of the day they were happy for an adventure. As for Clyde, he was thinking things would've been better if he'd kept his damn ideas to himself.

"I'm telling you," Clyde said to Garrick. "We shouldn't be charging in without a plan."

"Don't be a baby." Garrick's voice was still rough, and from the way he moved, Clyde knew he was feeling his lumps and bruises as much as the rest of them. Except for Eli, lucky bastard.

"I'm not a baby. You're as scared of that place as I am."

Fire flashed in Garrick's eyes, and Clyde knew immediately he'd stepped in it. Clyde instinctively drew closer to Eli, as if that beanpole could protect him. He'd be better off cozying up to Bert.

Of course if the lot of them had a brain between them they'd all turn right around and at least talk over their options before storming that building on Shepherd Street.

Clyde's heart stopped as Garrick gave him a long, hard stare. The pavement was heaving that day, though nobody seemed to pay the boys any attention. Two lorries had collided in the street, and cabs, traps, and two-wheeled hansoms were crawling around each other and over the pavement to get past them, while the drivers shouted at one another from their perches. After a moment Garrick turned his gaze forward and started walking again. Clyde let out a noisy breath of relief and began walking as well.

"You said it yourself," Garrick said loud enough for the other boys to know he was including them. "The nurse is behind it all. "

Clyde tried to stammer out a response over the grunts of agreement coming from Eli and Bert.

"That ain't…That ain't exactly what I said," Clyde said, walking faster to catch up with Garrick's long steps.

"What did you say, then?" Bert asked.

Clyde wanted to roll his eyes. "I *said* that the two times the Fiend showed up, it were because someone done something to the nurse. That Evans woman let herself into the back door of the clinic and helped herself to medicine, and we—"

"We know what we done," Garrick said.

"Conscience?" Eli asked under his breath. Garrick whipped his head around, his face balled up like a fist.

"You what?"

"You heard me," Eli said mildly.

Garrick narrowed his eyes, which would normally be enough to make any of them think twice. But Eli had been standing a bit taller since that lady had showed him his name in the Bible and told him he was someone important.

"We was hungry, if you remember," Garrick said. "You had a better idea you should have said somefin'."

"I always said robbing church ladies ain't right. And that one saved your life *and* fed us even after we—"

Garrick stopped again and turned. Eli licked his lips. He was a head and a half taller than Garrick, but Garrick was faster and meaner and better with his fists. Everything seemed to go quiet around them—so quiet that Clyde half expected to see the Fiend out of the corner of his eye in an alley or looking down from one of the dark windows above the shops on the street.

"So you think we got what was coming to us?" Garrick gestured to his bruised and battered face. He frowned and cocked his head. "Except you. That devil barely touched you. I wonder why that was."

"What are you saying?" Eli asked. His voice had a new tone. Calm. Not cold exactly, but calmer than Clyde would have been if he found himself facing down Garrick. "Do you think *I* set us up? Is that what you mean?"

Garrick glanced from Eli to Bert then stayed a bit longer with Clyde. Then he started walking again, head forward, shoulders angled into the crowd, going out of his way to elbow anyone who was even a little too close.

"Why would I do that?" Eli asked. Even with his long legs, he had to step to it to catch Garrick up. "I'm asking you a question. Why would I—"

Garrick stopped so fast that Clyde nearly walked into them. The wall of pedestrians split and streamed around them like they were a sand bar in the Thames, and Clyde had the strangest sensation of being invisible.

Garrick said, "I ain't sayin' you did and I ain't sayin' you didn't. What I *am* sayin' is that it's quite a…a…" He snapped his fingers at Clyde.

"Coincidence?" Clyde said.

"Yeah, that. You was against going after the nurse—not that you said anyfing about it—and when the Fiend attacked, you got away without a scratch."

"So…what…you think that gigantic thing was the nurse in disguise?" Eli asked. Bert guffawed. "Nice trick getting back to the clinic so fast in all that fog."

"The devil moves fast."

"How did you know where to find the clinic, Eli?" Bert asked reasonably.

Garrick turned back to Eli, raising his eyebrows.

"I…I don't know. I reckon I passed it sometime before."

"Another coincidence," Garrick said.

"Hold up," Clyde interjected. Everyone turned to him. He felt the weight of their eyes and shifted from foot to foot. "That nurse didn't know Eli from Adam. If she did, we'd have seen it in her face. She didn't know Eli, and she didn't know anything about the Fiend until we said it. And when we did say it, well, Garrick maybe you was a bit too busy choking to death to see as much, but that nurse went white as milk."

Bert nodded slowly. "He's right. Even after she recognized us, she was just annoyed. But when we started talking about the Fiend…"

"Maybe she's nothing to do with it," Eli said.

"Or maybe she sends it out to get her revenge, but she didn't think we'd figure it out," said Garrick.

"If that's the case," said Bert, "should we be looking for her at all? I mean, wouldn't we be better off counting our blessings and leaving the nurse and the clinic alone?"

"Better off?" Garrick snapped. "It ain't about being *better off*. That thing attacked us. She's tied up in it somehow, and I aim to find out how."

"Then…" Eli stroked his chin with his long fingers. "Then *why* are we going to some haunted house on Shepherd Street?"

"'Cause it's an evil place where evil things happen, and Bert says she has business there every week. And if the Fiend and that nurse are connected, I'd bet Nell Evans's good arm that everything comes down to that place on Shepherd Street. All right?"

No one had much to say about it after that. Garrick was right. There was a mystery and a monster, and even Clyde had to admit that if they were going to find an answer, a haunted building in the middle of Whitechapel was as good a place as any to start. So on they walked.

The crowds thinned out as they passed through the commercial area. Clogged streets calmed, then quieted. Busy shop fronts gave way to vast, dark-windowed tenements, and then to the falling-down-looking buildings that Clyde remembered that first night, when he'd seen the strange lights at Number 16.

Shepherd Street wasn't far now. Clyde couldn't see it, but he could almost *feel* it vibrating in his bones. A fish-scented wind pushed them from behind, swirling dirt and rubbish around their feet. Clyde jammed his hands into his pockets and pulled his thin jacket tighter around his shoulders. Then, suddenly, there the building was, as if it had appeared the moment Clyde had taken his eyes off the path before them.

Garrick stopped. "Right. *Now* we need a plan." He swung his gaze toward Clyde.

"Me?" Clyde squeaked. He cleared his throat and tried again. "You're asking me?"

Garrick shrugged. "You're the one said we needed one. Any bright ideas since then, or was it just talk?"

"Well..."

They had emerged from the mouth of an alley, then turned a corner onto Shepherd Street. There was still a short walk between their group and Number 16, and Clyde could see a small group of people—two men and a woman—in front of it. He couldn't hear what they were saying, but it looked like they were having an argument. The woman stalked away, mounted the stairs of Number 16, and slammed the door behind her. Then one of the men steamed off in the other direction. The second man stood for a minute, then followed him.

Then a hand grasped Clyde's elbow and pulled him back into the alley. Another hand—Eli's—clamped firmly over Clyde's mouth. The boys pressed themselves against the walls, willing the shadows to swallow them, as two women approached on the other side of the street.

"I'll be damned," Garrick whispered.

Bert said, "What's she doing here?"

"Bleedin' *coincidence*," Garrick answered. His expression went hard, and his eyes narrowed again. Clyde slapped Eli's hand away from his mouth and ventured an inch or two out of the shadows for a closer look.

It was the nurse, by God, and she'd brought someone with her. Not another Booth lady, but something similar. A bit younger, just this side of posh and dressed for slumming. They didn't see him and the others. Weren't even looking. They only had ears for their own prattle, and eyes, so it seemed, for each other.

Garrick snorted. He saw it too. He opened his mouth to say something rude. Clyde cut him off.

"I have a plan," Clyde said.

He did not.

Garrick tore his eyes away from the women, leaned back against the wall, and dramatically cupped a hand over one ear.

Clyde looked nervously from him to Bert, then to Eli on his other side. He cleared his throat again. "It seems pretty busy out front," he said. Eli nodded encouragingly. "So...I say two of us keep watch on the place from across the street, while the other two go around back to see what they can see."

Garrick stared for a moment. Then, slowly, he began to nod. "Who're you taking with you, then?"

Clyde swallowed hard. Of course it made sense for him to be doing the sneak-work. He was small and quick and, in a pinch, could play the poor, lost child really, really well. Still, he couldn't shake the feeling that Garrick was giving him the most dangerous part on purpose.

"Bert," Clyde said, just as Eli volunteered himself. Clyde glanced an apology at his mate. "It's just if there's trouble, I want Bert's fists."

Eli nodded, but his disappointment was heavy in the air.

"Right, that's settled then," Garrick said. He gave Eli a nod and jerked his head toward the street.

As Eli passed Clyde, he said, "You remember our signal?"

"Bark like a dog," Clyde said.

"That's right. You find trouble, you use it."

Clyde watched Eli and Garrick emerge from the alley onto the street. They crossed the empty pavement, glanced around, then headed for a patch of shadow just opposite Number 16. Clyde gestured for Bert to follow him out the other way.

The space behind Number 16 was wide. In fact, it was wide enough for some swell to be parking a hansom cab there. The cab was shiny, black, and new, and it had some kind of seal on the door: a snake wrapped around a stick, and...

"Pru—pru-denties Sick-cut..." Bert sounded out.

"That's good," Clyde whispered. "You're getting it, but whoever that belongs to ain't going to leave it sittin' here for long."

Bert nodded and pulled himself away. Of the four, Clyde was the best reader. Eli and Garrick did all right for themselves. Bert could get by, and he definitely wasn't thick, but it just seemed to come harder to him than to the others. Which was why, Clyde suspected, he was at it every time he had the chance.

The alley was tidy, for an alley. The windows were in good nick, and it even looked like someone was keeping the back stairs swept. It was more than you could say for the front of the building, for Number 16, that was. It was almost as if this were the real entrance, and they were trying to make the front of the place look abandoned. Clyde wondered why they would want to do that. The rear of the building, though, was just as Clyde remembered it. Right down to the basement window and the crack in the curtains.

"What are we looking for, now?" Bert asked.

"Anything that looks like it don't belong."

"Nothing looks like it belongs," Bert said, looking sidelong down the alley. "This entire place is *wrong*. I can feel it."

Clyde nodded. That foul-smelling wind picked up again, rattling the debris in the corners and crevices. It smelled rotten—not just rotting fish, but sewage, too, and the filth at the bottom of the Thames. Then he saw it.

"There," Clyde said, pointing.

Across the expanse of packed earth—an expanse that seemed to grow wider as Clyde considered scuttling across it—near the back door of Number 16, was a well. If Clyde stood on his tiptoes, he could just see the top of a window.

"I'm going to have a look in the cellar," Clyde said. "Watch my back."

Bert nodded. Clyde's heart pounded as he looked right down the alley, then left out toward the street. That expensive hansom cab was still sitting there with no one to guard it. That made him uneasy. It meant either no one had noticed it yet, or people knew it was there but knew better than to try their luck with its owners. Clyde swallowed. Then, before he could talk himself out of it, he darted across the alley and ducked into the stairwell. He peeped up at Bert and gave a little wave. Bert nodded. Clyde continued down the stairs.

The window was low to the ground but high up on the wall of the cellar. A dark curtain obscured most of it, but by pressing himself into the corner at just the right angle and squinting his right eye *just so*, Clyde could make out a table and chair, and on the wall above it, a set of shelves with numerous bottles. Some of the bottles had labels, and he tried hard to make them out, but they were too far away, and the light from the crack between the curtains was too dim to see much of anything.

The table had a small amount of equipment on it. A flask, a burner, and an arrangement of things to hold it. Just then a door on the far side of the room opened, and Clyde had all the light he needed.

Two men were carrying a third. Clyde watched as they brought him into the room. On the opposite wall from the desk was what appeared to be some sort of animal enclosure. One of the men set down the legs of the unconscious man and opened the door. Then they set the unconscious man inside the enclosure and secured the door with a padlock.

A scraping sound came from behind Clyde on the stairs. Irritated, Clyde said, "Damn it, Bert—"

"What have we, here?" a posh voice asked. As a well-manicured hand came down on Clyde's shoulder, he realized it wasn't Bert.

CHAPTER SIXTEEN

Meg

As they'd walked from the station, Meg and Abigail had fallen into a companionable rhythm. The initial awkwardness following their Moment had faded, and the ensuing relief had rendered them both chatty.

The streets had narrowed as they passed out of the commercial district, and long tenement walls had risen up on either side to block out the weak, grey sunlight. A chill had settled around them, and, perhaps inspired by their grim surroundings, Abigail had regaled her with a thrilling story about a group of street toughs that she had treated the night before. Meg had gasped as Abigail had told the story of how those same young men had set upon her just a few short hours earlier. Shock had turned to admiration when Abigail described how she'd bravely and cleverly treated the wounds of the young man who had held her at knifepoint then sent them off in the morning on an errand.

It was all so unexpected, coming from such a prim and straitlaced-appearing young woman. So unexpected that Meg had very nearly missed the part about a creature in the fog that the young men had blamed for their injuries. There hadn't been time to dwell on it, however, as the tale had grown even stranger from there.

Abigail was convinced that Number 16 Shepherd Street housed some sort of scientific facility. From Abigail's hushed tones when she spoke of it, and the way she kept staring directly ahead of them rather than meeting Meg's eyes, Meg surmised that something was illicit about the facility and the people who ran it, and that Abigail was caught between her instincts and her need for the medicine she traveled there, on a regular basis, to acquire.

When Abigail asked her about her own reasons for coming to Shepherd Street, Meg's own answer—seeking to make amends with Bernadette after Bernadette had quarrelled with Meg's abominable brother—had seemed disappointingly quotidian by contrast.

And then they had passed the marker for Shepherd Street and made the turn.

"Oh. Oh...*dear!*" Meg stopped, grasping at the euphemism for Abigail's sake, though in truth the situation called for much stronger language.

There on the other side of the street, standing in front a boarded-up building that, if it weren't condemned probably should have been, stood two men. Or rather one man and one rat named Nathaniel Herschel Eisenstadt. And the other? Meg couldn't be certain, but from the long hair tucked into the man's collar, his corset-altered figure, those *shoes*, and the look of aggravation blooming on Nat's face, Meg reckoned that the men were, or had been, on intimate terms.

"What is it?" Abigail slowed to a stop beside her.

"What the dev...what on Earth is he doing here?"

"Which one? Do you know those men?" Abigail asked.

The two men had reached a flamboyant impasse by that point. Nat had spun dramatically on his heel and was stalking in their general direction, fists clenched, his head forward like a bull. The other man was staring after Nat, looking flummoxed. Meg sympathized.

"The one storming off is my brother," Meg said.

"And the other?"

Meg shook her head. "I don't know. But I suspect they know one another."

"Doesn't look like they're friends," Abigail said.

"Not anymore at least. I wonder what they're doing here."

Meg threw a quick glance up and down Shepherd Street, then, grasping Abigail's wrist, started across to intercept him. The same pulse of energy passed between them, even through the wool of Abigail's coat sleeve. Meg ventured a look over her shoulder and was rewarded by a bloom of pink on the other woman's cheekbones and a shy smile.

"Perhaps...perhaps your brother came to apologize to Miss Kingsley himself," Abigail said as she stepped quickly across the cobblestones to catch Meg up. "And ran into his acquaintance."

Meg barked a short laugh. "Nat doesn't think it's necessary to apologize when one is right. And he's always right, at least to hear him tell it. But I do wonder who that other man is."

Meg was about to say something else, but Nat was upon them.

"My God, sis. What are you doing here?" he demanded.

"I'll give you some space, shall I?" Abigail said.

"No—wait—" Meg said, but by that time she was off. Sighing, Meg turned her attentions back to her errant brother. "Me? I would be mopping up after you. Again." Nat's brow furrowed, so she explained. "Bernadette is here, at Number 18, doing voluntary work with her animal charity. I came to take her to luncheon and to try to smooth over your abominable behavior the other night. Hopefully I'll be able salvage our friendship and some semblance of our family's social standing. Not that you care about any of it."

"I care," he said. Meg suspected he spoke more out of contrary habit than because he actually did. "And if you want Bernadette, she's in Number 16, not Number 18."

"Number 16? With the boards across the windows? Whatever for?"

Nat shrugged. "Whatever she's told you about voluntary work at Number 18 is a lie. She's some sort of office worker at Number 16." He glowered over his shoulder at the other man, who was watching from what Meg hoped was too far away to hear them. "With Jin and Algernon sodding Hathaway."

"Who? Wait, that's Jin? Your Jin?"

She craned her neck to see. As she did, she noticed that Abigail was already striking up a conversation with the man. What the devil? "What does she have to do with your Jin?" Meg wasn't quite sure if she was talking about Bernadette or Abigail. Nat's expression brought her back to reality. It was a strange, dark sort of triumph, and his eyes lit with righteous fury.

Nat said, "They were in on it together, my Jin and your Bernadette."

"In on what? Are you feeling—"

He batted her hand away from his forehead. "I am quite well, thank you, apart from being betrayed. I was right, you know. Bernadette stole my notes. *Scintillam vitae*?" he said when she frowned in confusion. "Or maybe Jin did. Who knows? They were in it together, along with that little…" He took a breath to compose himself. "Along with Algernon Hathaway."

"And Hathaway is?"

He shrugged that Gallic you-should-know shrug of his. "The head of the Academy of Occult Sciences, of course."

"That group that you wanted to join at university."

"Would have joined, had they not been a bunch of raving anti-Semites," he said.

"Or had your antics not resulted in your expulsion from university." Another shrug. "So your Jin is part of this academy, and so is…Bernadette?" Bernadette was clever, certainly, and Meg could even squint and see how she might insinuate her way into an all-male scientific society, but she'd never shown any interest in the occult before, and frankly, the theory just smacked of pharmaceutical overindulgence.

"Nat," she said gently. "Is it possible that some of those chemicals you've been working with might have gotten in the air or on your fingers, or—"

"And pickled my brain? Is that what you're saying?" He stopped for a moment and looked like he might actually have been considering the possibility. Then he shook his head. "No, though I might have wondered as much if I hadn't seen the two of them together just now." He punctuated the last two words with twin stamps of his feet and a thrust of his finger toward where…oh, my, his Jin and her Abigail were turning together toward the crumbling stairs in front of the dreaded Number 16. Out of the corner of her eye, she saw Nat take note of her expression and follow her gaze down the street. "And who the devil is that?" he demanded.

"Her name is Abi—that is, Miss Gordon. She's a nurse at a clinic in Shadwell."

Nat's nose wrinkled at the mention of Shadwell. Then a sly expression crept across his face. "Not your usual type," he said.

She started to sputter a protest, but her cheeks had gone hot and rendered any such protest moot.

Then he said, "Does she know my Jin?"

"Certainly not," Meg said haughtily.

Nat smirked. "She does now."

Meg wasn't quite sure what that meant, but she didn't like it. And she really didn't like the fact that Jin and Abigail were walking up the stairs of Number 16 together. "So," she said to Nat, "you say that Bernadette is in that building," she pointed to Number 16, "and not the other one."

"She rode her broom through that front door just before you arrived."

"Well." Meg crossed her arms over her chest. "I aim to find her. And if you're any kind of man, you'll come with me and make your own apologies."

He narrowed his eyes, but in his expression she could see that he knew she was right.

"Fine," he said. "But when we're safely back home with a proper meal inside us, you're going to tell me all about your new girlfriend."

"She's not—"

Nat raised his eyebrows.

"Fine," she admitted. "I'll tell you everything."

CHAPTER SEVENTEEN

Abby

"Are you certain you have the correct address?" the man asked.

He was a most unusual man, Abby thought. Tall and well formed, perhaps around thirty-five years of age, clean shaven, with unfashionably long hair tied back behind his head. He was standing outside, hatless in his shirt sleeves, which suggested that he'd rushed out of the building for some reason. He was shivering slightly and, in Abby's opinion, was probably regretting his haste. He was also wearing a corset.

"Yes," Abby said. "I've been here before. Just never without prior arrangements," she admitted.

She threw a quick glance over her shoulder to where Meg and her brother were engaged in an animated conversation. Meg's brother knew this man, which was the only reason Abby had not walked haughtily around him when he'd stepped into her path and addressed her. Perhaps, she thought, she should have, regardless.

"I should think not," the man said. He cocked his head. "Still, I've never seen you here."

"Nor have I seen you, but it's a large building. Perhaps we missed one another." She did step around him this time.

"Perhaps," he said, moving back into her path. "And you've been here how many times?"

"I can't see how that's your concern." She'd been there exactly four times, once per week, just before sunset. She'd met with two men, one older and one younger, but never with this one. She'd surely have remembered *that*. If this man didn't know about their meetings, he wasn't meant to.

The man's frown deepened. He'd shaved that morning, but the coarse hair beneath the still-smooth skin of his chin was showing dark. He stroked at it thoughtfully and tapped the toe of one very expensively shod foot.

"You're not a member of the academy," he said.

"No," she replied, though her ears pricked up at the word.

"Forgive me," he said. "I can't imagine what your business here might be."

"That's because I haven't told you. Excuse me."

Really, she thought, as she stepped firmly away. The cheek! He might have known Meg's brother, but her business was her own. She was worried about Gideon, and wasting time with this self-appointed gatekeeper was not about to help her find him. She half expected him to step in front of her a third time, but, thankfully, he did not.

Instead, as she approached the front steps, he called from behind her. "Perhaps I can help."

She stopped. Quick, surprisingly light footsteps, then he was by her side. Notes of bergamot and jasmine danced on the air between them. At the same time, a fetid rotting-fish smell rose to meet it.

"Dr. Wylie," he said with a little bow. "I'm sorry if I appeared rude. Our organization doesn't typically entertain visitors."

"Miss Gordon," she said. "Nurse. And I'm not seeking entertainment."

He kept pace with her as she walked up the steps of Number 16. "What is it you're seeking, then, Nurse?"

The way he said her title indicated a strong and specific interest. Professional, certainly, though he seemed a bit more intent than that. Ignoring him, she turned the handle of the door. The times she'd visited the building before, stout, stony-faced men had been waiting in the shadows flanking the staircase. No sooner would she knock than the door would open to her.

But that afternoon there were no stony-faced men, just the annoying doctor, and the door was shut fast. She took the knob as if she'd done it a hundred times before, only to find it embarrassingly locked.

"Allow me," Dr. Wylie said. He brought out a key and made quick work of it.

"Thank you."

The entryway looked exactly as it had every other time she'd been there: dark, save for the light from a pair of sconces on either side of a corridor extending to the left and right. The corridor and the entryway were both swept clean but bereft of rugs, paintings, or any other type of decoration. The door to the room where she made the usual transaction was shut and, she suspected, locked. Straight ahead, a hallway led toward the rear of the building, its terminus disappearing into shadow.

Footsteps creaked past overhead. They both glanced up.

"If you tell me who you've come to see," Dr. Wylie said, "I could fetch them for you."

She sighed, her patience beginning to fray. "The problem is, we've never exchanged names."

"Oh?"

He didn't intend to go away, Abby realized. At the same time, she thought, edging away from the shadows lingering in the corners and listening to the ominous creaks and bangs above them, she wasn't certain she wanted him to, now. She didn't trust him, exactly, but neither did he seem as if he wished to harm her. And she couldn't say the same for the people moving about upstairs.

That rotting-fish smell had followed them inside. Strangely, it seemed to be stronger here.

Something crashed overhead. Then the floorboards groaned. She watched Dr. Wylie's lips purse and a furrow form between his carefully shaped brows as he seemed to fight the urge to investigate.

"Perhaps you can help me after all, Doctor," she said.

He turned back to her. "Certainly, if I can."

"One of my patients has a...a somewhat disturbing condition. The usual remedies have proved insufficient. Someone here has been providing me with an elixir, which has been surprisingly successful in suppressing the condition."

Now his attention was fixed fully on her, his dark eyes intent.

"I understand how it must look. Secret meetings in an abandoned building, no exchange of names. And yet—"

"What does your contact look like?" Dr. Wylie asked.

"That's the thing," she said. "The meetings are always conducted in shadow, shortly after the end of the business day. I've met with two men on a total of four occasions, but I've never seen either of their faces clearly. They speak as if they've an education, however. And, from their speech, I believe them to be from a higher social class. Also, one is quite a bit older than the other."

The curiosity in Dr. Wylie's expression had turned, though to what, Abby was at a loss to say. His dark eyes had gone narrow, and the furrow at the bridge of his nose had grown deeper. Alarmingly, he seemed angry. Abby took a step back.

"They've been providing you with an elixir, you say?" She nodded. "And may I ask what payment they're taking in return?"

"No payment," she said. "They simply ask that I record the efficacy of the treatment and any side effects."

"You're experimenting on a patient?" Dr. Wylie demanded.

"No!" Abby cried. "No, absolutely not! The patient...he's a physician himself, and he's fully aware of the provenance of the treatment. It's...he's my fiancé, actually. It's a bit complicated."

Some of the anger left his expression. Curiosity quickly replaced it.

"He...we were desperate, Doctor," she said. "I can't break his confidence and discuss his condition with you, but I assure you that he is fully aware that this is an unsanctioned, and probably untested, treatment. But we had no other option."

"Dr. Spencer," he said.

Abby blinked. "How did you know that?"

"You must be Abby. And you and Dr. Spencer run the Cornwall Street Clinic together in Shadwell."

Abby took another step away, but Dr. Wylie's attention no longer fixed on her. Instead, he was beginning to pace. She followed his gaze up toward the ceiling.

"Gideon's here," she said. "Isn't he?" His expression told her all she needed to know. "Take me to him straightaway."

"I'm not sure…" Dr. Wylie said.

"I *am* sure. Gideon needs me, and I need to find him. He's upstairs. I can tell from the way you keep looking toward the ceiling. If you're holding him against his will—"

"I assure you that's not the case," Dr. Wylie called after her.

But Abby was halfway toward the back of the building by this point. The shadows seemed to part for her as she steamed through the corridor. Dr. Wylie's light footfall sounded behind her, but she didn't care. Whoever these people were, if they knew what was good for them, they wouldn't stand between her and Gideon.

At the end of the hallway was a door and, to her right, a staircase. A blood red wool runner ran up the stairs like a tongue. Abby wondered briefly at the contrast between such an expensive touch and the abandoned-looking front of the building. But this was no time to linger. She hurried up the stairs.

"To the left," Dr. Wylie said behind her as she turned to head right. She turned again and followed him. He seemed worried, now, as well, and walked quickly until stopping before an open door. Abby came up behind him.

"Dear God," Dr. Wylie said.

A struggle had taken place in the room. A dividing screen lay on its side, revealing an overturned wash basin and a pile of Gideon's clothing. A coffee table lay on its back in the middle of the room. Beside it was a smashed tea pot. Someone's carefully handwritten notes splayed across a Persian carpet like rain-swept leaves. The air was fragrant with tea and a strange, sweet chemical tang. And that rotting-fish smell was starting to become overpowering.

"He was here," she said. "But—"

"But now he's gone. And not of his own volition."

"What do you mean? Who took him?" Abby's mind raced. "What is this place? Who are you people, and what do you want with him?"

"I don't know who took him or why," Dr. Wylie said. Then he turned to her. "Do you trust me, Nurse Gordon?"

"Not even a little bit!"

He nodded. "That's understandable. Nonetheless, I believe your fiancé is in much danger. Will you at least trust me to help you find him?"

"I don't suppose I have a choice," Abby said.

CHAPTER EIGHTEEN

Garrick

"I don't like this," Garrick said. "They've been gone too long."

He and Eli were standing in the shadows between the two buildings across the street from Number 16. There had been a lot of action in front of that building. Normally the place looked abandoned during the day, but after Bert and Clyde had gone around the back, Garrick and Eli had watched two men have an argument right outside the front door. The boys hadn't been able to hear much, but the argument had had the look and sound of a lovers' tiff, and it had been very entertaining. Then the nurse and her friend had come along. The pairs had split up when one of the men recognized one of the women and went to speak with her. Then the other woman had joined the other man.

None of the four had looked like they belonged in this part of town. However, Garrick reckoned that if their affairs were so complicated, it was probably best they sort them out somewhere like this, with no one else around who wasn't up to something worse.

But now one of the pairs had gone back into Number 16, and the other had started to argue amongst themselves, and Bert and Clyde were nowhere to be seen.

"You want me to go look?" Eli asked.

"We'll both go," he said, thinking, if you want something done right, you gotta do it yourself.

Careful not to attract the attention of the man and woman bickering on the pavement, Garrick and Eli doubled back and made their way to the alley behind Number 16. They exchanged a nod. By all appearances, the alley was abandoned. But Garrick would have expected that. His boys were good at staying out of sight. Eli raised one hand to his mouth and barked.

"Nothing," Garrick said after a moment. Pins and needles rose along Garrick's neck. He might have expected one of the boys not to answer, especially if they'd found a way inside the building. But one of them would have been standing guard. Eli made his signal again.

This time there was a returning bark. Garrick sighed.

"Thank—"

"That wasn't Clyde," Eli said.

Before Garrick could tell him not to, Eli was jogging into the alley, danger be damned. Eli had brought Clyde to the group in the first place. Since then, the two had been as thick as the thieves that they were. For some reason Eli felt responsible for Clyde, though Garrick well knew that Clyde could fend for himself. Before Garrick could say anything else, Eli was hooting like an owl—the boys' signal to drop everything and come quick.

"It's Bert," Eli said when Garrick caught him up.

"I can see that."

Bert was sitting up, now, but it was plain that he'd been flat on his back until Eli found him. He was blinking and rubbing an impressive-looking goose egg on the side of his head.

"What happened?" Garrick asked. At the same time, Eli demanded, "Where's Clyde?"

"Over by the window," Bert said irritably. Garrick opened his mouth to speak, but before he could, Eli was sprinting back across the alley.

This was bad. Few things shook Garrick, but this time he was well shook. His fingers trembled as he helped Bert to his feet. Someone would have to have been very clever and quiet to have sneaked up on Bert, and very large to have subdued him.

"There's a set of steps going down in front of the window." Bert rubbed at his head and blinked hard a few times. "The curtains were open a crack, and Clyde was going down to have a look. Then a man came out the back door and saw him. I was about to shout to Clyde to leg it out of there…then the next thing I know, Eli's shaking me and calling my name."

How had it all gone so wrong so fast? They'd been in scrapes before but had always come out of them all right. Garrick felt like a heel. This was his fault, and if anything happened to Clyde, he'd never forgive himself.

"I'll go look for him," Bert said. It's what Garrick would have asked him to do, and even though he was hurt, he was ready to do it. This made Garrick feel even worse.

"Naw," Garrick said. "You sit tight. Keep watch. I'll go."

❖

Eli

The window was below ground level in a well that stood to the left of the back door. As Eli drew closer, he saw the narrow set of steps that led down from the alley. He stopped at the top of them.

Bert had said that Clyde had gone to peek through a space between the curtains. But the curtains were pulled tight, now, and Eli couldn't see even a hint of what lay beyond them. The steps, however, had their own story to tell.

First, there was no door at the bottom. Only the large window. So why would there be steps? Maybe it was a way out in case of fire. Or perhaps a way to bring things into the basement from the alley.

Whatever the reason for the steps, though, no one had used them in a long time. Dirt, leaves, and rubbish had blown in and formed a mucky carpet on them and at the bottom edge of the window. A seaweed stink rose from it. It reminded Eli of the night in the alley. He shuddered.

Crouching down, Eli could make out prints from Clyde's small shoes. Exactly two larger shoe prints stood behind them. Eli's stomach sank as his mind filled in the gaps. Someone had stolen up behind Clyde. A few scuff marks showed a struggle. But Clyde was scrappy. Eli would have expected him to fight a lot harder than this particular set of footprints showed. Someone had grabbed Clyde before he had even had time to react.

The carpet of muck beneath the window lay undisturbed. Whoever had taken Clyde hadn't brought him through the window. Eli took a few steps back and searched the ground for footprints. But the ground was hard and dry, and he couldn't see a thing.

"Well?" Eli jumped at Garrick's voice behind him. Bert was there, too.

"He was here. There, on the steps," Eli said. "Then it looks like someone grabbed him. After that, no idea."

"I've a plan," Garrick said.

"Oh?"

Garrick was too deep in his own thoughts to scowl at Eli's tone. He narrowed his eyes and turned his gaze toward the back door of Number 16. "Every blasted thing seems to come back to this building, including that nurse. One of our own is in there, and nobody's coming to the rescue. It's up to us."

CHAPTER NINETEEN

Gideon

For the second time that day, Gideon awoke the worse for wear. He was clean, at least. And indoors. He was also wearing another man's clothes. Faint traces of jasmine and bergamot rose to meet his senses. These were Dr. Wylie's clothes. Heat rushed to his face as he remembered his flood of realizations, the dread that Dr. Wylie might somehow have read them in his features, the charge that passed between them when Gideon's fingers had brushed against Wylie's skin, and the crushing mortification when Dr. Wylie had suddenly fled the room.

Another smell-memory: sweetly chemical, and on the tail of that, an eye-watering stench of seawater and decay. His mouth suddenly filled with saliva, and he rolled over just as his stomach emptied itself onto a pile of straw.

There was straw on the floor.

Heart pounding, head throbbing, he sat back, wiped his chin, and waited for his eyes to adjust to the shadows. He was in some sort of animal pen, but indoors. A wall of wooden slats split the room. Through the bars on top, he could make out a shelf with bottles, though without his spectacles the labels were dark scribbles on light. There was a split door along the wall, such that one might open the top half to observe without danger that the animal inside might escape.

Outside the wind was picking up, gently pelting the veiled window with sand.

The last thing Gideon remembered was that pretty young woman, Miss Kingsley, coming back with a tray holding the luncheon that Dr. Wylie had requested. In retrospect, of course, he should have registered her nervous smile, the tremor in her fingers as she set the tray on the little table. He shouldn't have allowed himself to become so distracted by the smell of the food and the thought of it, warm and comforting inside him. He should have registered the second set of footsteps behind him.

His wolf rumbled a growl of admonition. A second growl answered.

Gideon gasped. Another wolf was in the enclosure with him. How had he not smelled her immediately? Gradually her form took shape in the dim light pushing through the fabric of the curtains. She was about the size of a large dog, with a wiry build that could have used a few good meals. Her coat was full and lush, though. With a good bath, it would be the color of brushed silver.

She was staring.

Gideon wondered if he should be afraid. He supposed it depended on the nature of the beast. Was it a simple wolf, in which case he was in a perilous place indeed. Or was it a beast such as he had inside him? If this was the case, he'd still would be wise to be afraid, or at least to show a healthy respect. Could he, perhaps, reason with her?

He'd never encountered another like himself. Part of him had always thought that like would recognize like. But it didn't seem to be the case. The other wolf cocked her head, taking his measure.

Slowly and cautiously, Gideon pulled himself up to his hands and knees. The wolf stiffened. Gideon noted the delicate rise of hackles, the less subtle pull of a snarl, and froze.

Her nostrils flared, taking in his scent, the scent of his fear. Holding his gaze, she raised her head, her tail moving slowly from side to side.

"It's all right," he whispered.

A bit of the stiffness left her posture. She was cautious but didn't fear him.

So they knew what he was, this Consortium. What's more, they'd found another like him. Dr. Wylie had said he wanted an interview, but the animal pen suggested that whatever his organization's intentions, they were not altruistic. Had this been Wylie's idea all along?

Footsteps in the corridor. Voices. The smell of three people, none of them Wylie.

"We'll stash him in here for now," a man's voice said. "Careful!"

A crash, a grunt, and then two men entered from the hallway, bundling a third ahead of them through the door. One of the men was older, perhaps in his sixties. The other looked to be in his twenties. The third was a slight figure, an older child, perhaps, gagged and bound at the wrists, but not, unfortunately for the men, at the ankles.

"Ouch! Damn you!" the younger man cried as the boy landed a kick to his shin. The man's eyes narrowed behind his tortoiseshell spectacles, and he gestured toward the pen. "In there. That'll sort you out."

"Are you sure?" the older man asked.

"Teach the brat some manners." His expression turned thoughtful. "And answer one or two questions. Oh, hello," he said when he caught Gideon looking. "How's your head? You must be feeling quite wretched. Chloroform will do that. But I couldn't imagine you'd have come along willingly."

"Where's Dr. Wylie?" Gideon demanded.

"Not here, and not coming to your rescue. Or yours." He stepped to the side as the boy tried for another kick, then quickly maneuvered himself behind the boy, taking the child's head in a lock as the older man brought out a set of keys. "Step away from the door, and don't even think about moving," he said to Gideon. "It would be my pleasure to snap this little bastard's neck. As for you," he said, glaring at the silver wolf, "you already know what happens when you fight back."

The silver wolf stood her ground, but she'd lowered her head and tail and was beginning to tremble.

Gideon stepped to one side, putting himself between her and the men. A snarl rose in his own throat. Something was off about this man. Something *wrong*. His pleasant features somehow made it worse.

"What is this place? Who are you?" Gideon asked. He looked toward the older man, hoping for sympathy, but the older man, having unlocked the door, looked away.

"You, Dr. Spencer," the younger man said, as he pushed the child through the door, then quickly shut it and replaced the padlock, "have the fortune of taking part in a groundbreaking study in a world-class scientific facility."

"World-class?" Gideon scoffed before he could stop himself. The younger man's eyes blazed at the insolence in Gideon's tone. "I see Miss Chase hasn't eaten you. Yet. There's another question answered."

Miss Chase. Miss Emily Chase, having escaped from the Hanwell Asylum for the—

"What do you think?" The man continued. "Is it because she recognizes a member of her own species, or because she's simply not hungry enough?" The older man was taking notes. He met Gideon's eyes briefly, then glanced quickly away. "Or perhaps she was simply waiting for something a bit more…snack sized."

The boy, by this time, had wedged himself into one corner, his gaze darting from Gideon to the silver wolf and back. To Gideon's horror, his own stomach rumbled loudly.

The younger man laughed.

"Monster," Gideon said.

"No, you are the monster, Doctor. And you," he said with a nod toward the silver wolf. "I imagine you must be quite hungry after your run last night. The question is, are you hungry enough to change and answer another of the questions that's been on my mind?" He folded his arms, his expression turning thoughtful. "Or will you and Miss Chase fight over him? Who would win? I wonder."

The older man was scribbling furiously, keeping his head down. Gideon could smell his discomfort, though he was trying to hide it. Strange. From the older man's bearing, he'd thought him the senior of the two.

"Is this really necessary, Hathaway," the older man asked.

The younger man—Hathaway—turned toward him. "You promised me I could have carte blanche if I found the answers to the Consortium's questions. And you yourself told me, Sir Julius, that science is not for the squeamish or the timid."

"Sir Julius," Gideon seized upon the name as if it were a lifeline. "Where's Dr. Wylie?"

Hathaway turned back to him, his features sharp with malice. "Dr. Wylie doesn't have the stomach to do what needs to be done. Enjoy your meal. I'll be back to check on the survivors later."

CHAPTER TWENTY

Jin

"Only one other person knew that Dr. Spencer was here," Wylie said as Miss Gordon paced the length of his office, carefully avoiding his scattered notes with her heavy, flat-soled boots. "That was Miss Kingsley."

Miss Gordon stopped. "Miss Kingsley? Miss Bernadette Kingsley?"

"Do you know her?" Wylie asked.

"She's Meg's—that is, Miss Eisenstadt's friend."

"Miss Eisen—"

"Yes," Abby said. "You were just speaking with her brother."

Eisenstadt had a sister? Of course it was possible. Wylie had only thought of the man in the context of his basement and bedroom. He hadn't dwelt at all on the rooms upstairs. Eisenstadt might have had an entire family stashed up there, for all Wylie knew.

"And you know Miss Eisenstadt how?" It was as difficult for him to imagine Miss Gordon's association with Nathaniel's sister as it was to imagine her married to Dr. Spencer. Poor Dr. Spencer, who would have been there enjoying his tea when his fiancée came to collect him, if only Wylie had been able to keep control of himself for five minutes.

"Meg—Miss Eisenstadt—and I met earlier today at the train station," the nurse said. "Miss Eisenstadt and Miss Kingsley are friends, or were friends, but they had some sort of falling out. Miss Eisenstadt was coming to sort it out. But she said that Miss Kingsley worked next door, at Number 18, not here."

Wylie crossed his arms and frowned. "She certainly does work here. She brings my tea. As for what she does when she's away from the office, though, that's none of my affair."

"But she saw Gideon? And you think she did...this?" Miss Gordon gestured around the office.

Wylie shook his head. "I can't imagine that she could have overpowered Dr. Spencer, even in the state he was in. If that is, indeed, what happened."

Her head snapped toward him. "What else could have happened?"

"He might have left on his own steam. Or," he said, taking stock of the wreckage, "he might have fought off his attacker and escaped."

Even as he said the words, though, something told him that wasn't the case, as much as he desperately wanted Dr. Spencer to be safe and far away. Something told him that Dr. Spencer had been taken unawares and that he was very likely still on the property.

"But *who?*" Miss Gordon demanded. Rightly. "*Who* took him, and what did they want?"

As if on cue, the monotonous barking started again. Outside, the wind was picking up, pelting the window with light debris. That same odor of decaying seaweed that he'd smelled on the street hung in the air. It was stronger here than it had been outside. Stronger, especially as he drew closer to Nurse Gordon. Yet it didn't seem to be coming *from* her, exactly.

"You don't really think he escaped," Miss Gordon said.

"No." He shook his head. "I don't."

"Then someone must have done something with him. And Miss Kingsley was involved. But why?"

Wylie hadn't an answer. He hadn't, quite frankly, given Miss Kingsley much thought before then. She brought his luncheon and tidied his office. But she *was* educated. Anyone could tell that. Much more so than one might expect from a low-level functionary. And more than once she'd attempted to share her ideas with him.

His stomach sank. Dear God, had she read his notes while she tidied? What might she have done with that information? He winced as he remembered their interactions that day. She had approached him to speak of some idea. And it hadn't been the first time that he'd dismissed her. He had been quite rude about it, actually, this time. Unforgivably rude.

A sinking feeling filled him. Miss Kingsley might not have physically dragged Dr. Spencer away, but she might well have discussed his presence with the person who had. And Wylie had a definite idea about—

"What state was that?" Miss Gordon interrupted his thoughts. Her blue eyes were piercing, now.

"Excuse me?"

"I asked you, exactly what was Dr. Spencer's state?"

He considered her carefully for a long moment. "Nurse Gordon, what do you know about the nature of Dr. Spencer's condition?"

She stared back at him. He could see her weighing decisions behind her eyes, but her mind was closed to him. Not deliberately shielded. She was simply very, very strong and determined, two qualities that he suspected Dr. Spencer would have appreciated very much.

"I'm his fiancée, Dr. Wylie. There are no secrets between us."

Wylie wasn't at all certain about *that*, especially if she had agreed to marry him. It was probable, however, that Dr. Spencer had trusted her with the knowledge of his condition. They were both medical professionals, after all. And she had been the one, he'd said, that had sought out the medicine that kept it at bay.

He nodded slowly. "Then you're aware that you've been bringing your fiancé a medicine that suppresses the lycanthropic state. That is—"

"I know what that is," Miss Gordon snapped.

"I'm sure. But the fact is, Miss Gordon, I've been working on the study of lycanthropy for our organization. I've been studying the phenomenon in an abstract sense and from a medical perspective. But before I came across Dr. Spencer, quite by accident, as it happens, I'd never encountered an actual specimen."

"*Specimen?*"

"Forgive me. That was an unfortunate choice of words. I was actually on my way to Shadwell for a different errand—" She was now regarding him with a keen interest. He continued. "I've been asking the Consortium for my own research facility for some time, but we hadn't found a suitable property. One of my colleagues had found the property, a working medical facility—"

"Wait," Miss Gordon said. She brought a crumpled sheet of paper out of her coat pocket. "The Consortium, you say? This consortium?" She held the sheet up so he could see. "This is *you* attempting to leverage away my clinic by force of law?"

She had seemed so mild mannered. The new ferocity in her tone made Wylie step back.

"This was not my doing, dear lady, I assure you. I simply told the Consortium my needs, and they set about finding—they told me it was a medical facility. I assumed it was disused—"

"You assumed wrong!" she cried. "Gideon and I founded that clinic. And it is very much in use, thank you very much!"

"They never told me that," Wylie said. "I'll have them issue a retraction at once. In fact, *I* retract it. In fact—"

"That can wait," Nurse Gordon said. "We need to find Gideon. If he was still on or near the property, where would he be?"

Wylie didn't even need to think about it. All he had to do was follow the mournful, monotonous barking throbbing at the back of his skull. At the same moment, Nurse Gordon cocked her head as if she were hearing it, too.

"In the basement," she said.

"But—" He called after her as she turned and made her way out the door. "Nurse Gordon, there is no basement!"

❖

Abby

Abby flew down the stairs, barely registering Dr. Wylie's words as he called after her. There had to be a basement. Every building had one. Didn't it? Not necessarily. The clinic didn't. She paused at the bottom of the stairs, where she saw no door or further staircase. She went back through the corridor toward rooms where she'd come all those times for Gideon's medicine.

"One of these has to lead to a staircase," she said as Dr. Wylie appeared in the corridor. "These are all locked. Try the ones on that side. This building has to have a basement," she said as they tried the doors one by one. "I could swear I saw a ground-floor window as I was walking up."

"That belongs to the building next door," Dr. Wylie said.

"The animal charity?" Abby asked.

Dr. Wylie frowned. "They told me it was a charity, but now I'm not so sure."

That sad dog was barking again. It wasn't so much a sound, Abby realized, as a sensation in her bones, at the back of her skull.

"You hear it, too," she said to Wylie.

He nodded. "It's a lycanthrope, but it's not Dr. Spencer. He heard it too, before…That poor beast was carrying on for a long time before I brought Dr. Spencer to the premises."

"A werewolf? At an animal charity? Do they know?"

"I'm not sure. I've been meaning to—"

"But it's not exactly barking, is it?" Dr. Wylie's eyes narrowed. Abby had a tingling feeling across the top of her head. She shook it, and the sensation was gone. "It's more of a feeling, right here." She touched the base of her skull. "You feel it in exactly the same way. I can tell."

"Yes," he said, "but why do you?"

"Why does either of us? Why does anyone?"

He crossed his arms over his chest. "Not everyone does hear it, Nurse Gordon. Miss Kingsley doesn't. But Dr. Spencer did. Let me ask you—"

"Later," Abby said, returning to her search. "We have to find Gideon."

She cast a dirty glare at the doors. Then the gas sconce at the end of the hall flickered. From a distance, the sconce had looked like any other, but as she drew closer, she saw something strange about the angle at which it sat against the wood paneling. "How long has that been like that?" she asked.

Dr. Wylie frowned. "I couldn't say. I hope it isn't leaking."

"That was my thought, too," she said. It would have been not only a health hazard but a fire hazard, as well. She listened for a hitch in the normal hiss of gas, but the flow sounded normal.

The sconce was a bit too high for Abby to reach without a chair, but Dr. Wylie reached it easily. As he tipped it back into place, she heard a metallic *ping,* and the wall panel slid back by an inch. Abby put her fingers in the gap and pulled it all the way to the right, exposing a deep, black shaft.

"A lift?" Abby asked. She'd heard of such things but had never seen one.

"I didn't know there was a lift here," Dr. Wylie said.

"I think that's the point. Do you have a match?"

Dr. Wylie patted himself down. "Sorry."

"Never mind. The shaft goes both up and down from here." Abby pulled the panel back as far as it would go and squinted down into the darkness. "I think I can see the top of the box down below."

"So there is a lower level," Dr. Wylie said.

"But where are the cables? I thought lifts had cables."

Dr. Wylie took his turn at the entrance. "It could be a Siemens lift. Runs on electricity. I saw it at an exhibition once, in Germany. See the metal pole against the back of the wall?"

"Electricity?"

"Runs almost silently," Dr. Wylie said to himself.

"How do we call it?"

"There should be a switch or something."

Abby stepped back, watching Dr. Wylie examine the sides of the sliding panel. They reached for the sconce at the same time. Something whirred to life in the shaft below.

"Great minds think alike," Abby said.

The lift rose slowly, majestically, and all but silently, coming to a stop before them. For all its advanced technology, its appearance was disappointing: a wire box atop a platform of wooden planks, with a sliding metal gate. A box with a switch hung from the back wall.

Outside, footsteps scuffled up the building's front stairs. They stepped inside, careful to replace the wooden panel behind them before pulling the cage door shut.

"Down?" Dr. Wylie asked.

"Down," Abby said.

He pulled the switch. But just as the front door opened, the lift began to move upward.

CHAPTER TWENTY-ONE

Meg

Meg hadn't expected to need her picklocks that day. But one had to prepare for the unexpected, so into her inner coat pocket they'd gone. The expression on Nat's face alone had made the choice worth it.

"I can't believe you're breaking into a *building*," he said. The admiration in his voice might have warmed her, had she not been nearly frantic with worry. She couldn't put a finger on it, but something was very, very wrong with this situation. Abby had been inside far too long for a simple exchange of money and medicine. She must have found trouble, as well. And not the kind of comparatively silly trouble that Meg had come to iron out with Bernadette.

"We tried knocking. We tried the bell. What's a person to do? Besides, the place looks abandoned. What the devil is Bernadette doing in there, rather than next door…blast!"

The picks jumped out of her shaking fingers. She stopped to retrieve them and re-apply them to the tumblers.

"But this *is* technically breaking and entering," Nat said. "I thought you do-goods didn't go in for that sort of thing."

"If someone sends for the police, you can put on your best imitation Oxbridge and convince them it's a prank."

Nat barked a laugh. "Sister, dear, the tender blossom of new love has returned your sense of humor. I approve!"

"Oh, shut it," she said.

She might have laughed with him had she not been struggling with an acute case of the shivers. Nothing about this place added up. A scientific facility in a building that should have been condemned? And which shared a building with Nat's posh occultists' club? Not to mention that she couldn't shake the feeling—evidenced by nothing but the growing pit of dread in her stomach—that Abby was in significant danger.

At last the lock gave way. Cautiously, Meg and Nat crept into an entryway that appeared as abandoned as the building's face. The only light came from a pair of gas sconces, one on either side of a corridor that extended to the left and right, casting flickering shadows in the corners. A faint mechanical whir broke the silence, followed by muffled footsteps on the floor above them.

Nat sneezed. "Someone's been neglecting the dusting," he murmured.

"You'd think your rich-boy warlock club could afford better digs."

"It's a university club. Limited funds. And who taught you to pick *locks*?" Nat's words were brave, but he'd threaded his arm through hers and huddled close.

"A month ago, my club had a lady in from the Pankhurst Society. You never know what might come in handy in the fight for women's liberation."

Nat laid a scandalized hand over his chest. "Sister, dear, you're not telling me you're one of those harridans fighting for women to obtain the vote."

"You'd be disappointed if I weren't."

"With your fists, though?"

"If it comes to that. As you've seen for yourself."

His features darkened as he no doubt remembered the reward he'd reaped for interrupting her group's self-defense lesson.

"Well. I suppose if women had more freedom, they'd perhaps be a bit more free with their favors. Ouch!" He jumped back as she ground a heel into his foot. "Those man-boots hurt!"

"Quiet!" she said, though the last thing this blasted building needed was more silence. They'd been standing in the entryway for some time, and no one had come down to greet them. Or even to see them off. Her Abby and Nat's Jin had, seemingly, vanished into this silent interior. Part of her wondered if they would be next.

"I don't like this. We need to find Bernadette, apologize, and get out of here."

"Not so fast, sis," Nat said.

"What?"

Nat took a few steps into the gloom. He gazed up one corridor and down the other. Then he cast his gaze to the ceiling and frowned.

"You seem to have forgotten that I came with an agenda. To wit, this is the sanctum sanctorum of the Academy of Occult Sciences, which courted me for my genius and ideas and then threw me away for no good reason, without so much as a—"

"We're going to find Bernadette, and you're *going* to apologize," she said. *And we're not leaving without Abby.* He was glowering at her now, which she supposed was better than cringing at her side like a frightened child. "And then we can deal with your little club," she added. "Besides, if Bernadette has business here, it can only help your case if she's on your side."

He shrugged again. "I suppose you're right."

"I am right," she said. "But before we do any of that, we need to speak to someone who can at least point us in the right direction."

"Right."

"So I'll check the doors on this side. You go to the left. I don't want to barge upstairs without an invitation if we don't have to."

The doors on Meg's side were locked. She might have brought out her picks again, had she not felt they'd pressed their luck quite far enough already. Besides, no light shone beneath the doors, and the corridors were as preternaturally silent as the entryway.

"No one's here," she said as they emerged simultaneously back into the entry hall.

"My dear, you do have a magnificent grasp of the obvious," he murmured. But he appeared to have something else on his mind.

"What is it?" she asked.

He turned to her, his face contorted with an uncomfortable emotion that Meg was quite certain she'd never witnessed in the man. Dear God, was that…guilt?

"It's just…I have been a bit of a shit, haven't I?" Meg stopped, and he did too, apparently mistaking her utter amazement for agreement. "Where Bernadette was concerned, I have. It's just…she was so pretty and clever and easy to talk to, at least when the wine was flowing. And I was in such a state over Jin. Damn and blast him, anyway," he said under his breath.

"I can't imagine you being in a state over anyone," Meg said honestly.

"Don't be cruel."

"I'm not," she said. "I've watched you go through lovers like cheap handkerchiefs. I thought you liked it that way."

"I thought so too," Nat said. His frown lines looked deeper in the shadows from the gas sconces. Had the man secretly been growing a conscience? "In fact, I chose Jin with exactly that in mind. He was gorgeous, good for a bit of interesting pillow talk, and was happy to leave after we'd had our fun. But at some point I started not wanting him to leave right away. And then I didn't want him to leave at all. Good God, I can't believe that he and Bernadette and Hathaway…."

"Yes?" A voice came from somewhere near the back door. A young man emerged from the shadows. Tall, thin, and bespectacled, he was in his shirt sleeves and waistcoat, and had rolled up his cuffs. Looking closer, Meg saw three raised, red rows of scratches along one of his forearms. His hair looked like it had been attacked by birds.

Beside her, Nat stiffened and raised himself taller.

"Speak of the very devil," Nat said a bit too loudly.

The young man frowned. "Eisenstadt? What are you doing here?"

"Looking for you, actually, Hathaway," Nat said. "To tell you that I know what you're up to, you and Jin Wylie and—" he narrowed his eyes, "Miss Bernadette damn-her-eyes Kingsley."

The change in Hathaway's expression was subtle and obfuscated by shadow, but Meg saw it nonetheless. Good God, was Nat actually tilting at a relevant windmill? If so, he must have found it by accident.

Nat barreled forward. "I'd have been more than happy to share my research with you, if you'd let me into your little circle. I don't understand why you felt you had to come up with some Byzantine plot to steal it."

Was that a flicker of relief on Hathaway's face? "What on earth are you talking about?" he said. "I didn't steal anything. As for the academy, it was strictly for students, and you were expelled."

"A convenient excuse," Nat spat. "But—"

"Look," Meg said, "you boys can finish your squabble later. Right now, Nat and I need to find Miss Bernadette Kingsley."

"Miss Kingsley?" Now Hathaway looked bewildered. "What ever for? Who are you?"

"That's my sister, and you can keep your filthy eyes above chin level where they belong," Nat said.

"What?" Hathaway shook his head. The arrogance had returned to his expression, and whatever Nat might have caught him out at was lost for the moment. Meg made a note to herself to get back to it later. "Look, I can't help you with the academy, and I didn't steal your notes. But Miss Kingsley is my assistant, and I can spare her for a few moments if that suits."

His assistant? "That suits fine," Meg said.

"Good. This way, please."

Hathaway turned on his heel and walked back toward the rear of the building. At the end of the corridor, he turned right and ascended the staircase there.

Curiouser and curiouser, Abby thought, the words from a favorite childhood book percolating up from memory as if on cue. The facade was boarded up and looked for all the world as if it had been abandoned. The inside appeared habitable but not inhabited. But the stairs had a red wool runner, and at the top she could see a well-lit corridor with paintings evenly spaced along the wall.

But Abby was still missing, and so was Bernadette.

"Mr. Hathaway," Meg said as they reached the top of the stairs.

"Miss Eisenstadt?"

"A friend of mine arrived just ahead of us." Hathaway stopped and turned very slowly to face her. Meg continued. "I was hoping that after we spoke with Miss Kingsley, my friend and I might walk back to the train station together. Have you seen her? Her name is Miss Gordon. Nurse Gordon."

Hathaway frowned. The gesture accentuated a smudge of dirt on his forehead. "We seem to be having more visitors today than we have had in the past month," he said more to himself than to her. Now Meg knew that she hadn't been imagining the shrewd flicker in his eyes. His features seemed to go sharper, somehow. They reminded her of a fox. No, a wolf.

"Do you know her?" Meg asked.

"No," he said warily. "What's her business here?"

"Apparently someone in this building supplies her with a specific medicine for her clinic."

Hathaway crossed his arms, and his frown deepened. He tapped his fingers on his elbow. Next to her, Nat had a funny look on his face and was rubbing at his scalp as if something was annoying him.

"And she's here now?" Hathaway asked.

"Yes. She came in just ahead of us, with…with someone named Jin."

"Dr. Wylie?" Hathaway asked, as if he'd never heard the name before. Nat was now squirming as if he'd ants in his small clothes. Finally Hathaway spoke again. "I see. Miss Eisenstadt, and Mr. Eisenstadt, I think we can help each other."

"Oh, really?" Nat drawled. Meg gave his ankle a kick.

Hathaway didn't seem to have heard the insult at all. "Yes, really, Mr. Eisenstadt. All three of us. Come. Let's go to my office and talk."

"But what about Miss Kingsley?" Meg asked.

"Miss Kingsley will join us in time," Hathaway said. "But in the meantime, we have quite a bit to discuss. Starting," he said, looking meaningfully at Nat, "with a reconsideration of your membership in the academy."

CHAPTER TWENTY-TWO

Gideon

The standoff had lasted a lot longer than Gideon had thought it would, with the boy cowering in a corner on one side, the wolf staring intently from the other side, and an eye-watering stench somewhere between bog and brimstone rising around them. Outside, the wind was moaning softly, casting dust and debris against the windowpanes.

"For goodness sake, I'm not going to hurt you," Gideon finally told the boy.

The boy's eyes darted past his shoulder and settled on the silver wolf. A warning growl rumbled in her throat.

"I won't let her hurt you, either," Gideon said. The boy scowled, probably—correctly—doubting Gideon's chances against the wolf. "May I at least take off your gag?"

Slowly the boy returned his gaze to Gideon and nodded. The gag was hastily and inexpertly tied, and Gideon's fingers made quick work of it. The cord that bound the boy's wrists was another matter.

"My name is Dr. Spencer," Gideon said. "With your permission, I'm going to manipulate your wrists to loosen the cord."

"All right, then," the boy said. "But no tricks, or I'll kick the life out of you."

"Tricks?" Gideon asked.

"That man said his dog ain't et in three days. If I was you, I'd feed me to it to save yourself." He was trying to sound fierce, but his voice contained a tremor.

"Then I'm lucky our positions aren't reversed, aren't I?" Gideon said. He moved the boy's wrists to and fro, twisting them gently. The cord began to loosen, and soon the boy was able to work himself free.

"How'd you do that?" the boy asked, rubbing his wrists where the cord had bound them.

Gideon said, "You did most of the work. Our captors' lack of expertise did the rest."

"But how did you know what to do?"

Gideon allowed himself a small smile. "I'm not as boring as I look."

The boy let out a long breath. "Sometimes I think boring would be nice."

"Comparatively, I believe you're right. What's your name?"

The boy regarded him for a moment with wide, solemn, eyes. "Clyde."

"Nice to meet you, Clyde."

"What's...does that dog have a name?"

"Her name is Miss Chase."

"You mean like the escaped murderess? Is it *her* dog?" Clyde scrambled backward into the corner.

Not exactly, Gideon thought. The violent murder of which the asylum escapee had been convicted could certainly have been the work of a lycanthrope. At the same time, to his experience, the papers loved to linger on gruesome details while leaving out more pertinent, if less attention-grabbing ones—such as motive and circumstance. And there was always the chance that someone had saddled the wolf with that name as a joke.

"I'm sure it's just a coincidence," Gideon said.

"Funny name for a dog, though," Clyde mumbled.

The silver wolf let out a chuff.

"She's not exactly a dog."

Clyde frowned. From his expression, Gideon reckoned the boy thought it best to leave the subject at that. "So, what kind of place is this? Why do they have you locked up here with a…with her?"

Gideon glanced over his shoulder. Miss Chase was holding the same posture, her stare still burning a path across the straw-covered floor at them, but he could swear she'd moved closer. That woeful, monotonous barking had, at least, ceased. Gideon wasn't certain that the animal's silent vigilance was better.

"That I couldn't tell you," Gideon answered. "A more salient question, in my opinion, is how we're going to let ourselves out of here."

"*Salient*," Clyde said. "That means important."

Gideon blinked. "Very good."

"I like words."

"A good vocabulary is a valuable servant." Gideon gave the door an exploratory shake.

"They got a lock on it," Clyde said.

"I figured as much. Don't suppose you have any experience picking them?"

"A bit," said Clyde. "Ain't never had a crack at one like that, though."

Gideon said, "I just thought since you'd let yourself into the building—"

"I never!" he cried. "I like my heart beatin', thank you very much."

"What do you mean by that?"

Clyde said, "There's somefin' wrong about this place. It's falling down, right? No one's set foot in it for years. Then a few months ago, some folks move in. Slow, quiet like. Hardly know they're there. The way they leave it with the boards on the windows and stuff, you'd think they don't want no one to know they're here. But at night…"

"It's different at night?"

"Lights in the windows, strange sounds. What kind of business is it that they have to do it at night?"

"So you thought to take a closer look during the daytime when it seemed like no one was around," Gideon said.

"That's right. And that's when they…" The boy's eyes widened, and he took a step back. Gideon followed the direction of his gaze and jumped at the sight of the wolf nearly beside him. Pulse racing, he forced himself to stand his ground.

"Behave yourself, Miss Chase!" Gideon cried, surprise momentarily overcoming good sense. The wolf cocked her giant head. Emboldened, he added, "You heard me." The wolf regarded him for a moment, then gave an indignant whine and sat on her haunches. Suppressing a laugh—Gideon had truly thought that either he or the boy was about to become dinner—Gideon returned his attention to Clyde. "Go on, then."

Clyde looked like he wanted to smile, too, but as he returned to his subject, his nervousness reappeared.

"We prolly wouldn't have come at all except for the nurse."

Gideon's ears pricked up. "What nurse?"

The boy paused, as if suddenly thinking better of it. Or perhaps in order to come up with a suitable obfuscation for his misdeeds.

"We met this nurse the other day, see," he said carefully.

"What, here?" Gideon asked.

"Nah. Down by the Old Stairs."

Gideon drew in a sharp breath. He remembered how Abby had come running out of the alley the day before, as if the entire legion of hell were after her. The street behind that alley went past the Old Stairs at some point, if memory served. She hadn't told him the details of what had happened, but someone had been chasing her, that had been clear, and she'd been terrified.

"You didn't *meet* her," Gideon said slowly, as the story unfolded in his mind's eye. "You attacked her. Tried to rob her, didn't you?"

A low growl rumbled beneath the white wolf's throat, and Gideon felt a bit like growling himself.

"Twenty-four years of age, brunette, grey dress, wool coat, carrying a Gladstone?"

"H-how did you know?" the boy said.

"That was *my* nurse." Gideon's wolf stirred below the surface. "And you and your *mates*—"

The last few words sounded like he was speaking through gravel. Gideon's vision sharpened. He could smell the child begin to sweat. Miss Chase was a warm presence at his hip, her growl vibrating against his leg. Clyde's eyes went wide. Gideon could hear the boy's pulse, as rapid as a bird's.

"We thought she had money or medicine or somefin' we could sell. We didn't mean nothing by it! We—we was hungry!"

The air around them had gone thick with the smell of fear and blood and seaweed. A field of red clouded before Gideon's eyes. He took a step forward, and...

Miss Chase whined again. Gideon glanced down. She had put herself between him and the boy. Gideon's wolf hesitated, and Gideon blinked, horrified to find his fingers arched into rigid claws, the tips tingling in anticipation of violence. He let out a long breath and jammed his hands into his pockets.

"That woman is my nurse and my fiancée," he said quietly.

"She's here."

"What?" Gideon's heart began to race again.

Clyde said, "Me and my mates was watching from an alley when she come walking up the street with another woman. Right up the street toward this building."

"And then what?"

"Then I don't know. Then we hid because we didn't want her to see us."

The boy was still pressing himself into the corner as if hoping he might disappear into the walls. Gideon took a step back, ashamed.

"So how do you know she's here, in this building?" Gideon asked.

"Because she has to be! See..." He paused again, but this time his face bunched up with the effort of putting his thoughts in order. "After she...after we..."

"After Nurse Gordon escaped from your pack of—"

"The fog came, and then the Fiend," Clyde said.

Gideon stopped. It was the same word Abby had used the last time Gideon had lost control of his wolf. A new kind of dread crept up his spine.

"What?"

"The Fiend came. It attacked us!"

"What…what did it look like?" Gideon asked.

Clyde swallowed. "Like a man. Big, with long arms. Too long. They dragged the ground."

Gideon paused. "But it walked on two legs?" Clyde nodded. "Was it hairy? Did it have an animal's face?" It occurred to him that he'd no idea what he looked like in his feral state.

Clyde said, "It was too hard to see, with the fog and all."

"But it was more like a man, than like…"

"It weren't no dog," Clyde said.

Gideon let out a long breath of relief. "Well, thank goodness for that."

"Garrick thinks the nurse sends it out."

"Excuse me?" Miss Chase pressed against his legs again, and he absently rested a hand on her soft ruff.

"She controls it, like," Clyde said.

"Why would you think that?" The boggy stench that had been tickling at the periphery of his senses was overpowering, now. Miss Chase sneezed.

"On account of the Fiend attacked us, but before that, it attacked Nell Evans."

"Who?" Gideon demanded.

"She broke into your clinic two weeks ago to steal medicines. And then on her way home that night, the fog rolls in and the Fiend attacks *us*."

"The same fiend?" Gideon asked.

"You think there's more than one? Listen. Nell Evans broke into your clinic. We tried to…well, we met up with that nurse…and we wasn't very nice…and then the fog came, and the Fiend came for *us*. That's why Garrick said we had to check out this place."

Gideon shook his head, exasperated. "I don't see the connection."

Clyde let out an exaggerated sigh, as if Gideon were being deliberately obtuse. "Because Bert says he sees her here, at this strange place with strange people, every week, once a week like clockwork. It all has to be connected. Don't you see?"

Suddenly Gideon did see. His hand flew to his mouth, and his mind raced to keep up with the rapidly forming connections. This was where Abby came for his medicine. She'd returned to ask for more after Gideon had dropped the original phial. Dr. Wylie had found Gideon. Dr. Wylie studied lycanthropy, though he'd seemed surprised that someone had developed a medication to suppress the symptoms.

"Well, this is a puzzle," Gideon said.

"I'll say."

"A dangerous one. We need to get out of here."

And, Gideon thought, they had to find Abby.

CHAPTER TWENTY-THREE

Jin

The elevator traveled for much longer than Jin imagined it should have to simply reach the next floor. From the way the chill increased around them, he expected to emerge into a drafty attic. But when the doors opened, what they found was anything but. Far from some dusty storage space, the study was elegant and inviting. Light spilled into the elevator from brightly burning sconces as the wall panel slid open, seemingly of its own accord. Heat from a well-stoked fire followed.

"Where are we?" Nurse Gordon whispered.

Jin placed a hand on her forearm, and she fell quiet. This was the private office of someone important. How had he not even known it was here? It was a large, circular space, decorated like the planning room of a general with cosmic aspirations. An enormous globe stood near the wall, cradled in the arc of a curved bookcase. Unnatural colors marked the seas and land masses, and Jin didn't recognize the shapes of any of the continents. A series of maps lay unfurled across a large table. On the top was a sky map with peculiar constellations.

This had to be, he realized, the beating heart of the Consortium. And they'd not been invited.

Jin reached behind him for the lift switch, but just as his hand found it, the metal gate slid aside.

"Come in, my boy."

Sir Julius rose from behind a wide mahogany desk. Nurse Gordon stifled a little cry. How had they both failed to see the desk facing them from directly across the room, and the man behind it, who must have been watching them this entire time?

"Are you lost?" Sir Julius asked. Instinctively, Jin reached for his mentor's thoughts. The wall he found protecting them was high and wide.

"I...I think I might be, sir," he said. He began to stammer an apology, which Sir Julius amiably waved away.

"Never mind, never mind. Come inside, both of you." His tone was welcoming, but Jin noticed how he gracefully crossed to the table and folded away the maps. "What a fortunate coincidence," Sir Julius said. "I was meaning to speak to you today. There's good news."

"Oh?" Jin asked.

"But first, please introduce me to your companion." He turned to Nurse Gordon, who was holding herself confidently despite the nervousness rolling off of her in waves. Jin couldn't blame her. Her eyes had lingered on the globe, just as Jin's had, and she had to be aware that they weren't meant to be there. "I don't believe I've had the pleasure," Sir Julius said.

"Abigail Gordon," she said, clearing the tremor from her throat. "But I believe you already knew that, sir. After all, we've met once a week for some time now, in the rooms downstairs. Please forgive my forwardness. I know I've not gone through the usual channels this time, but it's an emergency. I must have more of the elixir."

Sir Julius frowned.

"There was an accident," Nurse Gordon continued. "The phial broke and the elixir was lost. I must have more, if it's not already too late."

Sir Julius glanced quickly at Jin, then said, "Young lady, you must be mis—"

"I'm certain it was you," Nurse Gordon said. "Your voice is very distinctive. There are two of you, no? A younger man as well. I apologize for breaking protocol, but this really is an emergency, and...well, I have money," she said, reaching into the inner pocket of her coat.

Jin's thoughts raced. Sir Julius had been providing the medicine that suppressed Dr. Spencer's lycanthropy, which meant that the Consortium's research in the area was a lot more advanced that they had let on. Why were they encouraging Jin to spin theories about the nature of the phenomenon and waste his time searching for a specimen, when someone had already—

"Put that away," Sir Julius said. Then, more gently, "It's not necessary, my dear. I'm certain we can sort this out. Tell me, have you been keeping track of the effectiveness and side effects, as I've asked?"

"Yes, as a matter of fact—"

"And I've no doubt that you've sampled the elixir yourself—just a touch, no need to be ashamed—to try to determine the formula? To make certain we weren't cheating you? I'd expect no less, of course," he said.

The remark seemed to fluster her, but she took a deep breath and refocused. "I'd be pleased to discuss all of these things with you at another time. But my patient he's…I have reason to believe he's in this building."

"*This* building?"

"As I said, we can sort this out later. But right now—"

"My dear Miss Gordon," Sir Julius said. "If such a creature were on the premises, don't you think I'd know about it?"

"He *is* here," she cried. "He is! I've heard him. Dr. Wylie *said* he was here, right in his office, but when we went there—well, I can't imagine you have more than one lycanthrope in your basement!"

Sir Julius turned to Jin and quirked a bushy eyebrow.

"I did come across Dr. Spencer, sir, quite by accident, on my way to Shadwell. Hathaway had arranged for me to visit a building there that he thought might be suitable for my facility." He tried to ignore the way Nurse Gordon's jawline hardened at the mention of her clinic. "Along the way, I came across Dr. Spencer, who was in need of medical attention. I realized what he…what was the nature of his affliction and transported him back, hoping for an interview. I asked Miss Kingsley to bring luncheon on a tray, and I stepped out for a breath of air, which was when I encountered Nurse Gordon. I led her back inside to reunite her with Dr. Spencer, but when I returned, Dr. Spencer was gone, and not of his own free will."

"What?"

"A struggle had taken place," Jin said. "Furniture was overturned, my notes were scattered everywhere, my inkwell—"

"Oh, dear," Sir Julius said. "I do apologize, dear boy. You know, I can't hear a thing all the way up here." He turned to Nurse Gordon. "But you believe your Dr. Spencer is still on the premises?"

"I hope so," she said.

"Then we shall find him. But first, we shall summon Miss Kingsley. After all, if she took Dr. Spencer his luncheon, she was probably the last one to see him."

Jin nodded. Nurse Gordon tapped an impatient foot on the thick carpeting as Sir Julius crossed to the bell pull that hung near the door of the elevator. He gave it a sharp jerk, then closed the elevator's gate and sent the platform back down the shaft.

"There, there, my dear," Sir Julius said to Nurse Gordon. "If your Dr. Spencer is here, we'll find him. And if there is some sort of animal in the basement, well, we'll deal with that, too."

"Thank you," Nurse Gordon said.

"Sir?" Jin asked. Sir Julius turned. "Why is it that you've had me examining theoretical perspectives on lycanthropy when the Consortium's research has advanced so much further than that? Why has no one told me that we've been distributing an *antidote*, for the love of God? I'm a doctor. In fact, my work at Hanwell—"

"Your work at Hanwell," Sir Julius said, "is exactly the reason I've kept you away from the practical applications of our research. That didn't end so well, your work at Hanwell, did it?" His tone was kind, but the words cut Jin to the core.

Before Jin could respond, a soft electrical whir heralded the arrival of the elevator.

"Ah, Miss Kingsley," Sir Julius said as Miss Kingsley pulled back the elevator's gate. "I'm glad you're here. We're about to go down to the basement."

"The basement?" Miss Kingsley asked.

Sir Julius smiled. "Yes. It's time that Dr. Wylie learned the truth about what we're doing, here."

CHAPTER TWENTY-FOUR

Garrick

This wasn't a quick butcher's anymore, Garrick realized, as he, Bert, and Eli scoped out the back of the building from the safety of their shadowy corner of the alley. It was no longer a fast in-and-out to satisfy his curiosity about the nurse and the dark deeds taking place inside the building on Shepherd Street.

This was now a rescue. No one was coming to help them, and if they wanted to get Clyde out of that building, it was down to him, Eli—who was becoming mouthier and more liable to mutiny by the day—and Bert, who'd taken a blow to the noggin. Bad for Bert, sure, but it also meant that someone knew they were there.

The smart thing to do would be to cut their losses, let Clyde take his own chances, and hopefully he'd catch them up later.

But for once the smart thing wasn't an option.

Garrick was worried about Clyde, worried about Bert and his head, and most of all, worried that they'd stepped into something a lot bigger than they could handle. For the first time, Garrick felt that the boys were more than his spying eyes and prying ears and thieving fingers. They were his responsibility, especially Clyde, who, for all his brains and talent, was so small and so young. If anything happened to any of them, it would be Garrick's fault. And, Garrick realized, he didn't know how he'd be able to live with that.

"There's definitely someone down there in the basement," Eli said. "I heard voices."

"How many voices?" Bert asked.

"Two? It was hard to tell, but at least two."

"Were any of them Clyde?" Garrick asked.

Eli shrugged. If Eli couldn't tell, then who could? Garrick wondered. "It's a bad idea to break into a room with two people and who knows what else," Eli said.

"You said the nurse is in there," Bert said, wincing as he touched the goose egg on his head.

"It weren't a woman's voice in the—"

"Eli?" Garrick asked. "What is it, mate?"

"That dog," Eli said.

Garrick didn't hear it. He also didn't tell Eli that the way he was squinting into the wind with his nose in the air, he *looked* like a dog.

"I don't hear it," Bert said.

"Didn't you tell Clyde to bark if he found trouble?" Garrick asked.

"It wasn't Clyde," Eli said. He frowned. "It's stopped now."

"If the nurse is inside, maybe she can help," Bert said reasonably.

Garrick tapped his toes impatiently. Leave it to a motherless lad to look to a woman for help. Wind spiraled into the alley from the street, bringing with it the dead-fish stink of the Thames. Strange. He'd never smelt the river so far from the actual water.

"She's not going to help us if she's a part of this," Garrick said.

"She helped us last night," Eli argued. "And that was after we—"

"Nothing doing," Garrick snapped.

Bert added, "Anyone who'd walk right into an evil place has to be evil too, at least a little bit."

Normally Garrick would give him an earful for being superstitious, but this time he felt in his bones that Bert was right. The wind was picking up dust and debris from the crevices of the alley. Garrick could make out its spiral now.

"Someone don't want folk seeing what they're doing in that basement," Eli said. "They snatched Clyde when he went to have a look, and then they pulled the curtains good."

"So whatever's going on there, the basement is at the center of it," said Garrick.

"Exactly," said Eli. "We have to get down there."

"But not through the window," Garrick said.

"No," said Eli. "Not through the window."

Bert made an annoyed sound. "I suppose we should just knock on the front door."

"That's the back door," Eli said. "And no, that's a terrible idea."

"Do you smell that?" Bert asked, crinkling his nose.

There it was again: that oily, dirty, river-stink. It had started as a tickle way at the back of Garrick's nose, but it was growing stronger, throbbing in his head as it rolled invisibly across the ground in the alley and surrounded them. The late-afternoon shadows were closing in on the corners and from above. But something else was happening, too. At first Garrick thought his eyes were playing tricks. The edges of the buildings rippled where they met the ground. The border where the wall met the pavement blurred. Then he realized what was happening.

"It's fog," Garrick said. His muscles started to feel liquidy, and he could suddenly taste and feel the mouth full of grainy, silty Thames mud that had almost choked him to death. He cleared his throat and spat out a gob of it. Eli and Bert were staring at the black, woolly mass as if Garrick had sicked up a three-headed baby.

"You all right, mate?" Bert asked.

Eli said, "I don't like this."

"Nobody likes it," Garrick snapped. Both Bert and Eli looked over sharply at the new croak in his voice. Garrick cleared his throat and stood up straighter. "But Clyde is in there somewhere, and you lot'd never let me hear the end of—well, we just can't leave him, can we?"

The other two blinked like idiots. They really had, he realized, expected him to abandon their mate at the first sign of trouble. In fact, Eli already had his fists up, ready to take a beating over it.

"We're not leaving anyone behind." Garrick looked from one to the other. "Something happens to one of us, nobody scarpers. You hear? We're in this together."

The other boys nodded, and Garrick was relieved to see the mutinous spark in Eli's eyes dim just a bit.

"Now, seeing as the front *and* back doors are out, and Eli's probably right about the window, anybody else have any bright ideas about how to get into that basement?"

They saw the drainpipe at the same time. There it was, thick and new and attached surprisingly well to the side of the building. And to one side of that, a window.

"No way I can make it up that," Bert said, breaking the silence. He wasn't wrong. Even if he hadn't taken a head-blow, he was too bulky to go shimmying up drainpipes.

"I can," said Eli.

Garrick nodded. "Then Bert can stay here and watch the window. Right, mate?"

Bert nodded.

"What if the people who attacked Bert come back?" Eli asked.

Bert's expression hardened. He folded his beefy arms across his chest. "I'll be ready."

"Right," Garrick said. As an afterthought he patted Bert's thick shoulder. "That's a lad. So we'll go up the drainpipe and through that window. It's too small to be a proper one, so it's probably a closet or something. Not the best place to start if we want the basement, but it's better than nothing. We'll go in, grab Clyde, and be on our way."

"And then that's the end of it," Eli said firmly. "We scarper and never come back."

"That's right," Garrick said.

Garrick glanced toward the end of the alley. The fog was definitely rolling in, now, and was starting to bank up. In a little while, Bert wouldn't have to worry about hiding from bad guys. The fog would conceal everything. He tried not to think about what else the fog might conceal.

"Right," Garrick said. "Eli, give me a boost up that drainpipe. Then Bert can lift you up."

CHAPTER TWENTY-FIVE

Meg

"This way, please," Hathaway said, and Nat followed along like a good little puppy.

Meg stopped as they rounded the corner onto a flight of stairs. A thick, crimson runner ran up a well-maintained stairway toward a wood-paneled corridor. The difference between it and the front rooms where they'd come in was jarring.

Like the two faces of Hathaway. Nat's apparently former nemesis spoke softly and had a mild, self-deprecating manner. At the same time, something dark seethed just below the surface. Meg couldn't put her finger on it directly, but she felt it all the same. She didn't trust him, and she didn't trust this building, which pretended to be one thing but was something quite different inside.

But Nat trusted it all. He was easily manipulated when he was in a lather and when he wanted something. Today it was both.

And where, she wondered, pulling her coat tighter around her despite the warmth she could feel coming from above, where had Abby gone?

The men had stopped to wait for her at the top of the stairs.

"Sorry," she said.

For all the building's sudden elegance—wood paneling, wool runner, a straight, evenly spaced line of paintings—the reek of the Thames hung, fishy and filthy in the air. She hadn't noticed the stench before. And wasn't the river a bit far away for the smell to be so strong? Fancifully, she thought that perhaps the stink was reflecting some inner rot of the organization.

Because while Nat thought it was simply a club for people who liked to chant and dance around in dark robes in candlelight, Meg was getting a really bad feeling.

"Mr. Hathaway," she said as she scrambled up the stairs to join them. They turned right and began to walk toward a door at the end of the corridor.

"Yes, Miss Eisenstadt?"

"Exactly what is it that you do here?"

"Don't ruin this for me," Nat murmured under his breath.

"If you don't mind my asking," Meg added.

"Not at all," Hathaway said genially. "Please, come through."

But it was a salient question. Hathaway was too young, for one, to be in charge. The decor, at least on this floor, spoke of money and the age required to accumulate it. Meg absently scratched at her scalp. A prickling sensation was creeping over her skull. She shook her head. The sooner they completed their business and left this place behind, the better.

At the end of the corridor, Hathaway let them into a well-appointed room with a wide table surrounded by chairs. A meeting room rather than a private office, then. A large envelope sat on the table, fat with papers. Hathaway had referred to Bernadette as his assistant. She wondered what, exactly, Bernadette assisted with. It couldn't be anything she was proud of, seeing how she had lied, even to her friends, about the nature of her work and even the address where she came to perform it.

"The academy, Miss Eisenstadt, is a club for university students interested in esoteric phenomena."

"That's odd, because Miss Kingsley told me that she works for an animal-welfare organization."

Hathaway cocked his head and frowned. "Perhaps she feared she'd not be taken seriously if she told the truth. After all, there's no shortage of skeptics. But there's nothing secret or shameful about our organization. It's a club for enthusiasts, that's all."

"And researchers," Nat added.

"Of course," Hathaway said, a bit indulgently, Meg thought. "We're always interested to hear about our members' independent research."

Meg had to admit that his explanation made sense. It wasn't exactly a sensible topic. Many, in fact, would find it silly. And if anything drove Bernadette demented, it was when she thought someone considered her silly.

"Perhaps," Meg said. "At the same time—Oh, thank you," she said as Hathaway pulled out one of the chairs and offered it to her.

"We were going to discuss my membership in the academy," Nat said.

"So we were." Hathaway, too, took a chair, and Nat, again the odd man out, scrambled to do the same. "Let me begin by apologizing for our callous and frankly ignorant treatment these months past."

Nat folded his arms and leaned back smugly in his chair. "I'm listening."

"You see, the academy is a university club. When you ceased to be associated with the university…"

"But somehow that's changed?" Meg asked.

"Indeed," Hathaway said. "The fact is, Dr. Wylie has conducted some groundbreaking research in his short time here. But you say, Mr. Eisenstadt, that you are the real author of that research—"

"I am," Nat said, his eyes alight. "He stole my notes—*scintillam vitae*—and I can prove it."

Satisfaction twitched at the edges of Hathaway's mouth. "I believe, Mr. Eisenstadt, that you just did. *Scintillam vitae* is the term at the heart of Dr. Wylie's research. You'll agree that it's not a phrase one hears every day."

"That's because I coined it," Nat said.

"Mmm. It was as I suspected. Dr. Wylie has a solid practical background, but his knowledge of the theoretical is somewhat lacking. You look doubtful, Miss Eisenstadt."

Meg *felt* doubtful. This was all happening too quickly and easily, and Nat was lapping it up like whiskey.

"Perhaps *you* can tell me if you recognize this handwriting," Hathaway said to her. He withdrew a few pages from the folder and slid them across the table to her.

"Those are mine!" Nat cried.

And so they were. "I'd know those scribbles anywhere," she admitted.

Hathaway said, "I recovered these from Dr. Wylie's desk. Plagiarism," he said with a sad shrug. "The last refuge of the incompetent."

"Indeed." Nat was seething.

"We owe you a debt of gratitude as well as an apology, Mr. Eisenstadt. Who knew that your expulsion from university would lead to the blossoming of one of the greatest scientific minds—"

"Exactly how has my brother's research been put to use?" Meg asked. Both men swiveled their heads to look at her. "Thanks and flattery have their place, but fine words butter no parsnips, Mr. Hathaway."

"Sis, please!" Nat cried.

Meg continued. "Someone at this address is making and distributing some sort of medication. And if my brother's research has contributed to the creation of a marketable product, then I think he deserves a portion of the profits."

Appreciation had replaced the horror in Nat's expression. "Well said, sister, dear! Yes, I do believe the girl has a point."

Hathaway's eyes widened and his features grew sharp. Then he blinked, and his features settled back into their pleasantly neutral configuration. "Of course. It's only fair, after all." He turned back to Nat. "Mr. Eisenstadt, I would like to apologize on behalf of the academy. If it's convenient, I'd like to introduce you to Sir Julius, our patron. You can tell him yourself about Dr. Wylie's theft and fraud. If you've nowhere else to be, that is."

"Oh, there's *nowhere* else I need to be," Nat said.

"Excellent. And although our rules about membership are fairly strict, perhaps we could come to some sort of arrangement, at least informally. As for you, Miss Eisenstadt," Hathaway said before she could interrupt, "if you'll kindly wait here, I shall send Miss Kingsley forthwith and try to find your Miss Gordon as well."

CHAPTER TWENTY-SIX

Eli

It had been a long time since Eli had scaled a drainpipe. But he was thin and had long fingers and feet, and that helped quite a bit. The hardest part, it turned out, was holding himself up while Garrick struggled. Garrick *struggled*, he realized. Just like the rest of them. It wasn't until Eli had begun testing his own power that he had started to think about the limitations of others. There, suspended in midair as the fog rolled in and the top of Bert's head started to disappear into it, it occurred to Eli that following Garrick was a choice. It had been a choice all along.

And if Garrick wanted the boys to continue making that choice, he was going to have to change a few things.

Garrick reached the window and leaned out toward it, holding onto the drainpipe with his legs.

"Nobody in there," he called down to Eli. "Just some old boxes and rags." Eli watched him attempt to pry open the window with one hand. For a heart-pounding second Garrick lurched out of balance before catching himself.

Eli wedged his skinny arm behind the drainpipe and held on with one hand while removing his cap with the other. "Use this," he said.

Garrick grunted a terse thanks. He wrapped the cap around his hand and struck fast. There was a tinkle of glass. Then Garrick, his hand still wrapped in Eli's cap, reached through the hole, raised the window by the frame, and slithered through. Eli followed quickly after.

The room was dark. Crowded shelves loomed on both sides. As Eli's eyes adjusted to the dim light, he saw buckets and brushes as well as boxes and rags. Supplies for the cleaning staff, then. Nothing important. He let out a breath he had apparently been holding. He was unsurprised that the door turned out to be unlocked. Garrick handed him his cap back, signaling for him to be quiet. Eli shook a piece of glass from his cap and screwed it back on, nodding, even though no one needed to tell him that.

Garrick cracked the door open. After a moment, he opened it wider and stuck out his head. Eli pressed close and looked out over Garrick's head. They were on the topmost floor. Aside from the closet, it appeared to be unused. The floors and walls were bare, and except for muffled voices below, it was silent. Cautiously, they stepped out onto a landing. A yard or so away, a narrow flight of stairs descended into darkness.

"Look at that," Garrick whispered.

One of the walls had been painted more recently than the others, and in a slightly different color. Plaster bulged beneath the paint in the shape of the doorway that had once stood there.

"I wonder if the room is still there," Eli said. "Or if it's been filled in."

Quickly, and as quietly as they could, they slipped across the landing to investigate. As Eli pressed his hands to the plaster, something huge rumbled behind the wall, vibrating the plaster and making the floorboards shudder beneath their feet. Eli skittered back.

"What the devil was that?" Garrick said.

"You got me," Eli said. He gulped a few deep breaths to calm his heart. "It ain't Clyde, though, so, whatever it is, I say we let it be."

Garrick nodded, and he didn't object when Eli took the lead and started down the staircase. Instinctively, both of them kept to the sides of the stairs, where the boards were nailed together. There was no runner to muffle their footsteps, and you never knew when a floorboard might decide to creak or pop and announce you to an entire building filled with freaks.

The staircase ended at a wall.

"What now?" Garrick asked. Eli laid his hands against the panel. It was thin and had some give. "Well?"

Eli frowned. "Clyde told me once about this house he cleaned a few times. A real queer customer. Said he had a secret little elevator built into the place." He pressed the panel gently, smiling when he felt the telltale flex. "See that?" He pressed the panel again, then, still pressing, moved his hands to the left. The panel slid open a crack. "There's a spring inside."

"Well, I'll be," Garrick said.

Eli pressed his eye to the crack.

Garrick said, "What's out there?"

This floor was a lot different than where they had come in. Red carpeting covered the floor. A foreign design. Expensive, Eli reckoned. The walls were wood, with a row of paintings extending from one side to another in an exceedingly straight line.

"Posh," Eli said. "Dead posh."

"In this neighborhood?"

Eli shrugged. "Gentlemen's club?"

Garrick nodded again. It made sense, Eli thought. At the same time, both Eli and Garrick knew that any gentlemen setting up in this area probably didn't want folk to know what they were getting up to.

"Have to be extra careful, then," Garrick said. Eli nodded his agreement. The hallway appeared deserted. The voices Eli had thought he'd heard had gone silent. He waited a minute more just to be safe. Then he pushed the panel back all the way.

"We'll check these rooms first," he told Garrick.

And again, Garrick seemed content to let Eli take the lead.

The boys crept through the opening, Eli careful to guide the panel silently back into place. There were several doors on this floor. They'd start with the first. Crossing quickly, Eli put an ear to the wood.

"No one," he whispered after a moment.

Garrick gave him the nod, and he eased the knob to the side and slowly slid the door open. He darted inside, with Garrick at his heels, then shut it.

It was an office. A rich man's office, with expensive furniture and a rug that Eli was fairly sure they shouldn't have been standing on with their dirty boots. A warm fire burned in a brick fireplace, and the walls were lined with leather-bound books, the titles in gold.

Yet someone had turned that office over but good.

"Cor," Eli said as he surveyed the wreckage. "What happened to this place?"

"I don't know," Garrick said. "But we'd best not get caught, or they'll think we done it."

Eli could envision the office as its owner had kept it: papers and books stacked neatly on the desk; blotter, inkwell, and other implements tidy and in their place. But now the papers were strewn across the floor like fallen leaves. A small table lay legs up beside an overturned teapot and broken crockery. Footprints decorated weeks of work or study with ink, cold tea, food scraps…and blood.

Garrick bent over and plucked a piece of paper from the top of the pile.

"What's this say, then?" He held the paper out toward Eli.

"You read it," said Eli, his attention caught by something else. Someone had stepped in the ink and left an inky footprint. It looked like a lady's shoe.

"I can read signs, but not this fancy stuff."

Eli glanced over, surprised by Garrick's admission of weakness. Of the four boys, only Eli'd had the patience to learn script from the church ladies. One of them, the one with the Bible stories, had even started to teach him a new set of letters. The ones, she'd said, that the Hebrews used to write with.

"Right," Eli said. "Give it here."

Garrick handed him the paper. He squinted at the loops and whorls. The letters were easy enough to make out, but the long, complicated words were something else altogether. He was so caught up in trying to sound them out that he barely heard the door open behind him.

"Well, hello, there," a woman's voice said.

Eli opened his mouth to speak, but before he could say a word, Garrick had the woman by the throat and slammed her against the wall with a force that left the plaster ringing.

"Who are you? Where's the nurse? What've you done with Clyde?" Garrick demanded.

"Mate," Eli began.

The woman's eyes bounced from Garrick to Eli. Eli took a step forward then stopped, caught between the instinct to help her and the fact that she probably did know where Clyde was.

"Well?" Garrrick gave her a shake.

"I don't know who Clyde is," she whispered.

"We ain't stupid," Garrick said. "You're with the nurse, and she's with them, and they've got Clyde."

"Clyde's our mate," Eli said. "Someone's took him, and they took him here."

Garrick kicked the door shut. The woman yelped as he feinted a punch toward her stomach.

"I swear I don't know anything about that!" she cried.

"Mate, I think she's telling the truth," Eli said.

When they'd seen this one walking with the nurse, the boys had figured that whatever the nurse's part in the goings-on at Shepherd Street, the two women were in it together. But watching her tremble like it was the Fiend holding her there and not just Garrick, who didn't even have his knife out, Eli reconsidered. It was a gut feeling, but Eli's gut had saved his life more than once.

Garrick glanced at him out of the corner of his eye. Eli nodded. Garrick let go of her throat and slowly stepped back, as Eli placed himself between the woman and the door.

"But you are with the nurse," Eli said.

The woman drew a shuddering breath and nodded. "We...we came here together. But we only just met today. Please..."

"What kind of place is this?" Eli said.

"I don't know." She exhaled and straightened her coat. "I walked here with Abby...Nurse Gordon...I was actually on my way to the building next door. We were going to walk back to the train together, but she took too long coming out, so I went in, and my brother was there, and then…" She took another deep breath. "I was looking for Nurse Gordon when I opened this door. But she's not here, as we can all see. And neither is your friend."

"That's right," Garrick said warily.

"You won't find him on this floor," she said. "I've checked the other rooms. They're all empty. And the floor below, as well."

Garrick sneered. "Where the devil did they go, then? They didn't just disappear."

"The basement," Eli said. Garrick and the woman turned.

She said, "There isn't a basement. There's only one set of stairs, from the ground floor to this one."

Eli shook his head. "There's another floor above. We came down from there through a hidden staircase. Maybe there's another staircase that goes down. It makes sense. Bert said Clyde was looking through the basement window when someone grabbed him."

"Perhaps whoever has your friend has my friend, too," the woman said.

Eli glanced at Garrick. Garrick narrowed his eyes. Then he nodded. "Someone catches us, you use your posh to talk us out of it."

"Fair enough," she said. "And if it comes to it, I'll be happy for that knife in your sleeve."

CHAPTER TWENTY-SEVEN

Gideon

"Sorry, Doc," Clyde said. Gideon was holding the boy's legs while the boy had a go at the lock through the bars. "It ain't no good."

Gideon gently lowered him to the ground. "Well, we tried."

Clyde made to toss the bit of wire to the side, then, thinking better of it, tucked it into his coat pocket instead. On the other side of the room, Miss Chase stood, turned around in a circle, and lay back down.

"Funny," Clyde said. "She don't look like no murderer." Miss Chase chuffed. "Don't act like one, neither."

"No," Gideon said.

Gideon had never seen a wolf, but the intelligence in this one's face gave him pause. Was she simply a very clever wolf, or had she retained her human intelligence? Gideon himself had no recollection of the time he spent as a wolf. When the wolf took over, Gideon went somewhere else, only to return as the wolf slunk away. Did these things vary from individual to individual?

"Wherever did they find you?" Gideon asked her. *And how is it that you haven't reverted to form?*

Miss Chase lifted her head to meet his gaze. Her silent, mournful bark throbbed at the back of his head.

Then suddenly she sprang to her feet.

CHAPTER TWENTY-EIGHT

Abby

The foetid, swampy smell grew stronger—as did Abby's apprehension—as the elevator traveled downward. Sir Julius was humming a happy tune. Miss Kingsley held her chin aloft and stared straight ahead. Dr. Wylie fiddled with a cufflink. Finally, the elevator stopped. Sir Julius pulled the gate aside and gestured for Abby and Miss Kingsley to precede him.

The smell in the basement was eye-watering. It had taken on an added barnyard dimension, as well. And that sad, monotonous barking pounded at the back of her head and in her temples. It didn't smell like dog, though. Whatever poor creature it was, was quite nearby. Then Abby heard voices.

Miss Kingsley frowned. "Sir," she said.

"In time, Miss Kingsley," Sir Julius said.

The voices grew louder. There were two.

"Gideon!" Abby cried.

"Miss Gordon, wait," Sir Julius called.

No. She wouldn't wait. This was all wrong, and she wouldn't let Gideon wait one moment longer. Abby pushed past him and ran down the hall. "Gideon, it's me," she cried as she threw herself against the door.

"Abby?" Gideon called.

She pulled and twisted the doorknob, but it held fast. "It's locked," she called. "Why is it locked?"

Footsteps slapped against the floor as Sir Julius and the others hurried to catch her up. A hand closed around her shoulder. Sir Julius said, "My dear, you're being—"

She slapped his hand away. "Open it! Open it right now! Gideon!"

"Of course," Sir Julius said. "But before I do, I need you to promise—"

"I promise you'll live to regret it if you don't open that door!" She struck her palm against the door. "Gideon!"

"My God," she heard Dr. Wylie say. "Are you holding Dr. Spencer prisoner?"

"Don't be ridiculous," Sir Julius said. "We'd never hold a man without his consent."

Abby whirled. "Well, you can't tell me he *volunteered* to be locked in a basement."

"Dr. Wylie can tell you," Sir Julius said. "Patients do sometimes voluntarily confine themselves when they're afraid they might hurt someone."

"He said no such thing to me," Dr. Wylie said.

"You're keeping animals down here," Abby said. "What the devil kind of place—"

"Sir," Miss Kingsley said again.

"Not now," Sir Julius said brusquely. But at least he produced a key. It seemed to take hours for him to fiddle the lock open, but the moment it did, Abby pushed past him and ran inside.

"Abby, thank God!" Gideon reached toward her through a set of bars.

"What happened? What are you doing here?"

She grasped his hands in hers, covering the fingers with kisses and tears. The very thought of him trapped down here in the darkness, and what was that *smell*? Not just the river-stink, but also urine and straw and fear, and what the very devil?

"Is this…some sort of *animal pen?*" Abby demanded.

"This is not a proper animal enclosure," Miss Kingsley said.

"Why are you keeping him in a *pen?* You said he *asked* to be here."

"I never did," Gideon said.

"Ladies," Sir Julius said. "I think we should all..."

Gideon squeezed her fingers through the bars. The rotten river stench had become almost unbearable. Something whined from the shadows. Abby squinted. Gradually a shape emerged from the gloom. It was the biggest dog she'd ever seen, with a thick, silver coat that would have been lustrous with proper care, and surprisingly intelligent eyes.

"Oh, my," Miss Kingsley said, drawing closer. "Is that..."

Dr. Wylie said, "Sir Julius, I demand to know why you're holding this man."

Abby turned. "Yes," she said, forcing a calm that she didn't feel. "You said you'd never hold a man without his consent."

"He's not a man," another voice said. Abby could make out a thin, bespectacled figure in shirt sleeves standing just outside the door. No, Abby thought as another backlit form took shape in the doorway; there were two of them. "And there's no law against keeping animals."

"Together?" Abby said.

"I ain't an animal! Miss! I ain't an animal!" Abby turned at the familiar voice. "Clyde," she said as she recognized the boy. "What are you doing in there?"

"This is all a terrible misunderstanding." The bespectacled man crossed the room toward her. "My name is Hathaway. Please," he said, reaching for her elbow. "Please, allow me to—"

"No!" She shook her arm free.

"Sorry, old chap," said the man who had come in with Hathaway. "I'm not sure what this has to do with my research."

"You're Nathaniel," Abby cried, grateful to see another outsider. He looked exactly as Meg had described him, right down to the supercilious pleasure that crossed his face at the sound of his own name.

"And you must be Meg's new little friend," he said delightedly.

"Where is she?" Abby asked.

Nathaniel frowned. "We left her upstairs to wait for...you. And *you*," he said as his gaze fell on Miss Kingsley.

"Hathaway, who *is* this person?" Sir Julius demanded.

"I am Nathaniel Eisenstadt, the author of the world-changing research for which *that man,*" he pointed at Dr. Wylie, "has taken credit."

Sir Julius turned to Dr. Wylie. "Is this true?"

"Sir Julius, I can ex—" A groaning gust of wind shook the window and spattered it with debris. The single gas sconce on the wall flickered as if the wind were there in the room with them. The dog gave a great bark.

"What the devil—" Dr. Wylie started across the room. When the dog saw him, it leaped to its feet, barking and dancing.

Gideon said, "They told me her name is Miss Chase."

Dr. Wylie turned, his expression fierce. "All this time?" He started toward Sir Julius. "You've been keeping her down here all this time? When did you find her? Why didn't you tell me immediately? I've been nearly out of my mind with guilt and worry—"

"You never had anything to worry about, dear boy," Sir Julius said.

"What?"

"Your Miss Chase has been safe, right here all along."

"But *why?*" Dr. Wylie demanded.

Sir Julius smiled indulgently. "You were never going to leave Hanwell of your own volition. And Hathaway needed a specimen for his own research. Research from which you, Miss Gordon, and your Dr. Spencer have all benefitted, if I'm not mistaken."

Another blast of rank air shattered the window and extinguished the light. The reeking wind blew through the room, rustling Abby's skirts and pelting her ankles with debris. Moist, silty earth followed, first in a trickle and then in a river, snaking toward the floor, then arcing into a roaring vortex in the center of the room.

Gradually, a shape took form. It was just as Nell Evans had said: the shape of a man, but not a man; long arms that ended in sharp claws that dragged the ground and glowing green eyes like malevolent stars—the only feature in a face of shifting sands.

Heart pounding, Abby skittered backward into Miss Kingsley.

"It's my fault," Miss Kingsley whispered to no one in particular. "It's all my fault."

Abby's heart pounded. She stepped to the side. The Fiend turned its head to follow her. On the other side of the room, a low mumble rose from the shadows. Squinting, Abby could make out the silhouette of Sir Julius through the swirling dirt, his hands tracing arcane symbols in the air.

With a roar the creature swept an arm in the direction of the noise. Sir Julius flew back against the wall in a shower of river-stinking silt. He cried out as he hit, then slid to the floor and lay still.

"Oh, God," Abby whispered.

At the sound of her voice, the creature turned. Behind her, Miss Kingsley whimpered. Abby spread her arms, putting herself between the young woman and the Fiend. The creature cocked its head, watching her. The sands of its face shifted, revealing some sort of glowing pictographs on its forehead. She turned as Dr. Wylie took a step forward. The creature turned at exactly the same time, releasing another blast of foul-smelling filth.

"Abby," Gideon whispered.

She jerked her head toward his voice. The creature followed with a gust that blew the wall of the animal pen into splinters.

"Gideon!" Abby cried.

The cloud of filth and splinters settled.

"He's all right," Miss Kingsley said. "Look."

Slowly, Gideon rose and turned, futilely brushing at the dirt and debris on his jacket. Then he helped Clyde to his feet. The Fiend watched closely, its green eyes never blinking, as they slowly moved toward the door. The dog shook itself off, then trotted after them.

Out of the corner of her eye, she saw Hathaway step forward to intercept them.

"I wouldn't if I were you," Dr. Wylie said. His fine shirt was covered in foul-smelling mud, but he was drawing closer to the Fiend, regarding it with scientific interest. Hathaway paused. Gideon ushered his charges past him. "What are you?" Dr. Wylie asked the creature.

Meg's brother cleared his throat. "If I may," he said, "I believe it's a golem."

"A what?" Hathaway demanded.

While the creature had been distracted by their conversation, Abby had moved along the wall, keeping Miss Kingsley behind her.

"A creature of Jewish folklore," Nathaniel said. "A protector. Fascinating. I've tried several times to call one into existence, but I've not yet succeeded." He frowned. "That's probably for the best."

"Who did call it, then?" Hathaway demanded.

"I don't know," said Nathaniel. "But I'd like to shake their hand."

Nathaniel and Dr. Wylie were circling the Fiend in opposite directions, shuffling the dust with their feet to form a ring around it. The golem whipped its massive head from side to side, trying to keep them both in its view. Abby herded Miss Kingsley farther along the wall, never taking her eyes from the creature.

"What do you think it wants?" Dr. Wylie asked.

"That," Nathaniel said, "I couldn't tell you."

"It doesn't seem too pleased with us," Dr. Wylie said.

Nathaniel frowned, venturing a bit farther inside the circle they were walking around it. "Speak for yourself, Doctor. It hasn't yet decorated me with filth."

"Never mind the filth," Hathaway cried from the corner where he was cowering. "Do you know how to get rid of it?"

"I do, actually," Nathaniel said. "If only your organization admitted people like me."

"For God's sake, Eisenstadt!" Hathaway said.

By this point, Abby and Miss Kingsley had reached the doorway. She glanced over her shoulder and sighed with relief. Gideon and the boy were nowhere to be seen.

"You see the characters on its forehead," Nathaniel said, taking another step toward the creature.

"Hebrew," Hathaway said.

Nathaniel nodded. "That's a *shem*. One of the names of God. Remove the shem, and the golem goes back to the dirt or clay or sand from which it came."

"Nat, no!" Miss Kingsley cried as Nathaniel darted forward toward the Fiend.

The golem roared, unleashing an eye-watering cloud of river-stench and a wall of sand that left Nathaniel stumbling blindly into the wall.

Abby skittered backward as Miss Kingsley surged forward toward Nathaniel. The two collided.

"This is my fault," Miss Kingsley said again. "I gave Dr. Wylie's notes to Mr. Hathaway. If anything happens—"

"Mr. Eisenstadt is fine," Abby said. She took Miss Kingsley by the shoulders. "He'll be fine." Abby wasn't at all sure about that, but whatever Miss Kingsley's role had been, it wouldn't be served by her rushing to her death. "Do you trust me?" Miss Kingsley bit her lip. Then she nodded. "Good."

Her arm around Miss Kingsley's shoulder, she took another step back and stumbled over a leg.

"Careful, miss," a voice said.

Abby turned. "Eli!"

The creature whipped its head toward them. Behind her, Miss Kingsley made a little sound like "Oh."

"Eli, turn around and run," Abby said, returning her attention to the hulking form. As long as she was watching it, the Fiend seemed content to leave the others alone.

"Don't worry, miss," Eli said. "I can do this." He darted forward, but Miss Kingsley caught him by the collar.

"No," she said.

"Why not?" Eli asked.

"Because," she said to Abby, "this monster is yours."

CHAPTER TWENTY-NINE

Bernadette

The monster was Miss Gordon's. Anyone could see it. Miss Gordon was an untamed force, a raw talent, and somehow, without knowing it, she had called this creature into existence.

Bernadette envied the other woman. If Miss Gordon managed to dismiss her monster, its damage would be limited. But the trouble that Bernadette had brought upon Dr. Spencer, the little boy, and that poor silver wolf—that trouble was only beginning. In turning over Dr. Wylie's research to Mr. Hathaway, she'd thought she was advancing her position. Instead, she'd been laying the groundwork for the research that had led to three souls imprisoned below ground and subjected to Heaven only knew what torments.

If she survived—if they all survived—she would spend the rest of her life trying to make amends.

CHAPTER THIRTY

Abby

This monster is yours.

The swirling, rushing air stilled as Abby stepped back into the room. The howling wind went quiet. The silence intensified, sharpened, until Abby felt it pressing in upon her from all sides. She saw Nathaniel's mouth move as he spoke, to her? To Dr. Wylie? To Miss Kingsley? She should have heard Dr. Wylie's footsteps as he inched past her, pulling Nathaniel toward the doorway. But all was oppressively, preternaturally silent.

This monster is yours.

The Fiend had stilled as well. The shifting, stinking river-bottom soil that made up its hulking form drifted in her direction until the golem was facing her, its green eyes glowing, unblinking, watchful. It didn't move as her feet broke the circle that Nathaniel and Wylie had traced in the dust around it. And, as she quieted her thoughts and allowed the tendrils of instinct to unfurl, she detected no ill will coming from the creature, nor any signs of hostile intent.

Perhaps it really *was* hers.

The Fiend was just as the boys had described it. It had arrived, they said, with the fog, not long after the boys had set upon her by the embankment. It had come from the river, called forth from the foetid soil at the bottom of the Thames.

Abby looked up. The creature turned its green gaze toward the ceiling. She looked down. It lowered its head. She held one arm out to the side, then the other. The fiend mirrored her movements.

"You *are* mine," she whispered.

The soil of its face shifted. Its eyes met her own—bright, intense green, a color like lichen and fire. On its broad, sandy forehead, characters pulsed and glowed with that same green light. The creature was beautiful in its own way, as every living thing was beautiful, animated as it was by *scintillam vitae,* the dancing spark of life.

Sir Julius stirred. A snarl rumbled in the Fiend's chest, and it reached an arm toward the noise.

"No," Abby said gently.

The creature hesitated, then lowered its arm.

Nathaniel had called it a protector. But Abby was no occultist. She'd not set out to call down supernatural protection. In fact, she'd always considered *herself* the protector—of Gideon, of the clinic and those who passed through it. How had this creature come to be? This great, hulking Fiend pulled from sand and soil and stinking river sediment, with eyes that glowed—like the elixir she fetched from Whitechapel, always putting a drop on her tongue to ensure it was safe.

Had the Fiend always been a part of her? Had it needed only a drop of the elixir—elixir, which, ironically kept Gideon's creature at bay—to manifest and come to her rescue in its own lumbering way?

Footsteps sounded in the hallway behind her. The Fiend's green eyes flicked toward a point beyond her shoulder before returning to her. And all at once she knew what she had to do.

Her heart thundering in her ears, Abby crossed the circle until they were standing toe to gigantic, seething, sedimentary toe, then reached toward the characters now glowing bright on the golem's forehead. She closed her hand around a clay tablet, and for one split second, the soil enveloped her hand in a gentle embrace.

"Thank you," she whispered. "Your work is finished. Now, rest."

Then she pulled back the shem, and the golem collapsed in a waterfall of dirt.

"Abby!" a voice called.

Abby turned to see Meg pushing past the others standing in the doorway. Meg crossed to her in five quick steps, and Abby sank into her arms, knowing at last she was home.

EPILOGUE

February 1886
Triskelion House

Abby

Once the boards had been removed from the front windows, new carpets laid, and a shiny new brass plaque screwed into the bricks beside the front door, the building formerly known as Consortium House had become a protective presence on Shepherd Street. It had taken nearly two months, but with all their help—and with both Sir Julius and Mr. Hathaway awaiting trial on a variety of charges—Triskelion House was building itself a new identity. It was now the home of the Triskelion Group, a cutting-edge research partnership and a budding cynosure of scientific inquiry into esoteric phenomena.

It was also a place where people with questionable histories and unconventional skill sets could find both shelter and gainful employment.

"Right," Garrick said, emerging through the doorway of the new front office. "Who's for tea, then?"

Bernadette glanced up from the papers arrayed before her on the wide conference table and raised a finger in response. Dr. Wylie, Eli, and Nathaniel quickly cleared away the piles of leather-bound volumes from the center, so that Garrick could set down a tray laden with cups, plates, a teapot, and the iced poppy-seed loaf that had been perfuming the air for the past hour.

Nathaniel shoved the end piece into his mouth and moaned. "Miss Chase has outdone herself," he said.

"Thank you, Garrick," Garrick mumbled as he poured Bernadette's tea.

"Yes," she said, meeting Garrick's eyes. "Thank you."

Pink rose to his cheeks at the sincerity in her tone, and he turned away, muttering under his breath. The young man still had a few sharp edges, but proper feeding up and a dependable roof over his head had brought out a nascent spirit of responsibility that Abby had suspected might have been lurking inside him all along.

Abby set another piece of fragrant wood onto the flames—an extravagance, to be sure, but so much more pleasant than a coal fire—and stole a glance at Clyde's stitching. She'd started him out with simple mending tasks, and from his progress, she reckoned he might one day make a fine tailor, among other things. But he still had plenty of time to make that decision himself.

"I'm still wondering, though, Bernadette," Abby said. "How did you know that the golem was mine?"

Bernadette drew breath to answer, but Clyde answered first.

"Anyone with half a brain could have worked that out, at least after a chat with Nell Evans."

"Oh?" Abby asked.

"Well..." Clyde held up his work to the firelight and squinted. Satisfied, he laid it back down in his lap. "Miss Evans had her own run-in with the Fiend...I mean, the golem...after she let herself in through the back window of your clinic. Then the Fiend attacked us after..."

"No need to remind us," Eli said without lifting his nose from the thick Hebrew language primer he held in his lap.

"That's right," Abby said. "Your assistance these past weeks has more than made up for your transgressions. All of you."

She looked around, including not only Eli, Garrick, and Clyde, but also Bert, who had proved to be an able and compassionate veterinary assistant during the weeks of Miss Chase's recovery.

"The point is," Clyde said, "the Fiend punished them what attacked you. Plus, Bert watched you come here every week like clockwork. And, as Garrick once said, this is an evil place."

"Was," Gideon said from behind his newspaper. The headlines read, *Escaped Murderess Exonerated*. Dr. Wylie had called in every last one of his professional favors to have Miss Chase's charges reduced and her care remanded to the Triskelion Group.

"That's right," Clyde said. "And all a person had to do was put one and one and one together."

Bernadette cleared her throat. "As I was *about* to say…"

Clyde's eyes went wide. "Sorry, miss."

"Think nothing of it. The thought occurred to *me* just after the golem manifested in the basement. Every time you turned your head, it did, as well. And when you directed it to knock down the wall of the pen, well, you might not have known that's what you were doing, but to the casual observer, it was all quite obvious."

"Speak for yourself," Nathaniel mumbled. "Some of us were just trying not to get sand-blasted into our next lives."

"Indeed, Miss Kingsley," Dr. Wylie said. "You see things that most of us miss. And the Triskelion Group would be nowhere without your research and observations. I hope that one day you'll be able to forgive me for underestimating you."

Miss Kingsley allowed herself a small smile. "Being made a senior partner was a good start."

Bernadette, Dr. Wylie, and Nathaniel made up the three arms of the Triskelion. Abby and Gideon provided occasional support, but from day to day, their newly renovated clinic took up most of their time. Which was just as well, Abby figured. The place would get a bit crowded if she and Gideon were spending their days at Triskelion House as well as their nights.

Nathaniel gave an exaggerated yawn and stretched in his chair. "Yes, and I suppose I shall one day find it in my heart to forgive *you* for having stolen my notes," he said to Dr. Wylie. "Especially since they led to the elixir. You're welcome, by the way," he said, giving Gideon's newspaper a flick.

"Eh? What's that? Yes, yes, brilliant work, Mr. Eisenstadt," Gideon said, his tone showing how many times he'd said it before.

"But what I don't understand," Abby said, "is how the elixir simultaneously held Gideon's wolf at bay, trapped Miss Chase inside her own wolf, and called forth my golem."

"*Scintillam vitae*," Nathaniel said, spreading his hands in a magician's gesture.

Bernadette rolled her eyes. "Ah, yes. You've stumbled upon your philosopher's stone. But now real scientists need to do some real work to figure out how to apply the knowledge to *real* situations."

Now Nathaniel rolled his eyes. "Details, details. I've been working too hard. What I really could use right now," he slid a hand up Dr. Wylie's thigh, "is a bit of distraction."

"Mm, me, too," Meg murmured. She laid a hand at the small of Abby's back. Abby stiffened, glancing toward Gideon, who was fortunately still engrossed in the *Times*. For Abby's sake, Meg had endeavored to be discreet. But Abby could tell she was growing impatient, and rightfully so, she supposed.

On the other side of the room, Gideon shook a crease out of his newspaper.

"Excuse me for a minute, love," Abby whispered to Meg. She squeezed Meg's elbow and gave her a meaningful look. "Gideon, might I have a word?"

"Certainly, my dear."

He laid his paper on his chair and followed her into the corridor.

"Gideon," she said. "There's something I've been wanting to discuss with you."

"We've all had a lot on our plates, lately," he said. His tone was good-natured, but his voice held a note of trepidation.

"This predates all of that. I'm pretty sure you know what I'm going to say."

He met her eyes. She balanced there on the precipice of the moment. If she said nothing, she could pretend away that which remained unspoken, and they could return to some semblance of the way they had always been. The way she thought they always would be. It would be the safe choice, and yet...

"I can't marry you, Gideon," she said before she could lose her courage. For one awful moment, the words hung there between them in the warm, pine-and-lemon-scented air.

He let out a long breath. "Thank God."

She laughed in surprise. "What?"

"Abby, I've been trying to find a way to tell you…I don't want to marry you, either." He took her hands in his. His grip felt exactly as it always had—soft, strong…and brotherly.

She laughed again, this time with relief. She felt light, suddenly, like a rising balloon. "I love you so much," she said.

"And I love you too, but—"

"But not in that way," she said, following his gaze to Dr. Wylie and Nathaniel.

Over the past months, the three men had formed a tightly bound molecule. Although just how tight, Abby hadn't been able to divine. They had knocked down the walls between two of the top-floor rooms to make one large living quarters for Dr. Wylie and Nathaniel, though Gideon maintained his own quarters on the floor below. Meg, Miss Chase, and Abby all kept rooms in Triskelion House as well, with the boys inhabiting the rooms below ground.

By the time she looked back, the red had almost left Gideon's cheeks. "No," he said quietly. "Not in that way. And it's the same for you, too, I suspect," he said with a nod toward Meg.

"Yes." Abby couldn't suppress her smile, and she didn't try to. "Oh, Gideon, I've never been so happy. You and I will always be special to one another, though, won't we?"

He smiled. "Like brother and sister."

"Speaking of brothers…" Nathaniel said, he and Dr. Wylie suddenly at Gideon's side. Nathaniel slung one arm around Gideon's shoulders, the other looped possessively around Dr. Wylie's waist. "Darkness has fallen, and my club in Holborn awaits the first visit of its newest member." Red bloomed on Gideon's dark cheeks, though his expression betrayed a secret pleasure at the idea. "Right," Nathaniel said, clapping Gideon's shoulder. "Get your coat, wolf-boy. Those hearts aren't going to break themselves."

THE END

About the Author

Jess Faraday is the author of the Ira Adler mysteries and several standalone novels. She lives in Scotland.

Books Available from Bold Strokes Books

Busy Ain't the Half of It by Frederick Smith and Chaz Lamar Cruz. Elijah and Justin seek happily-ever-afters in LA, but are they too busy to notice happiness when it's there? (978-1-63555-944-6)

Calumet by Ali Vali. Jaxon Lavigne and Iris Long had a forbidden small-town romance that didn't last, and the consequences of that love will be uncovered fifteen years later at their high school reunion. (978-1-63555-900-2)

Her Countess to Cherish by Jane Walsh. London Society's material girl realizes there is more to life than diamonds when she falls in love with a non-binary bluestocking. (978-1-63555-902-6)

Hot Days, Heated Nights by Renee Roman. When Cole and Lee meet, instant attraction quickly flares into uncontrollable passion, but their connection might be short lived as Lee's identity is tied to her life in the city. (978-1-63555-888-3)

Never Be the Same by MA Binfield. Casey meets Olivia and sparks fly in this opposites attract romance that proves love can be found in the unlikeliest places. (978-1-63555-938-5)

Quiet Village by Eden Darry. Something not quite human is stalking Collie and her niece, and she'll be forced to work with undercover reporter Emily Lassiter if they want to get out of Hyam alive. (978-1-63555-898-2)

Shaken or Stirred by Georgia Beers. Bar owner Julia Martini and home health aide Savannah McNally attempt to weather the storms brought on by a mysterious blogger trashing the bar, family feuds they knew nothing about, and way too much advice from way too many relatives. (978-1-63555-928-6)

The Fiend in the Fog by Jess Faraday. Can four people on different trajectories work together to save the vulnerable residents of East London from the terrifying fiend in the fog before it's too late? (978-1-63555-514-1)

The Marriage Masquerade by Toni Logan. A no strings attached marriage scheme to inherit a Maui B&B uncovers unexpected attractions and a dark family secret. (978-1-63555-914-9)

Flight SQA016 by Amanda Radley. Fastidious airline passenger Olivia Lewis is used to things being a certain way. When her routine is changed by a new, attractive member of the staff, sparks fly. (978-1-63679-045-9)

Home Is Where the Heart Is by Jenny Frame. Can Archie make the countryside her home and give Ash the fairytale romance she desires? Or will the countryside and small village life all be too much for her? (978-1-63555-922-4)

Moving Forward by PJ Trebelhorn. The last person Shelby Ryan expects to be attracted to is Iris Calhoun, the sister of the man who killed her wife four years and three thousand miles ago. (978-1-63555-953-8)

Poison Pen by Jean Copeland. Debut author Kendra Blake is finally living her best life until a nasty book review and exposed secrets threaten her promising new romance with aspiring journalist Alison Chatterley. (978-1-63555-849-4)

Seasons for Change by KC Richardson. Love, laughter, and trust develop for Shawn and Morgan throughout the changing seasons of Lake Tahoe. (978-1-63555-882-1)

Summer Lovin' by Julie Cannon. Three different women, three exotic locations, one unforgettable summer. What do you think will happen? (978-1-63555-920-0)

Unbridled by D. Jackson Leigh. A visit to a local stable turns into more than riding lessons between a novel writer and an equestrian with a taste for power play. (978-1-63555-847-0)

VIP by Jackie D. In a town where relationships are forged and shattered by perception, sometimes even love can't change who you really are. (978-1-63555-908-8)

Yearning by Gun Brooke. The sleepy town of Dennamore has an irresistible pull on those who've moved away. The mystery Darian Benson and Samantha Pike uncover will change them forever, but the love they find along the way just might be the key to saving themselves. (978-1-63555-757-2)

A Turn of Fate by Ronica Black. Will Nev and Kinsley finally face their painful past and relent to their powerful, forbidden attraction? Or will facing their past be too much to fight through? (978-1-63555-930-9)

Desires After Dark by MJ Williamz. When her human lover falls deathly ill, Alex, a vampire, must decide which is worse, letting her go or condemning her to everlasting life. (978-1-63555-940-8)

Her Consigliere by Carsen Taite. FBI agent Royal Scott swore an oath to uphold the law, and criminal defense attorney Siobhan Collins pledged her loyalty to the only family she's ever known, but will their love be stronger than the bonds they've vowed to others, or will their competing allegiances tear them apart? (978-1-63555-924-8)

In Our Words: Queer Stories from Black, Indigenous, and People of Color Writers. Stories selected by Anne Shade and Edited by Victoria Villaseñor. Comprising both the renowned and emerging voices of Black, Indigenous, and People of Color authors, this thoughtfully curated collection of short stories explores the intersection of racial and queer identity. (978-1-63555-936-1)

Measure of Devotion by CF Frizzell. Disguised as her late twin brother, Catherine Samson enters the Civil War to defend the Constitution as a Union soldier, never expecting her life to be altered by a Gettysburg farmer's daughter. (978-1-63555-951-4)

Not Guilty by Brit Ryder. Claire Weaver and Emery Pearson's day jobs clash, even as their desire for each other burns, and a discreet sex-only arrangement is the only option. (978-1-63555-896-8)

Opposites Attract: Butch/Femme Romances by Meghan O'Brien, Aurora Rey, Angie Williams. Sometimes opposites really do attract. Fall in love with these butch/femme romance novellas. (978-1-63555-784-8)

Swift Vengeance by Jean Copeland, Jackie D, Erin Zak. A journalist becomes the subject of her own investigation when sudden strange, violent visions summon her to a summer retreat and into the arms of a killer's possible next victim. (978-1-63555-880-7)

Under Her Influence by Amanda Radley. On their path to #truelove, will Beth and Jemma discover that reality is even better than illusion? (978-1-63555-963-7)

Wasteland by Kristin Keppler & Allisa Bahney. Danielle Clark is fighting against the National Armed Forces and finds peace as a scavenger, until the NAF general's daughter, Katelyn Turner, shows up on her doorstep and brings the fight right back to her. (978-1-63555-935-4)

When in Doubt by VK Powell. Police officer Jeri Wylder thinks she committed a crime in the line of duty but can't remember, until details emerge pointing to a cover-up by those close to her. (978-1-63555-955-2)

A Woman to Treasure by Ali Vali. An ancient scroll isn't the only treasure Levi Montbard finds as she starts her hunt for the truth—all she has to do is prove to Yasmine Hassani that there's more to her than an adventurous soul. (978-1-63555-890-6)

Before. After. Always. by Morgan Lee Miller. Still reeling from her tragic past, Eliza Walsh has sworn off taking risks, until Blake Navarro turns her world right-side up, making her question if falling in love again is worth it. (978-1-63555-845-6)

Bet the Farm by Fiona Riley. Lauren Calloway's luxury real estate sale of the century comes to a screeching halt when dairy farm heiress, and one-night stand, Thea Boudreaux calls her bluff. (978-1-63555-731-2)

Cowgirl by Nance Sparks. The last thing Aren expects is to fall for Carol. Sharing her home is one thing, but sharing her heart means sharing the demons in her past and risking everything to keep Carol safe. (978-1-63555-877-7)

Give In to Me by Elle Spencer. Gabriela Talbot never expected to sleep with her favorite author—certainly not after the scathing review she'd given Whitney Ainsworth's latest book. (978-1-63555-910-1)

Hidden Dreams by Shelley Thrasher. A lethal virus and its resulting vision send Texan Barbara Allan and her lovely guide, Dara, on a journey up Cambodia's Mekong River in search of Barbara's mother's mystifying past. (978-1-63555-856-2)

In the Spotlight by Lesley Davis. For actresses Cole Calder and Eris Whyte, their chance at love runs out fast when a fan's adoration turns to obsession. (978-1-63555-926-2)

Origins by Jen Jensen. Jamis Bachman is pulled into a dangerous mystery that becomes personal when she learns the truth of her origins as a ghost hunter. (978-1-63555-837-1)

Pursuit: A Victorian Entertainment by Felice Picano. An intelligent, handsome, ruthlessly ambitious young man who rose from the slums to become the right-hand man of the Lord Exchequer of England will stop at nothing as he pursues his Lord's vanished wife across Continental Europe. (978-1-63555-870-8)

Unrivaled by Radclyffe. Zoey Cohen will never accept second place in matters of the heart, even when her rival is a career, and Declan Black has nothing left to give of herself or her heart. (978-1-63679-013-8)

A Fae Tale by Genevieve McCluer. Dovana comes to terms with her changing feelings for her lifelong best friend and fae, Roze. (978-1-63555-918-7)

Accidental Desperados by Lee Lynch. Life is clobbering Berry, Jaudon, and their long romance. The arrival of directionless baby dyke MJ doesn't help. Can they find their passion again—and keep it? (978-1-63555-482-3)

Always Believe by Aimée. Greyson Walsden is pursuing ordination as an Anglican priest. Angela Arlingham doesn't believe in God. Do they follow their vocation or their hearts? (978-1-63555-912-5)

Best of the Wrong Reasons by Sander Santiago. For Fin Ness and Orion Starr, it takes a funeral to remind them that love is worth living for. (978-1-63555-867-8)

Courage by Jesse J. Thoma. No matter how often Natasha Parsons and Tommy Finch clash on the job, an undeniable attraction simmers just beneath the surface. Can they find the courage to change so love has room to grow? (978-1-63555-802-9)

I Am Chris by R Kent. There's one saving grace to losing everything and moving away. Nobody knows her as Chrissy Taylor. Now Chris can live who he truly is. (978-1-63555-904-0)

The Princess and the Odium by Sam Ledel. Jastyn and Princess Aurelia return to Venostes and join their families in a battle against the dark force to take back their homeland for a chance at a better tomorrow. (978-1-63555-894-4)

The Queen Has a Cold by Jane Kolven. What happens when the heir to the throne isn't a prince or a princess? (978-1-63555-878-4)

The Secret Poet by Georgia Beers. Agreeing to help her brother woo Zoe Blake seemed like a good idea to Morgan Thompson at first...until she realizes she's actually wooing Zoe for herself... (978-1-63555-858-6)

You Again by Aurora Rey. For high school sweethearts Kate Cormier and Sutton Guidry, the second chance might be the only one that matters. (978-1-63555-791-6)